God, Jed thought, *but she was so beautiful,*

with her dark hair tumbling wildly down her back and curling about her face. He reached up to gently wipe the tear away with the back of his forefinger. "It's all right to cry," he told her softly.

Victoria shook her head stubbornly. "No, it isn't. I haven't cried since the day my parents were buried. Tears are not to be shed for little things."

He could only stare down at her, his heart slamming against his chest in reaction to the pain revealed by her statement. "You are so brave. So beautiful," he whispered.

She caught her breath, those gray eyes growing dark with an emotion he did not want to acknowledge, even as he felt an answering reaction stir in himself.

He could no longer pretend to deny the desire she felt for him. That he felt for her...

Dear Reader,

The heroine in Catherine Archer's *Lady Thorn*, Victoria Thorn, is a descendant of the characters from Catherine's first book for Harlequin, *Rose Among Thorns*. It's the story of a Victorian heiress who is being pressured to find a suitable husband. Instead, she falls in love with a sea captain who promises her protection in exchange for her help in locating his son. Don't miss this touching story from this gifted author whose tale we hope you'll find, as *Affaire de Coeur* did, "impossible to put down."

Josh Colter and Alexandria Gibson discover they are both looking for the same man in Susan Amarillas's new Western, *Wyoming Renegade*. Susan's last two books have won her 5★ ratings from *Affaire de Coeur*, and fans have been eagerly awaiting this tale of two people who must choose between family, and love and honor.

USA Today bestselling and multiaward-winning author Ruth Langan's new series, THE JEWELS OF TEXAS, moves into full swing with this month's *Jade*, the story of a small-town preacher who surrenders his soul to the town madam. And in Kate Kingsley's new Western, *The Scout's Bride*, a determined young widow decides to accept the help of a rugged army scout who has made himself her unwanted protector.

Whatever your taste in reading, we hope you'll keep an eye out for all four titles wherever Harlequin Historicals are sold.

Sincerely,

Tracy Farrell
Senior Editor

Please address questions and book requests to:
Harlequin Reader Service
U.S.: 3010 Walden Ave., P.O. Box 1325, Buffalo, NY 14269
Canadian: P.O. Box 609, Fort Erie, Ont. L2A 5X3

Catherine Archer

Lady Thorn

Harlequin Books

TORONTO • NEW YORK • LONDON
AMSTERDAM • PARIS • SYDNEY • HAMBURG
STOCKHOLM • ATHENS • TOKYO • MILAN
MADRID • WARSAW • BUDAPEST • AUCKLAND

ISBN 0-373-28953-7

LADY THORN

Copyright © 1997 by Catherine J. Archibald

This edition published by arrangement with Harlequin Books S.A.

® and TM are trademarks of the publisher. Trademarks indicated with
® are registered in the United States Patent and Trademark Office, the
Canadian Trade Marks Office and in other countries.

Printed in U.S.A.

Books by Catherine Archer

Harlequin Historicals

Rose Among Thorns #136
*Velvet Bond #282
*Velvet Touch #322
Lady Thorn #353

*Velvet series

CATHERINE ARCHER

has been hooked on historical romance since reading Jane Eyre at the age of twelve. She has an avid interest in history, particularly the medieval period. A homemaker and mother, Catherine lives with her husband, three children and dog in Alberta, Canada, where the long winters give this American transplant plenty of time to write.

This book is dedicated to my brothers,
Russell, Michael and David, who are heroes in the
rough, as most interesting heroes are.

I must thank my daughter Katie for her inspiration for
Jedidiah McBride. She loved him before I did.

Lastly I wish to thank Dave at the Soft Shoppe, for
the help he has given me with my PC, and all
things related.

Chapter One

England, 1855

Jedidiah McBride traveled slowly over the road from Westacre. He held the reins firmly, feeling their smooth leather against his palm, as he tried not to acknowledge the unaccustomed feelings of despondency that were prodding at the back of his mind, ready to overtake him.

Not since he was a boy had Jed allowed anything to affect him this much. Not since his mother's death, some few months after Nina's desertion. It had been an untimely death that he knew had been hastened by Nina and her high-and-mighty family's cruel treatment of him.

An owl hooted in the trees to his right, and Jed shifted around in his saddle, his sea-green eyes searching the inky darkness for a glimpse of the night bird that sounded so alone. As alone as he would feel if he allowed himself that luxury, which he would not.

Nothing stirred in the cluster of young oaks that grew behind the hedge of hawthorn. Yet he had no doubt that the creature was there, among the dense growth of late spring, watching him. If he was capable of reason, would he think Jed was a fool to have come all this way from America with only the content of one vague and confused letter to go on? Then, even as Jed watched, he saw the dark spread of the owl's wings as it swooped from the highest treetop, across the greening open field, in search of small prey.

If only his own life were so simple. He would like to be able to swoop down on Nina, take what was his and go. But even though twelve years had passed since the last time he'd seen her, she could still manipulate him by saying only what she wanted him to know and nothing more.

His gaze flicked across the sky, where the half-moon was partially obscured by gauzy iron clouds. Find her he would, no matter what the cost. He must succeed in what he had come to England to do. There was no reasonable alternative.

Over the course of the past twelve years, he had faced worse odds and won. Jed had started his nautical career as a cabin boy at the age of seventeen. He was now co-owner of a thriving shipbuilding firm, master of his own ship, and master of his own life.

Or so he had thought until he received the letter from Nina some two months ago. It was then that he had learned she'd left Bar Harbor with his unborn child inside her. Pain sliced through him, and his knees gripped the horse more tightly, causing it to prance beneath him. Deliberately, calling on the strength and determination that had sustained him all these years, he forced himself to relax those muscles and the ones in his shoulders and prodded the animal on.

He would find Nina, and his son. Nothing, not even her cruel theft of the boy's childhood, would prevent him being a better father than his had been to him.

The night closed in around him as his mind centered on that one most important need, using it to block out any thought of possible failure. Again he went over the minimal clues he had to help him locate her. He knew that Ni-

na's name was now Fairfield and that she had borne him a
son. Little else had been said, other than that she was finally telling him about the child out of a need to salve her
own conscience. It didn't even enter his mind that the claim
might be false. Some inner sense, the same one that fore-
warned him of a squall before it came, told him she was
telling the truth.

Jed's lips tightened. How very like Nina to say she was
telling him in order to salve her conscience. She had always acted to preserve her own pretty hide. His chest tightened as he remembered the ache her rejection had brought.
It hurt all the more because of the fact that he had actually
believed she loved him. Why else would a girl from one of
the foremost families in Maine show an interest in him?
He'd lived in a hovel not far from the docks. After his father left them, he and his mother had subsisted on the
meager income she earned from doing laundry and mend-
ing, and whatever he might bring in from laboring on the
local fishing boats.

Only fate could have brought Jed into contact with the
fragile and darkly lovely Nina. One day when the housekeeper had fallen ill, Nina had gone to the market with her
maid. The handle of her basket had broken, and Jed had
stopped to help her retrieve her purchases. Their hands had
inadvertently brushed. Their eyes met. After that, there had
been no holding back the force of their youthful desire.
He'd actually believed she loved him, until there came a
time when he went to their meeting place night after night,
with no sign of Nina. In desperation, he had finally gone
to her home. The harried housekeeper had given him an
impatient look and informed him that Miss Nina had been
married the previous day and was at that moment making
ready to board a ship that would take her to the estates of
her husband, Squire Fairfield, in England. So shocked had
he been that Jed could only back down the steps in disbe-

lief when she closed the door in his face. Clearly Nina had
cared nothing for him, for never had she even hinted at any
of this. In a short time, his devastation had turned to rage,
and he'd vowed never again to allow himself to look to any
woman for anything other than physical release, and never
to one of Nina's social class. They cared for nothing beyond their own comfort and position.

His devastation had come to the point of near madness
when his mother died, some few weeks later. That had been
when he signed on as cabin boy for a voyage that was to
take him from Bar Harbor and the pain of his life.

During the ensuing years, he'd learned much about the
world, including the fact that the only person he needed was
himself. It was a lesson he would not soon forget.

Yet Jed knew that in this instance there was one great
obstacle in his path, despite his self-reliance and determination to find his son. He had no access to the very society
he scorned. His confidence in himself and his abilities
would not gain him entry to the salons and morning rooms
of London society. And that was where he must certainly
begin his quest. But how?

He pushed aside this core of doubt, prodding his horse
to a faster pace. He had no intention of returning to his ship
at Westacre, where its cargo of cotton was being unloaded,
without his son. He'd not told his first mate, David Orsby,
the details of his quest, but he had informed him that he
might be gone for some time. David had shrugged, saying
he would do whatever Jed asked of him, and that the crew
would wait, because they were well paid.

Jed turned his attention to the road ahead. He had just
rounded a sharp bend when he took note of the vague shape
of a coach up ahead. He shifted his mount to the far side
of the lane, which was wide enough for both his horse and
the vehicle. As the clouds passed away from the moon,
casting more light down upon the scene, he paused.

The halted carriage swayed wildly ahead of him, and the four matched black horses danced in the harness. Atop the conveyance, two men struggled violently. *Surely one of them must be the driver,* Jed thought as he dug his heels into the bay's flanks and it started forward. At that moment, from inside the carriage, he heard the sound of a woman's scream.

Jed rose in the saddle and slapped the reins against the horse's rump. His urgency was immediately transferred to his mount, for it reared up and ahead at the same time. They were near to traveling at a gallop when he drew the horse alongside the swaying coach and pulled himself up onto the platform.

For a moment, he hesitated, as he studied the grappling men. Then one of them cried out, "Please, help me, sir!" That was all Jed needed to help him decide which was defender and which attacker. The taller of the two turned, as if meaning to jump from the vehicle, just as the other finished calling out to Jed. But he had acted too slowly to protect himself, for Jed grabbed him by the back of his coat and spun him fully around. The man swung wildly, and Jed ducked. He countered the blow with one of his own and sent the thug reeling over the side of the coach.

The other man, whom Jed was now certain was the coachman, flinched as another scream sounded from inside the carriage. He looked to Jed with eyes rounded in panic. "We must help my lady."

Jed pointed to the fallen man, who lay still upon the ground. "Watch him. I will see to her."

Without waiting to see if his order was obeyed, Jed leapt over the side of the vehicle and reached for the elaborately emblazoned door. As the woman cried out again, he reached into the belt of his breeches and withdrew his pistol. Then he was inside.

A man's voice addressed him immediately. "Blazes, Lloyd, let's be off, shall we?"

Both tone and inflection proclaimed this man a member of the upper class. At that moment, Jed had little time to wonder why a gentleman would be accosting a woman in her coach. He took in the fact that this man was so busy wrestling with the pile of blue silk skirts and other female apparel he held that he had not even bothered to see who he was addressing. Jed could only assume there was a woman beneath all that tangle. He was assured that this was true when an arm appeared from the mass, and her assailant grunted as a blow landed on the side of his head.

With a grunt of irritation, the man renewed his efforts to restrain her, nudging her hooped skirts so far forward that he unwittingly exposed a tantalizing section of female anatomy. The decidedly shapely bottom, encased in soft white bloomers, briefly caught and held Jed's undivided attention. The fine fabric stretched taut as the muscles in the unknown woman's buttocks flexed in her efforts to free herself.

Her attacker's gasp of rage, as the woman's heel connected with his chin, brought Jed to his senses. What kind of rescuer was he, to be leering at the poor woman's backside? What would his mother say, especially when it was she who had taught him to offer help to those in need?

At that moment, the man cried out again in exasperation. "I say, Lloyd, can you hear me? What is the hold up?"

Self-directed amusement colored Jed's voice as he spoke. "I'm afraid that won't be possible. Lloyd is...well... resting."

The man swung around, and his expression was astonished when he saw Jed. "What have you done with Lloyd?" The look in his light gray gaze changed from anxiety to haughtiness as he took in the sea captain's attire. His expression said quite plainly that Jed's snug black pants, white open-necked shirt and black overcoat proclaimed him to be other than a gentleman. Which Jed understood would certainly mark him an inferior in this fool's opinion. He was dressed in a tight-fitting cutaway coat, brown trousers and a multihued brocade vest.

The dapper fellow frowned again as his eyes came to rest on the pistol in Jed's hand. "Now see here, my good man. Just be on your way, and I will forget that you interfered in something that was not your concern." His scowl deepened. "That is, if you have not been so foolish as to kill my friend."

Jed merely smiled. This man was in for quite a surprise if he thought he could intimidate Jed with his superior manner. "I do not know, nor do I care, if your friend lives. And forgive me—" he glanced down at the pistol "—if I point out that, although I'm sure you believe you are being quite magnanimous in regards to myself, you are really in no position to do so."

The blond man looked down his narrow nose, even as he renewed his grip on the woman, who had ceased to struggle when Jed spoke. She jerked away in response, and he spoke to Jed with irritation as he tried to draw her closer to him. "How dare you! Obviously no one has taught you how to treat your betters. I am a member of the English peerage, sir!"

Jed simply shrugged, raising the pistol and bringing the attacker's attention fully to himself. "I think now that you will release this lady."

With obvious reluctance, the man loosened his hold on her. Immediately she rolled away, pressing her back against the opposite door of the coach even as she raised her head to look at them.

As her face became visible beneath the rim of her slightly askew beribboned blue bonnet, time seemed to halt. Jed found himself forgetting for one heart-stopping moment that he was holding a pistol on a member of the British peerage in a strange coach in the middle of the night. He could think of nothing besides the strange, brave beauty of the woman before him.

Because it wasn't just that she was beautiful that gave him pause. Though there was no denying that she was, with her aquiline features and haughty expression. It was the pure defiance in her gray eyes, the look of outrage and regal condemnation she turned upon the man who had dared accost her. Not even a hint of fear was evidenced in those heavily lashed eyes.

She spoke with open contempt, drawing Jed's gaze to her mouth. And in its lushness he glimpsed an unexpected hint of womanly softness that stirred him more than he would have imagined possible. He forced himself to concentrate on her words. "What can have possibly come over you, Reginald Cox? Did you really believe you would succeed in abducting me?"

Jed settled back to watch as Cox shrugged, nodding to him. "I would have done quite well, if it had not been for this brave lothario here, interfering in things." His face took on a petulant expression as he went on. "Though really, Victoria, must you refer to what I was trying to do as abducting you?"

"And what then would you prefer I call it?" She barely glanced toward Jed as the other indicated him, rising with surprising grace, considering the circumstances. She perched, ladylike, on the seat and righted her bonnet with unruffled aplomb, and he began to wonder at the sheer depth of her bravado. Did the woman have no understanding of what had nearly happened to her?

It was when she brushed the dark curls away from her face, even as she continued to eye Reginald Cox with disdain, that Jed noted a barely perceptible trembling in her slender, white-gloved fingers. Sympathy stabbed at his chest. Obviously she was more shaken by what had happened than she would have them know. Obviously she was acting out of true bravery, rather than because of a foolish sense of invulnerability, as some did. He felt a growing admiration that surprised him, since he would not have expected to feel that way about anyone of her class.

Surprise at his own reaction kept Jed silent as Cox shrugged again and said, "I did mean to make an honest woman of you, Victoria. I had nothing less than marriage in mind, and would still continue toward that end, if you would only come to your senses."

The beauty's arched brows rose with haughty contempt. "I wonder that you would not take my repeated refusals as reply enough to convince you to leave me be."

Reginald pursed pouty lips. "Dash it, Victoria, that was what drove me to compel you. I am at my wits' end to have you."

Neither Cox nor the lady took note of the fact that Jed leaned toward the other man. "To have me," she sputtered. "More like to have my wealth and property."

Her remark served to cause the man to flush with embarrassment, but it did not stop him from trying to convince her she was wrong. He reached toward her. "Victoria, you must know how I feel. . . ."

He was halted by Jed's firm grip on his shoulder. The sea captain could now feel the undivided attention of both centered wholly on him. He focused on the man. "That will be enough Mr. . . . Cox."

Clearly, Reginald Cox was not going to give up on this easily. He made a move to pull away from the hold on his shoulder, but Jed's grip held firm. Cox's frustration was apparent even when he raised his nose and tried for a superior expression as he lifted his gaze to Jed's. "Unhand me, you madman. This is really none of your concern. Be

on your way, and I will forget that you intruded where you
were not wanted.''

Jed made no effort to hold back the mocking smile that
curved his lips. ''How very good of you, but again I must
decline to accept your generous offer.'' His expression and
voice then hardened as his grip became what must be painfully tight. ''Get out of the carriage.''

Cox paled, as if finally understanding that he was completely in Jed's power. Slowly, and with clear reluctance, he
followed the larger man without another word.

Victoria Thorn found herself blinking in surprise as she
realized that the two men had exited the carriage. She sat
back on the seat with a groan of self-derision. What in
heaven's name had come over her?

She could not have said. All she did know was that she
had not had a coherent thought since first looking into the
face of her rescuer. Surely, she thought, pressing her hands
to her heated cheeks, her odd sense of disorientation was
nothing more than a strange reaction to nearly being kidnapped, then just as suddenly finding herself safe once
more.

Again she envisioned those heavily lashed sea-green eyes,
that mobile mouth, which had been thinned with dangerous intent as the man spoke to Reginald Cox. He had radiated a kind of hard strength that had nothing to do with
the gun in his hand. Here was a man who knew how to at-
tain what he desired, who knew how to command respect
because of what was inside him. If he had no weapon at all,
Reginald would still have been forced to heed him. It was
equally obvious that he was a man of honor or he would
not have come to her aid.

She did not want to think that her awareness had anything to do with the fact that he was incredibly handsome,
a valiant liberator who had come dressed all in black ex-

cept for his flowing white shirt, as a reckless buccaneer might. That kind of breathless fantasy was for chambermaids and debutantes. Not for mature women, women for whom the well-being of hundreds of people was a daily concern.

But it could not be denied that he was handsome, with his strongly cut features, the angles and hollows having been clearly outlined by the light from the carriage lantern. That same light had played on the pale golden streaks in his dark blond hair. His hard jaw and lean cheeks had not kept her gaze from drifting down to the strong, tanned column of his throat, which was exposed by the open neck of his white shirt.

A shiver rippled through Victoria, though she was not the least bit cold. Her gaze strayed to the now closed carriage door through which the men had passed, even as her ears picked up the sounds of their voices.

It was not difficult to differentiate between her rescuer's tone and the other's. His was rich and authoritative, even without being raised. It was apparent that he was accustomed to giving commands—and having them obeyed. She also noted as he continued to speak that the man's English was strangely accented. Surely, she thought, he must be American.

American. Her own grandfather's brother had gone across the sea to make his fortune there. It was said that he had been a great adventurer who could not be contained by the small islands of Britain. The Thorns had never again heard from him, nor from any family he might have. Would his descendants have the same intractable courage and confidence that this man had displayed thus far?

An angry retort from outside roused her from these thoughts, and Victoria sat up straighter, running her hands over her blue silk skirts. Taking note of the fact that they were trembling, she then clenched them tightly in her lap. She must get hold of herself.

Victoria could only hope that neither Reginald nor her rescuer had taken heed of her upset. It was quite unlike her to become so distraught, and she disliked any sign of weakness in herself. As she was the last surviving member of the Thorn family, it was her duty to meet every challenge with fortitude and heroism.

She could not help casting up a silent prayer that Reginald had indeed given up the notion of abducting her. She could still hardly give credence to the fact that he had been so foolish. Did he actually believe he could whisk her, Lady Victoria Thorn, sole heir to the duke of Carlisle, off to Gretna Green or some such place and marry her against her will?

Victoria had been rejecting his proposals for weeks, and had known that he was growing impatient with her refusals. Never had she imagined that the fortune-hunting Reginald would have the audacity to kidnap her. Regally she raised her finely sculpted chin. The very impudence of him.

Yet in spite of her bravado she did know a flutter of fear at realizing that he might well have succeeded, had it not been for the stranger. The man with eyes the color of a frothy sea.

The fluttering came inside her again, but this time it had nothing to do with fear. There was much that was compelling about the man who had aided her. He was quite unlike any she had ever chanced to meet. Such a mixture of strength and chivalry was definitely unusual and gave Victoria pause for thought.

She was again pulled out of her reverie, by the sounds of angry voices from outside the clarence, and her heart thudded in reaction when they were followed by the retort of a pistol. There was then more shouting, and the sound of hooves thundering off into the distance. What could have happened, she wondered?

Deciding that she must see for herself what was taking place, Victoria reached for the door handle. But she sat back in surprise and sudden unease as the door opened.

Pray God, she murmured silently, it not be Reginald. A sense of relief coursed through her in the next instant as she saw that it was the very man who had rescued her.

He was rubbing the back of his neck gingerly. "I'm afraid they have gotten away. The other one had managed to overpower your driver while I was binding Cox. He hit me over the back of the head with a branch, and they escaped. I am going after them, but I am going to tell your driver to take you directly home."

She held out her hand to halt him. "No, please, let them go. I do not believe Reginald will be of any threat to me now. He would not risk the scandal."

"But . . ." The man's expression was incredulous.

"Please," She broke in. "I wish nothing so much as to put this whole episode behind me. Reginald is really quite a harmless fool, and he will never find the courage to attempt such a thing again."

He frowned in consternation, but she pressed on. "I assure you that this is all for the best. I have no wish to make this incident public. Nor will Mr. Cox, or Mr. Jenkins."

He hesitated as his gaze met hers. "Is there no way that I can convince you? They should be punished."

She shook her head.

As he was obviously not happy with her decision, she breathed a sigh of relief when he shrugged. "As you will." He nodded toward the seat across from her. "May I at least suggest, then, that I see you safely home?" He looked at her questioningly, one dark brow quirked rakishly over those compelling green eyes.

She took a deep breath to steady herself as she realized anew just how attractive he was. The feeling of being safe in his presence had not abated. And in spite of what she had said to him, there was a lingering trace of fear in her at what might have happened if he had not chanced upon them. She gave a barely perceptible nod. "I would be grateful."

He nodded. "I'll tie my horse to the back."

Victoria nodded in return, wondering why she was being so faint of heart as she watched the man leave the interior of the carriage. A moment later he was back, opening the window and instructing the driver to go on. He then settled himself on the seat across from her.

The carriage started off with a slight jolt, momentarily distracting her. It was well sprung, and the motion smoothed out quickly, and her attention was soon drawn back to the man who had come to her aid. Try as she might, Victoria could not help noticing the way the lanternlight set his dark blond hair agleam with golden highlights. Coupled with the deep tan she had previously noted on his face and throat, this evidence made her certain he spent long hours in the sun.

Who was this man? And what strange twist of fate had placed him on this lonely stretch of road so late at night? And just when she needed him? She asked none of the questions dancing through her mind, something telling her he would not welcome her queries.

He leaned forward, drawing her gaze back to his eyes, which were watching her with concern. "Are you all right Miss...?"

"Victoria Thorn, and of course I'm all right," she answered hurriedly as she willed herself to stop the blush that was stealing up from her own throat. It did no good. She could only hope her bonnet would conceal it.

Surreptitiously she ran her gaze over the considerable length of him. As she did so, she realized that his long legs, encased in snug black breeches, were mere inches from her own. He shifted, and she could not help noticing the flexing of the hard muscles in his thighs.

Victoria forced her gaze away from the amazingly stirring sight. What was the matter with her? she asked herself in exasperation. Carrying out her duties as mistress of all her deceased father's lands and finances had given her a maturity far beyond her twenty-three years. Why was she now acting like a schoolgirl?

Obviously concerned at her renewed silence, he asked again, "Are you sure you're all right?"

She nodded slowly as she met that green gaze. Her breath caught in her throat as something powerful yet indefinable passed between them. She felt protected and cared for beneath that steady regard, as she had not since her parent's deaths, three years gone by. Victoria felt a sudden and inexplicable wish for him to hold out his arms and take her into them, as her father would have done. But, she reminded herself as she dropped her gaze to her clasped hands, this man was not her father. Her own reactions to his maleness were reminder enough of that.

Silently she berated herself for her own mad thinking. She had known many handsome men. Victoria had in fact been courted by some of the most attractive bachelors in England on her coming out. Her own unmarried state was due more to a desire to put the matter off than to lack of opportunity. But as she risked a quick glance at him from the corner of her eye, she realized that that did not change what was happening to her now. None of those men had been as devastating to her senses as this one.

In a manner quite unlike her usual direct one, she continued to look at her hands as she answered him. "I am fine, sir. I must thank you now for having come to my aid, though I should certainly have done so sooner."

"There is no need to thank me. Anyone would have done the same."

The modesty of his tone made her look at him. As she answered, her voice was filled with sincerity. "No, I do not believe that *anyone* would have. You must certainly be a man of good character and a brave heart, else *you* would not have done so." He appeared decidedly uncomfortable with her gratitude, which drew her to say, "You must allow me to reward you in some way."

He shrugged offhandedly. "I will accept your thanks as reward enough."

She watched him with growing approval. What a rare man he seemed! Strong, chivalrous, modest, and apparently without greed. Again she tried, feeling compelled to do something for him in return. "Is there nothing I can do for you? You have no idea how much good you have done me. I fear I would have had the dubious distinction of being Mrs. Reginald Cox by morning if you had not happened along."

He laughed ruefully, his teeth flashing white, his eyes sparkling in the lanternlight. "Maybe a reward *is* in order. The crown jewels just might equal a debt of that magnitude."

Ah, a sense of humor as well, Victoria thought as she watched him. The husky sound of his laughter sent a tingle of awareness down her spine. "Truly," she found herself asking, "is there no small thing I can do for you in return for your kindness? I do not even know your name."

Jed sobered as he studied her. His expression was thoughtful, assessing. For into his mind had come the realization that this might just be his opportunity to try to learn something of Nina, or at least to get some idea of where to begin to find her. Yet he hesitated.

As he watched Victoria, saw her gray eyes earnest on his, he felt a strange reluctance to tell her anything about himself or his problems. Some part of him said to get on his horse and never look back. Another part, the one that was bent on locating Nina and his son, told him his resistance had solely to do with the fact that Victoria Thorn was just the type of woman he so wished to avoid.

The crest on the carriage door, the woman's clothing, her regal bearing, all were evidence of a certain social standing. Yet in spite of all that, he had not been able to let her ride off into the night alone, especially knowing that those two men might be lurking about with that hope in mind. After the way Jed had watched his father mistreat his mother, he could not bear to see anyone abused by someone of greater strength.

His discomfort had nothing to do with the way her dark hair curled softly about her delicate cheeks, nor the expression of interest he saw in her undeniably lovely gray eyes—which he knew was only a trick of the light. Surely his wariness was not connected to the way his body tightened when he remembered the view he'd had of the lady's sweetly rounded bottom.

And because his discomfort was not caused by any of those things, he would be a fool indeed to pass up this chance to gain some knowledge of Nina and his child. So thinking, Jed looked at her squarely, not allowing his gaze to stray to the distracting curves that were exposed by the tight-fitting bodice of her blue gown. "My name is Jedidiah McBride. I was on my way to London from the port of Westacre, where I left my ship."

He couldn't help seeing the way her interest quickened at the mention of his ship. Her words confirmed his thought. "You are a sea captain?"

"Yes, I . . . have some business in England."

There was curiosity in her tone as she said, "You are an American, are you not?"

He nodded. Jed continued to face her, not liking to be anything but direct. Still, it was a moment before he could bring himself to say what he wanted to, as she was looking at him with those wide, questioning gray eyes of hers.

Jed forced himself to look away from the hypnotic attentiveness in her gaze. He had to know if she could tell him anything that might help him find Nina. That was all he wanted from her.

He spoke with cool remoteness. "There is a possibility that there is something you could do for me." He could not quite keep the slight hopefulness from his voice as he went on. "Would you know of a family by the surname of Fairfield?"

She frowned as he glanced at her, and he saw that she seemed somewhat surprised by the question. Slowly she shook her head. "Fairfield? I do not know. Is there any more you can tell me?"

Jed frowned himself. "Squire Fairfield."

Her expression grew even more pensive. "Squire Fairfield." After a moment, she looked at him regretfully. "I am very sorry. Are these people some relation of yours?"

He was disappointed, but he tried not to let it show as he shook his dark blond head. "No, no relation of mine." She was watching him very closely, and Jed had the feeling that she was seeing more than he would have liked.

She held up her hands in a gesture of helplessness, confirming his suspicions when she spoke. "I can see that this is important to you. Is there not some other clue you might give me? I feel quite useless in not even being able to help with this small matter."

Their gazes met and held, as Jed found himself thinking that she was indeed very lovely with the gentle glow of the lanternlight on her face. The delicate curves of her cheeks and jaw beckoned a man's lips, as did her sweetly shaped mouth. For one arresting moment, he could have sworn that he saw attraction in those fathomless gray depths. But he knew that could not be. Never would a woman of her world be interested in him, a simple man of the sea.

Yet she seemed genuinely concerned that she had not been able to assist him. She did in that regard appear different from the other women of her kind he had known. For some inexplicable reason, he found himself wondering if he should reveal to this stranger, this English lady, his reason for being here. If she knew more of the story, might then she be able to help him find Nina—and his son?

Yet even as he made the decision, it was almost against his will that Jed found himself reaching into the inner pocket of his coat. He watched her eyes widen as he withdrew the letter and handed it to her.

"What is this?" she asked.

He took a deep breath and exhaled slowly. "It is a letter from a woman I knew when I was quite young. I received it about ten weeks ago. If you would be good enough to read it, I think it will explain itself."

Victoria could only look on the handsome man seated across from her with amazement. Never had she expected this. Realizing that she was staring, Victoria turned her attention to the letter.

Carefully she opened the wrinkled page, which bore the evidence of having been read many times. The message was simple.

Dear Jedidiah,
I hope you will be able to find it in your heart to forgive me for what I am about to tell you. For that is the one hope that has given me the courage to write to you at all.

You see, I am very ill. I am, in truth more painful to
admit even to myself, dying. In order to go to my rest
with conscience clear, I must then tell you something
that I have kept hidden from everyone, including my
husband, for twelve years. You, Jedidiah, are the father of my eleven-year-old son. I ask you not to try
contacting him or myself. As I said, all I ask of you is
your forgiveness. Please try to find it in your heart to
give me that much, though I understand you do not
owe it to me.

Nina

Victoria looked up at the man, not knowing what to say.
"I take it you are the Jedidiah she mentions?"

He nodded. "Yes."

She hardly knew what to say. "How very dreadful for
you! But I did not understand how I can be of assistance. I
do not know anyone by that name. And if you do not mind
my asking, how do you know that Fairfield is her surname? She did not sign it on either the inside or the outside of the letter."

His jaw flexed as he answered her. "I have known the
name of her husband for some time."

Victoria had the impression that he would say no more
on that subject, and she didn't ask. It seemed there were
many long-held resentments at work here. Obviously this
Nina's husband was the Squire Fairfield he sought.

She found herself asking. "Do you have any other information that might help?"

He grimaced. "I know that the letter was posted from
London." His wide shoulders drew her gaze as he shrugged.
"Other than that, I know nothing. I have no leads, no
contacts, not one thing. I only know that to find her I must
gain entry into the circle she inhabits. When you asked if
you could help me in some way..." He shrugged again.

She looked down at her hands, then glanced back to his face as she wondered why this woman had not told him of the child all those years ago. Had she feared that he would not marry her? Victoria could not even imagine that any woman who could have the man before her as her very own would not do so. Thus, the reluctance had to have been on his part.

Although Victoria felt that Jedidiah McBride was in fact a good and decent man, she also thought there might be a hint of ruthlessness in him. She sensed that he would do nothing against his own indomitable will. And, likewise, that nothing he desired could be denied him.

What would it feel like to be desired by this man? A shiver of awareness raced down her spine and she could only pray that he had not seen it.

She tried to focus on what Jedidiah McBride had said to her. Obviously he was determined to find this woman and his child. Doing so might prove very difficult for him. As he had said he knew no one who might assist him. Though she knew many people socially, Victoria could think of no person she would trust to assist a man like Jedidiah McBride with his problem. She, in her own way, was as isolated from London society as he. The responsibilities of her position made it impossible for her to waste time in the frivolous entertainments the London season had to offer. Truth to tell, Victoria cared more for being at her country manor house, Briarwood. It was where she had spent most of her time as a child, where she had lived with her beloved mother and father.

Previous to this night, she would have believed that nothing would threaten the peace of that existence. This attempt to kidnap her gave evidence to the false nature of her security. It seemed that, without a man to protect her, she was vulnerable indeed.

Her searching gaze ran over the man across from her, taking in the wide set of his shoulders, his strong hands, his confident demeanor. The sea captain would have no need to fear anyone. He wore his strength with an easy grace that made him all the more intimidating.

An idea was beginning to insinuate itself into her mind. It was an idea she could not dismiss, though she did make an attempt. Surreptitiously Victoria studied the man seated across from her. He seemed lost in thought, and the tightness of the hands clenched around his knees gave away the tension inside him, his desperation to find this woman. Was he desperate enough to agree to her plan?

There was only one way to find out.

"Mr. McBride," she began, feeling his attention come back to her face. "I have a proposition for you to consider."

She glanced at him and saw that he was looking at her with a puzzled frown. "Yes?" he replied somewhat warily.

She centered her gaze on the hands she held clasped in her lap. "What has happened this evening has made me realize that there is a matter which I have been putting off for far too long." She paused and took a deep breath, then went on, determined not to let him see that she was nervous. "The matter of my marriage." Facing him directly, she wondered what his reaction might be to her blunt statement.

"I see," he told her. But it was obvious that he truly did not see what connection this could have to him.

Quickly Victoria went on. "I have been quite occupied with running my father's estates in these past years since my parents were both killed in a boating accident at Bath—" Her voice broke for a moment, as the years between had hardly dulled the pain of being without them. She forced herself to continue in an even tone. "My father was the duke of Carlisle, and . . ."

He interrupted her, scowling darkly. "Duke—?"

"Yes," she said, not liking the way he was staring at her now. She continued, wondering what had brought about this reaction. "And as his heir I have been left with a great trust in my keeping. I have realized that I should have married long before this. If I had, none of the events that took place this very night would have happened."

His expression grew puzzled. "You obviously have a problem," Jedidiah McBride told her, "but I do not see what it has to do with me."

A frown marred her own brow. "I am getting to that. It seems clear, Mr. McBride, that I have need of a husband, but it seems equally clear that I have need of a protector until such a man is located. I am asking you, sir, to be my protector." She hurried on before he could reply. "In return, I am offering to introduce you to London society. There, you would be able to make inquiries about these people named Fairfield, and your child."

She raised her head and saw that his face was even more thoughtful than before. He looked up at her, his eyes assessing. "Are you sure that you know what you would be doing here? You do not know me, or anything about me. I have just told you that I fathered an illegitimate child. Doesn't that concern you in any way?"

She watched him, her gaze never leaving his as they measured each other. The moment stretched on, and she felt a strange stirring inside her as she looked into those clear green eyes, with not even a hint of fear. Feeling an unexplainable breathlessness that she could only put down to her anxiety that he might refuse, Victoria answered him softly. "No, I am not concerned. That was many years ago, and I do not know what happened between you and this woman. But you have come to do right by your child as soon as you learned of his existence. That is not the action of a dishonorable man. In fact, everything that has occurred this evening has made me sure that you would discharge the duty of protecting me with great diligence. I will not judge you by something that must have happened between you and this woman when you were a boy."

"I was seventeen, and what happened between us was she did not want me," he supplied dispassionately.

Heavens, she thought, *but he had been little more than a child himself!* "More fool she," was all she said in answer.

He seemed more than slightly taken aback and, dared she think it, pleased by her reply. She soon wondered if she had imagined the look of pleasure, for he shrugged noncommittally. "And how long do you believe this business association would last?"

She said, "I have no idea of the exact timing, but I can assure you that I should be able to find myself a husband from among the eligible bachelors who will be attending the season without a great deal of delay. I am not without assets." Her wealth and position were well-known, and were the very things that had made her a target of Reginald's greed.

"I would not deny that," he said, causing her to look at him again. She flushed when she saw the assessing glance he cast over her. Although she realized the man had misunderstood her comment, she did not feel that she could clarify the matter. Not with him studying her like that, those cool green eyes of his making her feel warm in a way she did not understand.

Victoria decided to simply go on with the rest of what she wanted to tell him. "For your part, I would be willing to give you my backing until your parties are found. You will, of necessity, go with me wherever I go. Thus, you may make your inquiries at will." She paused, then went on,

"We shall say that you are my cousin, come from America."

He quirked a brow, the side of his mouth turning up at the same time, and her heart tripped a double beat. "Your cousin?"

She squared her shoulders, doing her best to concentrate on the conversation, not on his mouth, or the way it made her stomach flutter. "My grandfather's brother went off to search for adventure there. We have not heard from him or any descendants he might have, but you see, there is no other way to explain your presence in my home. I simply could not entertain any man who was not a relation to me. It would be completely unacceptable."

"Of course, your kind would expect you to adhere to all the conventions." She sensed a hint of disdain in his tone, and wondered at it. An unpleasant flash of disquiet darted through her.

When he went on, she momentarily forgot that faint unease. "I accept your offer. I will watch over you and make certain that no harm is done to you while you find a husband. In return, you will introduce me to the people who can help me find my child."

She nodded. "It is agreed."

Yet now that they had settled on it, Victoria could not dismiss the tickling feeling of apprehension that lingered as she looked at him. He was watching her, as well, and she had to force herself not to look away from the intensity of his gaze. It was as though he were searching, trying to see if there was something about her that did not please him.

The mere idea of such a thing rankled, but Victoria did not remark on her suspicions, as she had no reason for them. When she went over his actual words in her mind, there was nothing in them to cause her worry.

The sea captain had been nothing but gallant in his rescue of her, a perfect stranger. But the notion that something was wrong could not be totally dismissed, no matter how she told herself that she was being absurd.

Determinedly Victoria pushed her anxiety down, far into the recesses of her mind. She had found a solution to her problems in meeting Jedidiah McBride and was now reacting to him in this way because it put off her real cause for concern—that of finding a husband who would care for her and her father's estates as they should be.

Victoria had no illusions about love. That was not something she expected or even hoped to find. The oft-lauded excitement and fulfillment of that emotion were not for her.

Duty and responsibility must stand in their stead. Then she realized that even as she told herself this, her gaze had strayed quite unaccountably to the handsome stranger who now sat silent on the other side of the carriage.

Chapter Two

Jedidiah opened his eyes and surveyed the elaborately corniced ceiling with a strange sense of displacement. He reared straight up in the huge four-poster bed. As he took in the blue-paneled walls, the heavy oak furniture and the long brocade curtains at the tall windows, the events of the previous night all came back to him in a rush of memory.

He was at Briarwood. The name of the sprawling mansion had been supplied to him by the liveried manservant who had seen him to his room. Even in the soft glow of the moonlight, Jed had been able to recognize that Victoria's three-story sandstone manor house was remarkable in size and structure. The main section was decorated by heavy cornice and sculpted window frames. It was flanked by two equally impressive wings that jutted backward over luxurious lawns. He realized that Victoria's house must certainly rival any of those owned by the queen herself.

Lady Victoria's manor house, he reminded himself as he threw back the covers, then strode across the room to take up his pants from the beige-striped satin chair where he had left them. He would be wise to keep things on a formal footing between himself and the beguiling mistress of Briarwood manor. When he agreed to protect the woman until she found herself a husband, he'd had no idea what he was getting himself into.

She'd said her father had been a duke, and Jed knew that having a title meant something significant here in England. But, being American, he had not been completely cognizant of the implications of the term.

Seeing the house, the liveried servants, the sheer grandeur of the manor's interior, which had been obvious even in the dim glow of the candles that lit the way last night, Jed understood that he had stepped into deep water. He had the feeling Victoria Thorn was someone at the very height of her social class. This realization did not please him in any way. Because of what he had agreed to do, he would be forced to mingle with the most arrogant and useless members of English society. In his experience, the more important the wealthy and highly placed felt, the more thoughtless and ignorant they were.

He wanted to find Victoria Thorn and tell her that he'd changed his mind, that she hadn't made the situation clear. But he knew he wouldn't do that. He'd given his word, and that was that.

What he could do was get on with the business of getting her married as quickly as possible. Once he helped Lady Victoria find herself a suitable husband, then located Nina, he would be on his way with his son. With that thought firmly fixed in his mind, Jed held out his pants in preparation for stepping into them.

At that same moment, there was a soft scratching at the bedroom door. He looked toward it, then down at his own bare length, with a frown of discomfiture. He called out, "Wait one—"

The door swung open.

A female, obviously a serving woman, judging by her dress and the fact that she held a wide silver tray in her hands, stood in the opening. Behind her, her eyes going wide even as a dark flush rose up to stain her cheeks, was none other than Lady Victoria herself.

Jed hurried to cover himself, but not before he took note of the fact that Lady Victoria's wide gray gaze came to light on that most male part of him. Even though the expression of curious wonder and amazement in those eyes was short-lived and quickly replaced by shock, his body's reaction was immediate and unwelcome. He told himself that the forced celibacy of the ocean crossing was the reason for his physical response. It had nothing at all to do with the unseemly fascination in that fleeting glance.

To his further dismay, Jed felt the heat of a blush rise up to color his own cheeks. He had no memory of the last time he had blushed at anything, let alone at having a woman see him without his pants on.

Determinedly he clutched his pants tightly to him, hoping he had moved quickly enough to keep the lady from seeing the evidence of his arousal. He was fairly certain she had never beheld a man in the buff before.

What she might make of it, he had no idea. Judging from her behavior last night, Victoria was not like the women he had known of her class. Her mature manner, undeniable courage, and poise in the face of nearly being kidnapped were proof of that. But he would be willing to bet that she was completely innocent in the carnal sense.

Yet what could he do? Jed looked into her face, quirking a brow as he shrugged. "Is there something I can do for you?" This seemed to at last bring her out of her dazed state.

"Oh, dear," she muttered, raising her hand to cover her mouth, then turning her back to him. "Please forgive me. I had no idea. I did not consider...Clara and I will leave you alone now."

Jed's gaze went to Clara, who was watching him with unconcealed appreciation in her blue eyes. For some reason, he had forgotten the maid, who he now saw was quite attractive, with her golden-blond hair peeking out from beneath her mobcap to curl around her fine features. To his surprise, he felt no pleasure in seeing her appreciative reaction to him, only indifference.

This caused him to scowl anew, though he was not prepared to question the cause of his disinterest.

Victoria Thorn spoke again, drawing his attention to her. The rigid line of her slender back was not alleviated by the soft yellow fabric of the gown she wore. "I will await you in the drawing room. The footman at the bottom of the stairs will direct you."

With that, she grabbed an arm of the obviously reluctant Clara and left without even shutting the door. As Jed moved to close it, he saw the servant throw one last peep over her left shoulder. He slammed the tall oak portal, then leaned back against it as he drew on his pants.

It was only a few minutes later that Jed left the room and made his way down the wide hallway, with growing discomfort. Last night he had had the vague impression of high ceilings and thick carpets. Now, in the light that streamed through the tall windows at either end of the hall, he was struck by the sheer magnitude of the wealth that had bought so much luxury. The walls were lined with fine works of art, which had no doubt been painted by great masters. Grecian statues graced velvet-lined recesses, and rested atop small carved tables that must be considered works of art in themselves.

It was becoming clearer by the moment that he had gotten himself into a position where he would be surrounded by a world that was the epitome of all that he despised. Such possessions set the extremely wealthy apart and made them feel somehow superior to others. How could Victoria, surrounded by all this opulence, be any different? In spite of his first impressions of her as being somehow more genuine and unpretentious, Jed knew that she could not be.

Again he reminded himself of why he had agreed to stay. Firstly for the purpose of finding his son, and secondly because Victoria Thorn needed his help. It was increasingly clear that her incredible affluence was one of the very things that made the lady the target of greedy suitors.

Men such as Reginald Cox were not as scarce as they should be. Though Jed had foiled the bastard's attempts to abduct Victoria, he could not abandon her now.

His mother had taught him better than that. She had always reminded Jed that it was important to help those who needed it. Margaret McBride had herself often shared what little she had with others even less fortunate than herself.

Though she had so much, Victoria had said she needed him. He recalled how visibly shaken she had been last night, despite her efforts to hide her fear. No, he could not abandon her.

Jed could only hope he would keep his own attraction to the lady under control. The memory of the rush of heat he'd felt only minutes ago, when she came to his room and found him without benefit of his trousers, was an intense one. Shifting his shoulders inside his black jacket, Jed shook his head. He was no inexperienced boy, he assured himself with forced confidence. His feelings would be kept at bay.

His boots made no sound on the plush carpet that ran the length of the corridor, but as he stepped onto the wide double staircase that lead to the foyer below, the sound of his heels clattered against the highly polished wood and echoed above him. This drew his gaze upward, where he saw a ceiling exquisitely painted with cherubs and clouds that were so real they looked as if they would be soft and billowy to the touch.

At the foot of the stairs, a footman, uniformed in royal blue, bowed and pointed to a door across the marbled floor. ''You are to go into the green sitting room, if you please, sir." The man rushed to open the white-paneled door for him.

Jed nodded. "Thank you." He was not used to receiving such deferential treatment from servants, was in fact not used to servants much at all. He preferred to wait on himself. When he was in Bridgeport, where the ship building firm was located, he generally stayed with his partner, Peter Cook, and his family. Peter's wife, Jane, and his young sister, Leanne, managed the household chores with the help of an authoritative older woman named Mrs. Muldoon. She was not the least bit servile in her manner, running the house with an iron hand.

With brows raised at the irony of this whole situation, Jed moved past the man and into the chamber beyond. The long room was resplendent with white-paneled walls and plush carpeting. The intricate trim on the walls and ceiling was lavishly bathed in gold. Settees and chairs in various shades of green, ranging from a yellow spring green to deepest hunter, were arranged about the room. Portraits of what Jed was certain were long-dead relatives in wigs and pantalets adorned the walls. The tall windows that ran along the length of the outside wall let in enough light to give the place a warm, cheery feel, despite its grandeur.

All this Jed took in as he made his way to the opposite end of the chamber, where Victoria sat on a light green sofa. She did not meet his eyes as he came to a standstill a few feet from her. All her attention appeared to be centered on the tea tray which lay on the table before her.

While her gaze was trained elsewhere, Jed had a moment to study her more closely than he had the previous night. Then he had had an impression of beauty and courage. Today he was hit with the full force of the femininity of the woman he had agreed to protect.

Her hair was quite dark, nearly black, in fact, and to his surprise seemed to be somewhat unruly. In spite of the tidy bun that had been arranged at the base of her neck, stray wisps had escaped to curl about her forehead and nape. Fringes of thick, dark lashes were outlined against her high cheekbones, which were flushed a healthy peach. Her nose was narrow and finely formed, her jawline clearly but not sharply defined. She wore a gown of some soft gauzy fabric in a delicate butter yellow. The high neckline did nothing to detract from the femininity of her figure, the bodice cut close over her sweetly rounded breasts. Inside him he felt a definite stirring that had nothing to do with wanting to safeguard this woman.

His lips thinned as he recalled his own certainty that he could put aside his interest in her. God help him, Jed thought grimly, he hoped he didn't end by having to protect her from himself.

Victoria did not look at Jedidiah directly as she heard him come to a standstill before her. She could not stop thinking about her own unexpected, and most unwelcome, reaction to seeing him in the altogether.

Yet neither could she ignore him. Trying with all her will, but with little success, to vanquish the memory of his tall, lean, muscular form from her mind, she picked up a blue patterned china cup. "Would you care for tea, Mr. McBride?" To her annoyance, her fingers quivered slightly, and she could only hope that he was not aware of it.

"Do you have coffee?" he asked politely.

She looked up at him. Of course he would want coffee, she told herself. He was an American. "I am very sorry," she told him hurriedly. "I do not. I will ring for the maid."

He stopped her with a raised hand. "No, don't bother. Tea will be fine."

Feeling suddenly awkward and not knowing why, Victoria told herself she must make certain that Mrs. Everard even had the beverage the sea captain preferred. She did want him to be comfortable while he was with them. Hastily she filled a delicate Dresden cup and held it out to him.

Jedidiah McBride reached out, and for a brief moment their fingers brushed as she relinquished the cup to him. A completely unexpected jolt of heat passed from his hand to hers and up her arm. Without thinking, she jerked back, folding her trembling fingers together in her lap.

Heavens, whatever was the matter with her? Although he was the first man she had ever seen without benefit of his clothing, the glimpse had been fleeting and inadvertent. It was quite unfortunate that she had been in such a panic to make certain the sea captain told no one, including Clara, of his true identity that she had accompanied the maid to his chamber. It had been that silly goose Clara who opened the door before being granted entry. The whole thing had been quite hapless, and would not be repeated.

Even as Victoria told herself this, she was again assaulted by the image of the stirring she had glimpsed, in his, well . . . there . . . as she looked at him.

She risked a glance at the man from beneath her dark lashes. He seemed to be stirring his tea with intense concentration, judging by the determined expression on his face. She couldn't help noticing that the delicate china looked even more so in his strong hands.

Because of his preoccupation, she was emboldened to look at him more closely. Goodness, but he was more handsome than she had remembered. Last night, there had been only the lanternlight in the carriage, and then candles when they reached Briarwood. She'd also been more shaken by what had happened than she cared for anyone else to know even now.

Sunlight did nothing to diminish Jedidiah McBride's attractiveness. If anything, he was even more compelling with the sunlight bringing his sun-streaked dark blond hair to vibrant life. Her gaze dipped lower, to where his lean jaw was lightly stubbled with dark gold hair. It looked coarser in texture than that on his head, and she wondered if it would feel so to the touch. Her curious eyes moved on. The black coat he had donned over his open-necked white shirt was rumpled from his altercation with Reginald, as were his close-fitting black breeches. His high black boots were scuffed and dusty, but the relaxed arrogance of his stance told her that Jedidiah McBride was not in the least concerned about his disordered state. To her surprise, Victoria did not find his slightly unkempt appearance distasteful, but somehow strangely appealing.

Before she could even begin to contemplate the reason for this, Jedidiah looked up at her, his brow quirked in an impatient query. Victoria felt a flush stain her throat. Heavens, she was being rude beyond imagining. Hurriedly she indicated the settee opposite her. "Please forgive me, it seems I have completely forgotten my manners today." Her blush deepened as she remembered anew what had occurred upstairs earlier.

After he was seated, she took a deep breath, knowing she had best put the matter to rest as soon as possible. Victoria began, "Mr. McBride, let me begin by apologizing for what happened.... I had no intention... What I am trying to say is that I had no right to come to your room this morning. I was simply eager to talk with you. I meant to make certain that you did not give away your real identity to anyone. Not even to the members of my household. For the purpose of keeping our secret, all must believe you to be my cousin." She stopped, then started again. "I had no idea Clara would just open the door. You see, the servants are accustomed to having few people here besides myself, and have grown less formal than they might otherwise be...."

She glanced at him and found him looking as uncomfortable as she felt. He did not meet her gaze as a dark flush colored his strong throat. She found her eyes lingering there. For some reason known only to whimsy, Victoria suddenly wondered what it would feel like to touch the ridge of muscle that ran down the side of his neck and disappeared beneath the collar of his shirt.

He cleared his throat, drawing her bemused gaze back to his face. Thankfully, the man appeared totally unaware of her madness. She forced herself to concentrate on what he was saying. "Lady Victoria, please don't go on. I will not tell anyone anything other than what we agreed to last night." He paused. "As to the other matter, there is no need to apologize. I understand, and it is already forgotten by me. I hope that you will forget what happened, as well."

As Victoria listened to the delicately put reply, she found herself thinking again what a very gentlemanly man he really was, despite his lack of noble birth. Her wayward attention wandered over the length of him once more. She found herself regretting the fact that Jedidiah must change his mode of dress to a more formal one in order to fulfill their purpose. There was something very stirring about the casually masculine cut of his captain's attire. There was no denying that he wore it with unexpected elegance. Many a man of her own acquaintance could benefit from emulating Jedidiah's nonchalant attitude toward his appearance. For all the money they spent on their perfectly tailored coats, trousers and highly polished boots, they could not compete with his effortlessly graceful masculinity.

Again she realized that Jedidiah McBride was waiting for her to answer. She blushed to the roots of her hair. "I... Then it will be as you ask. We will forget what happened, and start afresh." But even as she said the words, Victoria knew it would not be as easily done as said. Never had she thought that a man could be so very interesting, even handsome, without his clothing. The brief glimpse she'd had of him had been enough to show Victoria that the way his smooth skin lay over the hard muscles of his body was quite pleasing to her. Nor had she been completely blind to Clara's reaction to the man. As these thoughts ran though Victoria's mind, she was doubly careful not to allow her gaze to stray to the area at the top of his thighs.

Determinedly she concentrated on Jedidiah's face as he nodded and gave her a crooked half smile. Unexpectedly, her heart turned over in her breast. Was there no end to the effect he had on her?

She nearly sighed aloud with impatience toward herself. Jedidiah McBride was here to help her with her problem. He had his own life and future. There would be nothing more between them when their bargain was met. She would remember that, if she knew her own good.

In the three years since her parents had died, she'd learned to control herself and her emotions. It was the only way she could have gotten through her grief, then accepted the enormous responsibility of running her father's properties and business interests. She called upon those skills of self-control now. She must begin her efforts to find a husband as soon as possible.

Almost as if he had read her mind, Jedidiah McBride looked up from his cup, his expression filled with determination, and said, "Well, where do we begin to look for a husband?"

Victoria gave a start, his question disturbing her for some unknown reason. Then she told herself that this was completely ridiculous. She should be grateful that he was anxious to get started. It was further proof that he was not some charlatan bent on taking advantage of her. But the feeling of irritation remained, even as she answered in a matter-of-fact tone. "We will, of course, be going up to London. It being May, the season is on, and most of society's eligible bachelors will be attending."

He nodded in approval. "Nina's letter was sent from London. It seems the best place to begin looking for her, as well."

"I'm glad that both our needs will be so well served," she replied smoothly. Victoria reached to pour herself a cup of tea before continuing. "There is much to be done before we can go on to London. The first thing we must do is see you outfitted as a gentleman. That will mean new clothing. Toward that end, I have sent for the man who tailored much of my father's attire. Although he lives in Carlisle, which is the local town, he is a superb tailor and will turn you out very nicely."

Jedidiah's cup clattered in his saucer, making her look with surprise into a pair of stormy sea-green eyes. "I cannot agree to that," he informed her curtly.

Her delicate brows raised in irritation at his unexpected brusqueness. "But I must insist. How can I introduce you into society as my cousin from America if you are not dressed as one of them?"

He scowled in displeasure, setting his cup and saucer carefully on the tray. "Lady Victoria, I had not realized that I would be expected to purchase a dandy's wardrobe in order to fulfill my obligations to you. What good would it be to me to spend hundreds of pounds on clothing I will never wear again?"

She smiled at this. The funds that would be necessary to purchase his clothing would not be missed by her, and quite fairly could be considered her responsibility, since it was she who required his changed manner of dress. "That will not be your concern," she told him. "I myself will see to that expense."

"You will not!"

His vehemence caused her to pause, but then she went on, trying to be reasonable. "Please, you must realize that you will be accompanying me to whatever social functions

I need to attend in London. We must not appear to be anything other than the cousins we have agreed upon. As I told you last night, it would not do for me to have you in my home without benefit of a chaperone if you are not related to me in some way. I have no female relation who could act as such. If I did, I might not find myself in this precarious position. The fact that I am alone is what gave Reginald the impression he might kidnap me without fear of retribution. As my cousin, you will be required to present yourself in a certain way, even if you are from America."

His eyes narrowed as he listened. "And what does that mean? Would it be too much for your snobbish society matrons to believe that a mere sea captain could be the cousin of the noble and wealthy Lady Victoria Thorn?"

Victoria watched him closely, hearing again the tone that had so disturbed her last night. This time she could not put it off to some other cause. His disdain for society could not be missed.

"Are you all so very democratic in America, then? Is everyone treated equally regardless of their social or financial situation?"

For some reason, her question appeared to irritate him far more than she would have imagined, for a muscle flexed in his jaw, his hands clenched and unclenched in his lap and his gaze was trained on the blue sky outside the window. It was some moments before he seemed to relax enough to reply. And when he did, she could hear the mocking irony in his tone. "No. It is not different in America. There, too, who you are and what you have is more important than anything, including loyalty."

Victoria could only study him for a long moment, realizing that he had just given her a clue as to the reason for his poor estimation of her kind. She wondered if this unfavorable opinion was connected to the infamous Nina. Had she rejected him because she felt she was better than he? She could not help thinking that this woman must indeed be a fool. Jedidiah McBride was handsome, intelligent, well-spoken, strong, and master of his own ship. One would need to have keener eyes than hers to find some flaw in him, other than the fact that he might be too obstinate and bent on keeping others at a distance.

What in heaven's name was she to do with the man in London? They would, in their search for a suitable mate for her, be moving among the very highest orders of English society.

He spoke, interrupting her thoughts. "I . . . Forgive me. I had no right to talk to you that way. You have done me no wrong, have in fact agreed to do me a great service in helping to find my child. I will do whatever is necessary."

Victoria felt a rising sense of compassion for this strong, intractable man. He must feel a great sense of longing for his child, if he was prepared to do something so unpleasant in order to find the boy.

She said, "I am very sorry for what this woman named Nina did to you. It was wrong, and had little or nothing to do with her social station. She was obviously just a foolish and selfish woman."

He looked at her with an expression of displeasure and surprise, clearly not happy that she should broach the subject. To her amazement, he did answer her, though the words caused her to frown. "She was a product of her class."

"The nobility are like everyone else. Some work hard and care about doing good, others live their lives for nothing but their own pleasure."

"I'm sure you are right," he told her, but the set expression on his face gave the lie to the words.

She wondered if there was more to this than a woman's rejection. Jedidiah McBride did not seem the type of man to let such a thing color his thinking so completely.

Victoria's thoughts returned to their original subject. "As we were discussing, you will have need of a new wardrobe. The very fact that it is for my benefit makes me feel I must certainly pay any expenses incurred in attaining it. You have already done much to help me, and I do not wish to inconvenience you further."

His expression grew obstinate as he scowled at her. Victoria could not help frowning in annoyance herself. What had she done now?

He spoke slowly and distinctly, leaving her in no doubt as to the fact that this would be his final word on the matter. "I will purchase my own clothing. I will buy only what is absolutely necessary to get me through the next weeks. When I am finished with the garments, they can be given to someone who has an interest in such foolishness. You will not be paying for them."

His dictatorial tone rankled. Yet, as her wayward gaze traversed the masculine length of him, Victoria had an unconscionable desire to tell him his garments would be of no use to anyone of her acquaintance. She knew no one with such wide shoulders, flat belly and slim hips. Victoria forced herself instead to concentrate on the fact that the stubborn man was being so very unpleasant. With a great force of will, she made herself answer with cool irony. "Thank you. I appreciate your amenability." But as she rose to her feet, she could not prevent herself from adding, "I can only hope that our purpose is accomplished quickly, so you can rid yourself of *everything* you find distasteful with all possible haste."

He stood as well, looking decidedly uncomfortable with her veiled sarcasm, but he made no reply. Obviously he felt it was better to allow the matter to rest.

But he had one last thing to say. "Your gratitude, although flattering, is somewhat misplaced. You are doing a favor of equal value for me. This is a business arrangement between us. You owe me nothing besides that which we've already agreed on."

She watched him for a long moment, then nodded. "Very well." Jedidiah was simply echoing her own sentiments. She ignored the tiny jab of regret in her chest.

Forcing a smile of deliberate civility, Victoria changed the subject. "I would assume you are hungry. I have asked that breakfast be held for you in the informal dining room. I hope you will find it to your liking." She met his eyes briefly. "Now I ask you to excuse me, for I must attend to some business matters myself. We will be having luncheon in the informal dining room. Later this afternoon, Mr. Randsome will arrive to see to your new wardrobe." She paused, then added, "I hope you will not mind if I meet with the two of you."

He nodded, his sea-green eyes cool, expressionless. "Not in the least."

It was clear that he meant to accept whatever was necessary to get the matter settled. With nothing more to add, she turned to go, but his voice halted her. "Lady Victoria?"

Victoria swung around to face him.

He said, "I will need to send a message to my first mate. I have to inform him of my whereabouts, in case he needs to contact me."

"Of course. My servants are at your disposal."

He grimaced, but made no other comment than to say, "Thank you."

Chapter Three

With that, Victoria left him and went to what she still thought of as her father's study. From behind that enormous black lacquer desk, he had directed not only his continued financial success, but also the well-being of the people he was responsible for.

She was accountable for doing the same. She would not allow thoughts of Jedidiah McBride and his stubborn American independence to distract her from her work. Many people depended on her being clear in her thinking. Victoria seated herself at the desk and rang for her estate manager, with whom she had a standing appointment.

As she waited, she thought about the many hours she had spent at this desk, the efforts she had made to fill her father's proficient shoes. In the beginning, she had been frightened and uncertain about fulfilling his responsibilities with even a modicum of competence. In the end, she had come to realize that she must trust in her own judgment. After all, there was no one else. It was because she had learned to trust herself that Victoria told herself to accept her first impression of Jedidiah McBride.

Her parents would have approved of the American. Her father had always said a man must be judged by his action and not by his title. And Victoria knew that anyone who came to her aid so gallantly would have earned no criticism from her mother.

Once more she asked herself what it was about Jedidiah McBride that awakened her. Perhaps, she told herself hopefully, he was not the cause. She recalled the start of awareness she had felt when his hand brushed hers. Perhaps it was her own realization that she must marry that made her begin to feel more awareness of the opposite gender.

A discreet cough brought her attention back to the present. The estate manager, Robert Fuller, stood waiting for her. His quiet demeanor and conservative brown attire did not disguise the keen intelligence in his brown eyes. Victoria knew him to be a man who missed little, a man able to read most people and situations quite accurately. It was one of the reasons he was so valuable to her, but today, especially when she considered what she had been thinking, those skills seemed less desirable than usual.

Victoria flushed, clearing her throat and feeling decidedly grateful that the man could *not* read her thoughts. She also felt a trace of irritation with herself. She had no cause to think of the obstinate sea captain in any but the most impersonal of ways. As the man had told her himself, theirs was a business arrangement.

Refusing to even acknowledge any hint of regret, Victoria forced her mind to concentrate on the present. Her duty must not be forgotten. "Mr. Fuller, please be seated. I'm sure there is much to be seen to, as I have decided to go up to London for at least a part of the season. Shall we get to it?"

If he had indeed noted her agitation, Mr. Fuller gave no indication of it, for with a nod he sat down and opened his case. Victoria felt herself flushing again. Of course he had seen nothing. It was her own ridiculous fascination with

Jedidiah McBride that made her think otherwise.

Determinedly she put him out of her mind.

Some two hours later, Victoria had seen to innumerable matters, including her approval of the distribution of extra funds to the orphanage she supported. She had also refused to increase the amount paid to the greedy blackguard who transported the coal from her mines to the railroad. She'd done some checking and found that the man already earned more than most of his counterparts. Victoria had an innate sense of fairness that would not allow her to cheat others, but she was equally careful about not being swindled herself.

When Mr. Fuller had gathered up his books and notes, she left the study and went to her own bedchamber to freshen up before luncheon. Victoria's room was adorned in ivory and varying shades of rose. She and her mother had decorated the room together when she was sixteen. Even if it hadn't been such a pleasant and peaceful decor, Victoria did not think she would ever be inclined to change it. Just waking up and seeing the deep rose hangings above the bed called to mind her mother's delicate floral scent and the sound of her gentle voice as they had viewed bolt after bolt of fabric, until they found just the right shade to match the rosebud centers in the brocade upholstery on the chairs.

Victoria sighed with unconscious longing. The wound of her parents' passing was not so fresh as it had once been, yet she still missed their loving presence in her life.

Enough, she told herself. There was no sense bemoaning her fate. It was fortunate that she had little time to dwell on her loneliness. Besides, she would soon have a husband to lessen the sadness, she reminded herself with determination, though the thought did little to soothe her.

Going to the dressing table, Victoria sat down and viewed herself in the gilt-edged mirror. For the first time since she

was a young girl, she found herself wondering how she
would appear to a man.

There was certainly no hint of fashionable beauty in her
regular features. She lacked the pursed lips, blue eyes and
sweetly rounded face that found such favor in the eyes of
those who decided such things.

Her own gray eyes, though pleasant enough and thickly
lashed, were too direct, her mouth was too full, her cheekbones were too high. No, she thought, shaking her head
regretfully, there was not a hint of great beauty in her. Then
her full mouth thinned in irony as she acknowledged that
this lack did not mean she was completely undesirable. The
vast fortune and social position she had been left were attractive enough for many to seek her out.

Since her very earliest realizations that she would someday marry, Victoria had wished to be treated as a woman
first and the daughter of a duke second. No man besides
Jedidiah McBride had ever done that. For that was exactly
what he had done by coming to her aid with no notion of
who she was or what she stood for.

Her hand drifted of its own accord to smooth the soft
dark curls at her temples. What would Jedidiah have done
if he had not found out that she was a noblewoman, one of
the breed he so clearly disdained?

For a brief moment last night in the carriage, when he
looked at her, she'd thought... But no. Not since discovering who she was had he given any hint that he might be
attracted to her.

She frowned at her reflection, her fingers tracing the lace
collar that edged the neckline of her yellow gown. Even
though the hooped confection was of the very latest design, with its wide lace-trimmed sleeves and multitiered
skirt, it certainly was not her best color.

Surely she had something more... But she resisted the
urge to summon Betty to her chamber. The maid would

wonder what was amiss if her mistress changed for the midday meal. She never did so.

She stood abruptly, knowing there was no time for such frivolity, and absolutely no need for it. There was no reason to worry about her appearance simply because a man happened to be in residence, even if he was undeniably handsome and made her heart turn over when he smiled at her. Victoria already was overdue in meeting with the head cook to go over the next week's menus. By the time she was finished with that, the luncheon would be ready to serve.

It would not be polite to keep either the servants or Mr. Jedidiah McBride waiting. She felt a strange fluttering in her belly at the thought of seeing him again. Her immediate attempts to still the sensation were not as successful as she would have wished.

Victoria was just giving the cook one final suggestion for a change in menu when there was a knock on the drawing room door. She called out, "Enter," then turned to finish what she had been saying as one of the footmen came into the room. "Beef on Tuesday, I think, Mrs. Everard, rather than the usual chicken." Something about Jedidiah McBride told her he was a man who preferred beef to chicken.

The cook looked at her mistress in obvious surprise. "Beef on Tuesday, my lady?"

Victoria was aware that they had been eating chicken on Tuesdays for as long as she could recall. "As I'm sure you are aware, my cousin from America is visiting us. I wish to make him comfortable and content while he is here. His visit comes as a welcome surprise to me. Who would have thought that Great-uncle Lionel's grandson would make an appearance here in England. For years no one had any clue as to what had become of the family adventurer."

Mrs. Everard smiled at her mistress with the proper mixture of fondness and deference. "It is a true wonder, and very good to see that you have family again." The cook lowered her blue eyes and nodded her gray head. "I will see that there is a nice roast laid on that day."

Victoria nodded in return, glad to have the housekeeper accept her explanation for Jedidiah McBride's presence so readily. She could only hope it would go so well once they began to introduce him to society. "Thank you, Mrs. Everard. You are, as ever, most accommodating. Also, I wish to inform you that there will be no need to prepare a menu list for the next week. We will be going to the London house to attend some of the events of the season."

The head cook curtsied and turned to go with a self-satisfied smile at the compliment. Victoria halted her. "One last thing, Mrs. Everard."

The robust woman swung back to face her. "Yes, my lady."

"Coffee."

"Yes, my lady?"

"My cousin prefers coffee to tea. I would appreciate your seeing that he has some of that beverage each morning."

Another curtsy. "As you wish, my lady." She left the room.

Victoria then turned to the footman. "Yes, Charles?"

"I have been sent to inform you that Miss Mary has arrived."

Victoria made a soft noise of surprise even as she stood and hurried across the room to the door, which the footman opened for her. She had forgotten having asked Mary to lunch with her. Which, she told herself, was not completely irresponsible of her, considering the events of the past twelve hours.

Should she tell Mary the sea captain's true identity? Not since they'd become friends as children had Victoria kept any secret from her.

Hurrying across the foyer to where her best and only true friend awaited her, Victoria held out her hands. "Mary, how good it is to see you. How is your father?" She studied her friend with true concern. There were faint shadows beneath her golden-brown eyes, and Mary sighed as she removed her straw bonnet and ran a hand over her gold-streaked brown hair. The hat was prettily decorated with dried flowers from her garden, and was simple in design, as Mary preferred things to be. She wore no hoop beneath her dark blue skirts, having told Victoria that she had no use for such conceits when the device made its appearance the previous year. She felt it did not offer her enough freedom in her walks across the moors, but there was little of the accustomed energy in Mary's movements as she turned back to her friend.

Victoria knew that the reverend's illness was beginning to take its toll on his daughter, though she would never complain. Mary's unstinting devotion to the sick man was one of the very reasons she insisted on having her friend to luncheon on a regular basis. Knowing how important this weekly outing was to Mary's well-being made Victoria flush with shame at having forgotten it.

Victoria tried not to show how flustered she felt as she listened to Mary, who replied with sad resignation. "Father is the same. Mrs. Withers was good enough to agree to sit with him for a few hours so I could come." She paused, studying Victoria with those unwaveringly direct golden eyes of hers, then said, "Why, Victoria, you had forgotten I was coming." As ever, she had been able to read her mind. Her tone was more amused than upset, effectively alleviating some of Victoria's remorse.

Despite her troubled preoccupation with Jedidiah Mc-Bride, Victoria gave a self-deprecating laugh. "I am afraid you have me there."

Mary's father was the vicar of the church in Carlisle, and a very learned scholar. Victoria had gone to him for lessons for years, and Mary had been present at those lessons. The bond that had been forged from the first day at the age of six was stronger than iron. Under no circumstances could Victoria keep a secret from her, and that included the truth about Jedidiah McBride's identity.

Mary was the one person with whom she must not stand on ceremony, which made Victoria cherish their friendship all the more. Even after the decision to tell all was made, Victoria felt an unexpected sense of shyness at the idea of speaking of Jedidiah to her friend.

Not wishing to question the cause of this feeling, she leaned close to the slightly shorter Mary. "I have so much to tell you."

Even as Mary's eyes widened, displaying her obvious curiosity at her friend's words, Victoria took her arm and pulled her into the library. After first making sure it was vacant, she pushed the other woman down into one of the leather chairs that sat before the lacquered desk.

Victoria remained standing, feeling too agitated to sit. She only hoped that Mary would not think she had gone mad. In spite of her self-professed disregard for propriety and convention, Mary was quite levelheaded, and Victoria very much respected her opinions on all matters.

As Victoria began her story, Mary settled back in her seat to listen. Only when the attempted kidnapping was mentioned did she make any sound, interrupting with a gasp. "Victoria, how can you stand there so calmly and tell me this? Have you called the law?"

Victoria shook her head. "No, but really, there was no need. You do not know Reginald Cox, but believe me, he is a coward of the worst order. The only reason I have any kind of acquaintance with him is that his mother and mine were friends as girls. When we were children, he sometimes visited Briarwood with her.''

When Mary opened her mouth as if to say more, Victoria stopped her with a raised hand. ''If you'll allow me to finish, you'll understand why he is no threat to me.'' The woman subsided, folding her hands in her lap, though she appeared no less concerned.

The horrified expression on her face was soon replaced with satisfaction when Victoria went on to tell of her unexpected rescue by the sea captain, Jedidiah McBride. As she continued to describe the events that had taken place since that fateful meeting, Mary began to smile.

Only when Victoria had finished did she speak. ''My, Victoria, but you are a dark horse.''

Victoria frowned at her. ''And what do you mean by that? It seemed like the most natural solution to ask him to be my protector. He had already proven himself quite capable, and he did have need of my help in return.''

Mary shook her head, eyeing her friend closely. ''That is not what I mean, and you know it. What I mean is that you are attracted to him.''

Far too quickly, Victoria reacted. ''I am not.'' But she knew that the words were a waste of time for she had never been able to hide anything from the other woman. The truth was that she did find him quite handsome, but there was no more to it than that. ''Well, not in the way you think. Besides, it wouldn't matter even if I was. He has quite a dislike for any person of high rank or social position.''

Mary was thoughtful, her finger worrying her full lower lip. ''I wonder why? You say he is well-spoken and has a gentleman's understanding of good manners.''

Victoria perched on the edge of the other chair. ''He did inadvertently tell me something that makes me think this woman, this Nina, rejected him because she felt he was beneath her. Yet I think there might be something more, something he doesn't want to disclose.''

''It seems there is some mystery to this man, this handsome paragon of bravery and intellect,'' Mary said. ''I can hardly wait to see him for myself.''

A blush stained Victoria's cheeks. Had she really described Jedidiah that way? No wonder Mary had come to the conclusion that she was attracted to him.

At that moment, the bell sounded to announce the midday meal. ''Heavens!'' she cried. Standing, she took Mary's hand. ''There is no more time to discuss it. You'll be seeing for yourself in a few moments.''

''I am most anxious to do so,'' Mary said, her golden eyes growing brighter with curiosity and anticipation as she followed her friend from the library.

Victoria paused outside the small dining room, smoothing her hands over her full skirts and taking a deep breath. As she looked at Mary, Victoria saw the expectant expression on her pretty face and could not help wondering what *she* would make of the American. Clearly her friend was willing to keep an open mind so far. If she thought him anything but the decent man Victoria believed him to be, the vicar's daughter would not hide it.

She realized she could not put off the moment any longer, knowing the man was very likely waiting for them. But she could not help interjecting a note of warning. ''Not a word, now, until we are alone. Then you can feel free to say whatever you like about him.''

With a frown of consternation, Mary answered her, ''But of course, Victoria. Am I not the soul of propriety?'' Only the sparkle in her golden eyes gave away her amusement.

Victoria would not be drawn. She was far too nervous.

On entering the cheerful room, with its bright yellow walls and dark walnut furnishings, Victoria saw that Jedidiah was just coming through the door opposite them. He paused in seeming surprise on seeing Mary standing there beside her, then greeted them both with a slight bow. "Ladies."

"Mr. McBride," Victoria responded, feeling decidedly disturbed at the way her heart thudded at the sight of him. It really was quite silly of her to react so every time she saw the sea captain. She also knew she could not allow her interest to show in the slightest of ways without Mary taking note of it.

Victoria turned to her friend, purposefully keeping her tone cool. "May I present my guest, Mr. Jedidiah McBride?" She then turned to face him. "Mr. McBride, my dear friend Miss Mary Fulton."

He bowed again, with a show of elegant manners that would have given any nobleman cause for pride. "How do you do, Miss Fulton? I am very pleased to meet you."

Victoria watched Jedidiah McBride with scrutinizing eyes. She was beginning to realize that there was more to the man than he had alluded to. Last night he had been a gallant soldier rescuing her in the darkness; this morning he was a stubborn man holding his disdain for the social elite before him like a proud flag. And now, meeting Mary, he appeared the consummate gentleman.

Which man was the true Jedidiah McBride? Perhaps all. And that, Victoria realized, made him even more fascinating.

Glancing at her, Victoria saw that Mary was staring at the sea captain with her mouth agape. She gave her lovely friend a surreptitious nudge.

Mary immediately recovered herself enough to form an equally formal rejoinder. "As am I . . . Mr. McBride." The brief glance she cast toward Victoria from the corner of her eye told the taller woman that she would indeed have much to say when they were alone.

Victoria motioned self-consciously toward the table, which had been laid with her grandmother's favorite silver and the Dresden china. "Please, won't you sit down?" She went to the head of the table.

Even as Mary took the seat to her left, Victoria could feel her penetrating gaze. Victoria deliberately trained her attention on Jedidiah. Facing him proved only slightly less uncomfortable than facing Mary. He was watching her with that one mocking brow arched over his right eye.

For some reason, Victoria had the distinct feeling that he was aware of her discomfort with the situation and was amused by it. That prickled, and she raised her chin in regal defiance.

No matter how uncomfortable this meal became, she would not allow Jedidiah McBride to get the best of her. Or, at least, she amended as he smiled and her heart skipped in response, she would not allow him to know that he had.

Jedidiah studied the two women while trying to appear not to. Victoria appeared to be completely occupied with filling her plate from the silver dishes that were presented to each of them in turn. The one Victoria had introduced as Mary seemed equally interested in him.

She smiled at him openly when she caught him glancing her way, and he could not help smiling in return. There was something very refreshing about the pretty woman, with her golden-brown hair and her eyes the color of a chunk of African amber he had once seen. There seemed not the slightest hint of artifice or pretension in her. "So, Mr. McBride," she began without hesitation, her curiosity apparent. "How long have you been in England?"

Taking a sip of the wine that had been poured into the crystal glass in front of him, Jed smiled. "Two days."

She nodded thoughtfully. "I wonder, is it very different from where you are from?"

He could feel Victoria's gaze upon him as he answered. "I am not really from anywhere. I live on my ship, the *Summerwind*. You could say that I am based out of Bridgeport, Connecticut. That is where our shipping firm, Cook and McBride, is located."

"Our?" she asked.

Jed scowled. He wasn't sure now that he wanted to answer all these questions, didn't want this situation to become personal. He glanced over at Victoria, and the way she was watching him made him wonder if she knew of his reluctance to talk about himself.

"Well?" Mary prodded unashamedly.

Jed told himself it didn't matter if they knew some things about him. It wouldn't really change anything. He and Victoria Thorn had a business arrangement, but he continued to be aware of her intent gaze as he went on. "'Our' refers to myself and my partner Peter Cook. His father, Sebastian, was the founder of Cook Shipbuilding. I... When I was eighteen, I went to work for them in the factory. As the years passed, the firm wasn't doing well. The type of vessel they were producing was being phased out by the advent of the steamship. I, well... I came up with a design that Sebastian claimed brought them out of the red. It was a sailing ship with a large hold, but a narrower hull that increased its speed. When Sebastian died..." He hesitated for a moment as he thought of the kindness of the man and how good he had been to him. "When he died, he was generous enough to leave me a half interest in the business."

Mary watched him with round eyes. "You relate it all so modestly Mr. McBride. Surely you are quite brilliant to have come up with such a design. How proud you must be."

Jed could not restrain a satisfied nod as he thought of the ships. "Those ships are beauties, all right. Peter and I own the first two of that model, the *Summerwind* and her sister, the *Winterwind.*'' Building those ships, having Sebastian and his family accept him, those things had changed Jed's life. Yet he'd never quite gotten over feeling as if he were an interloper, no matter how they behaved differently.

And the Cooks had come to accept him on his terms, understanding that he could not allow himself to come too close to anyone. That would all change now that he had a son. His child would be the recipient of the love he had kept locked inside himself.

He looked up then, with a self-conscious expression, feeling as if he had already given away too much. "Enough about me, Miss Fulton. Why don't you tell me something about yourself?" He smiled at her with as much charm as he could summon up.

He was surprised to hear her laugh. "Why, Mr. McBride, are you trying to change the subject?"

This time he could not restrain a genuine grin. "Yes, Miss Fulton, I am."

Her eyes sparkled as she replied. "Then I shall allow you to do so."

His gaze went to Victoria, who had said nothing throughout the exchange, simply listening with avid interest. When their gazes met, she flushed and turned her attention to her meal. As he looked at her, he realized that though he found Mary Fulton quite attractive, with her delicate features and direct gaze, she seemed somehow to fade next to the regal beauty of Victoria Thorn. This realization did not please Jed in the least.

He had no desire to find Victoria Thorn exceptional in any way. It was sheer madness on his part to do so. She represented everything he disdained, extreme wealth and social position, not to mention her titled status.

Yet he cast a surreptitious glance from her to Mary Fulton and back. Did the fact that this refreshing woman was Victoria's friend say something about her? Something that gave lie to his beliefs?

This very morning, she had told him that not all aristocrats were the same. That they were both good and bad, like anyone else.

Jed gave himself a mental shake as he turned his attention to the roast pheasant on his plate. What Victoria said might have some validity where she was concerned, but he did not think for a moment that she was being truly honest with herself as far as her peers were concerned. The power and privilege of their circumstances held them above reproach.

And God help those who had not been born to that same lofty state. Or those who had been cast out for some perceived offense against the rules of society. Cast out and forgotten, no matter how young and foolish they might have been.

As his mother had been by her own family when she had fallen in love with and married his father.

Chapter Four

Victoria was apprised of Mr. Randsome's arrival later that afternoon. She thanked the maid who came to inform her and sent her to fetch Jedidiah.

She hadn't seen him since luncheon, when he had chatted so amiably with Mary. Jedidiah had been far less cryptic and jealous of his privacy than he appeared to be with her. Victoria was sure she would never have learned so much about him if Mary had not arrived for luncheon. He'd even come to the door with them when the vicar's daughter left.

What she did not know was why this bothered her so much. Apparently without even trying, Jedidiah McBride was driving her to distraction. One moment he could be intractable and stubborn. The next he could be charming and attentive, as he had proved himself to be with Mary over the midday meal.

Victoria did not know when she had last heard her friend laugh so much, which of course was very welcome, considering the strain she was under, caring for her father. The reverend was not expected to recover from the consumption that had ravaged his once robust frame, and Mary worked tirelessly to keep him comfortable.

Why, then, did Victoria not feel more cheery?

Squaring her slender shoulders in preparation for the coming meeting with Jedidiah McBride, Victoria went directly to the green drawing room, where the tailor and an employee were waiting.

Mr. Randsome's assistant had already taken the opportunity to lay out several lengths of fine fabric. They ranged in color from a subdued buff to a deep, vibrant blue. Victoria eyed the royal blue with a frown. For their purpose, she felt, it would be best that Jedidiah dress as conservatively as possible. They had no wish to draw too much attention to the sea captain. She very much hoped the stubborn man would not be bent on having the blue.

The very man she was thinking so uncharitably of made his appearance only a few moments later. Every time she saw him, Victoria was struck by his sheer masculine presence. He walked into every room as if he belonged there and was ready to take control of any situation. As before, Victoria found herself thinking how well his captain's garb suited him. The snug-fitting black breeches hugged his lean hips, and the loosely cut black coat, with its gold buttons, gave him the freedom to move with that untamed grace that was so much a part of him.

As Jedidiah strode toward them, Victoria watched the tailor to gauge his reaction to the sea captain. If Mr. Randsome thought there was anything amiss with Jedidiah's appearance, he made no comment. The only evidence of his curiosity was one raised brow as he seemed to size up the younger man.

When Jedidiah stopped before them, looking at the many bolts of fabric with a decided frown, she said hurriedly, "Mr.... Cousin Jedidiah, this is Mr. Randsome. As I told you, he was my own father's tailor. I am sure he can be of assistance to you."

She turned to the tailor with a smile. "Mr. McBride is my cousin from America."

"America?" The older man looked to Jedidiah in obvious surprise.

"Yes." She nodded emphatically. "It is a well-known fact that my Great-uncle Lionel went to America in search of adventure." She turned to Jedidiah with a forced smile. "My cousin has journeyed all this way to find his family. I hope he is not too disappointed at discovering that I am the only remaining Thorn."

Jedidiah answered quickly, his gaze catching hers with an expression she could not name. "Not at all, Cousin...Victoria." Her name on his lips had a strangely intimate sound that she had not expected and left her feeling somewhat vulnerable.

She dragged her eyes from his and looked to the tailor once more. "My...cousin will need some new things. You see, we are going up to London for what remains of the season. I am most anxious to introduce him to society."

Jedidiah made a soft noise that sounded like a choking cough, and Victoria had the distinct impression that he was laughing at her. And for some unexplainable reason she felt like joining him, though the feeling stemmed more from nervousness than from actual amusement. She could hardly believe herself, standing here lying as if she'd been born to it.

But it must be done. She'd known that from the beginning.

"I see." Mr. Randsome nodded quickly, though he continued to watch Jedidiah with poorly concealed interest. "I'm sure I can help you with whatever you might require." He gestured around them as he focused his attention on Victoria. "Your message said to bring some samples of cloth that would be suitable for a gentleman's garments. I hope these meet with your approval." He turned to Jedidiah and bowed politely, making a better show of containing his curiosity. "And yours, sir."

Victoria replied with equal civility, though she could feel the force of Jedidiah's resistance. Clearly he was still not happy with the notion of purchasing clothing to wear in London. Yet something told Victoria he would not admit to this. Jedidiah McBride seemed a man of his word, and he had agreed to do this. It would be done.

As if he had read her mind, the American came farther into the room, his features set with determination.

The next few minutes passed in surprising tranquillity. Victoria did not try to lead Jedidiah in his choice of fabric. He just seemed to prefer the more subdued colors himself.

In point of fact, he chose only dark colors when he began. It was Mr. Randsome who suggested some of the lighter tones, to add contrast to his new garments.

Jedidiah seemed uncharacteristically content to follow the older man's lead. Only a short time had passed before they began choosing specific cuts of jackets and trousers from the sketches Mr. Randsome and his assistant had brought with them.

Victoria was beginning to feel she did not have to be there at all. There was other work she was neglecting. Still, she stayed on in case she was needed. Not because she liked seeing Jedidiah relaxed and as at ease as he seemed now with Mr. Randsome. Not because she liked the deep sound of his voice as he talked. Not because of the way the light gilded his hair every time he passed in front of the tall windows.

It was not until the tailor began to speak of the quantity of coats and other clothing that Jedidiah balked, shaking his head. "I will not require so many coats, nor—"

She interrupted, addressing Mr. Randsome directly. "We will take all of those items you mentioned, and a riding jacket of the dark gray, as well."

The American swung around to Victoria with a forbidding scowl. "Do you realize that you have ordered fifteen coats in all?"

Victoria turned from speaking to Mr. Randsome, with a frown of her own. The very fact that she had been surprised by his ready compliance with everything thus far had left Victoria somewhat prepared for this reaction.

Yet she could not help feeling frustrated by it. She had no wish to discuss this in front of the tailor. She tried to answer with careful courtesy. "Yes, of course, Mr.... Cousin."

He shook his head. "That is too many."

Victoria could feel the interest of both Mr. Randsome and his assistant. She moved closer to Jedidiah, telling herself that he was likely very pleased to have found something to disagree with her about. She answered him through tight lips. "Please, Cousin, might we discuss this later?" She raised her eyebrows meaningfully.

Jedidiah McBride paid her signals no heed. He only looked down at her with clear disapproval, his own brows raised in reaction to her expression. "I will not have it, Lady Victoria."

She forgot the other two men, in her amazement at those words. Victoria was not in the least accustomed to being spoken to that way. She sucked in a deep breath, raising her chin. "You . . . you will not have it."

To her utter stupefaction, his reaction was to take her by the arm as he addressed the two men. "Excuse us for just a moment." Jedidiah then half pulled her to the other side of the room, next to one of the tall windows. So shocked was she that Victoria made no effort to resist him.

But as soon as they came to a stop with the long brocade drape partially blocking her view of the room, she recovered herself enough to jerk her arm from his grasp. "How dare you!"

He stared down at her in abject surprise. "How dare *I*?"

She resisted the urge to rub the spot where his fingers had held her. "You are not to lay your hands upon me again."

Jedidiah had the grace to appear chagrined. "I . . ." His lips thinned, and he took a deep breath, letting it out slowly. It was clear that it cost him dear to admit, "You are right, I had no reason to grab your arm. I only wanted you to listen to me."

Now that Jedidiah seemed to have found his right mind once more, Victoria, too, began to calm down. As she looked up at him and into his stormy green eyes, she realized that she was not really angry. In fact, what she was feeling was a very different emotion. One she would not even hazard to try to name. The tightness in her breast, the thumping of her heart and the quickening of her breathing were all clear signs of this unknown emotion.

It was quite unusual for anyone to even dare raise his voice to her, let alone physically lead her about. Jedidiah had not actually hurt her, and for some reason his resistance only gave her a stronger sense of respect for him. Her position meant nothing to the tall, lean man. He thought of her as nothing more than a woman who had driven him to the point of forgetting himself.

Victoria could not help liking the notion of being thought of as a woman. For was she not just that?

She looked up at him from beneath her lashes, her gaze grazing the lean line of his jaw, the irate curve of his supple lips, his straight nose, those stormy green eyes. He really was very handsome, this proud sea captain of hers. She stopped herself, glancing away from him even as the words formed in her mind. Jedidiah was not now, nor would he ever be, hers.

Victoria's gaze came to rest on Mr. Randsome's assistant, who was now openly peering at them from across the room. Dear heaven, but they were making a spectacle of themselves.

Chancing another glance up at Jedidiah from beneath her dark lashes, she saw that he, too, had noticed how the other men were staring. He scowled with chagrin.

Biting her lip, Victoria took a deep breath before whispering, "Mr. McBride, I realize that it might appear as if I am being overly extravagant." Her gaze locked on his, her eyes pleading with him to heed her. "I assure you that I am not. When we go to London, we will be attending many social gatherings. It is the only way I am to meet a man so that I may marry. It is equally important for you to accompany me in order to search for your child. You do recall that those reasons are why you are here? Why we are going?" She halted, feeling unexpectedly cheerless at the idea of her future marriage. A fact that puzzled her greatly, for it was unlike Victoria to bemoan her fate once she had accepted it.

She brushed the thoughts aside, concentrating on the moment as she willed Jedidiah to see her position. "You must have the proper clothing to take me to these social gatherings. It would not do for you to be seen in the same coat day after day, or even from morning to evening. Have you forgotten you are my cousin? You must appear to be so in all things, in order to remain in my household without the benefit of some other chaperon. It is absolutely necessary for everyone to accept you as who we say you are."

He continued to stare down at her, but Victoria could see the wavering in his eyes. Then, as he stood there, a strange sort of light came into those compelling eyes, and for a heart-stopping moment, Victoria nearly forgot that they weren't alone.

He smiled, a slow, knowing smile. "Very well, then . . . Victoria."

It took her a moment to realize that this was the second time he had called her by her Christian name. It was even more intimate in tone when he said it so deliberately. No one besides Mary called her Victoria.

Then she was distracted by that light that was still there in his eyes. She pursed her lips, wondering what had brought it on. He answered her unspoken question mockingly. "I suggest that you call me Jed, even when we are alone. That is what I usually go by."

She blushed. Really, he was going too far. The nickname was just too familiar, especially without the appellation "cousin" to formalize it. And there was no need, when no one was around to hear them. "I could not—"

He stopped her with a raised hand. "Haven't you just said that I am to appear to be your cousin? That we can't do anything to make anyone doubt I am what you tell them I am?"

She frowned, feeling as if she had just stepped into quicksand. "Yes, but—"

He interrupted again, though politely. "Please, excuse me. Do you really think people will be convinced that I am your cousin if you go around calling me Mr. McBride, which you do most of the time? It's just a bit formal for such a close family tie. If you call me by my given name all the time, perhaps you'll begin to remember."

She bit her lip, realizing that he had her there. She really could not call him Mr. McBride. It would cause comment. But then, neither could she bring herself to call him Jed.

She could tell from the expression on his face that Jedidiah McBride felt he had found at least a small way of getting back at her for all the indignities he felt he was suffering at her hands. Victoria would not allow him to best her so easily. She smiled, and had the pleasure of seeing a trace of unease creep on to his face. "Very well, *Cousin*

Jedidiah. You make a very valid point. We must learn to address one another less formally.''

He scowled down at her. ''I prefer Jed.''

She raised her chin. ''As I said, *Cousin Jedidiah.*'' She then turned and moved across the room to the tailor and his assistant.

Jed watched Victoria with a pained expression as she flounced away from him, that slender backside of hers having the same effect on him that a rudely protruding tongue would have produced. Damn, but she was one stubborn woman.

He heard her telling Mr. Randsome he could make up everything they had discussed. Looking extremely pleased, the tailor hastily began to gather up his goods, as though he feared Jed might countermand her if he lingered. As he did so, the lady added, ''And do remember that there will be a bonus for every garment that is ready by the beginning of next week. Anything that is finished after that should be sent directly to the London house.''

''Very good, my lady.'' The tailor bowed.

Jed turned to look out the tall, narrow window, no longer interested in the exchange. He did not want to think about Victoria or his having given in to her. He did not want to admit that he had been pleasantly surprised to learn that the tailor had talked of elegant but conservative fabrics and clothing. The garments would be fashionable, but comfortable for Jed to wear.

He did not know why he had objected in the end. Maybe it was because he liked to see the light of battle enter a certain lady's gray eyes.

She'd been far too subdued over luncheon, making Jed wonder why. Even though he'd told himself it was best for them to remain distant from each other, he couldn't help wanting her to show some of that spirit that drew him so.

* * *

Victoria watched Jedidiah turn his back to them with an odd sense of abandonment. Was he thinking of the time when he would be gone from Briarwood—gone from her? With a sigh, she swung back to the tailor, who was clearing his throat loudly.

Seeing that he had her attention, Mr. Randsome bowed apologetically. "Oh, forgive me, Lady Victoria, I nearly forgot about that other matter you had mentioned in your note. About the matter of contacting Sergeant Winter."

Quickly she nodded, only now recalling that she had asked him to contact the valet. Sending a fleeting glance toward Jedidiah, she saw that he seemed completely unaware of them. His gaze remained trained on the view outside the drawing-room window.

Victoria focused on Mr. Randsome. "Yes, and were you able to do as I asked?"

The tailor nodded. "Yes, my lady. Sergeant Winter was most happy to hear that he would be needed. He agreed to come to Briarwood as soon as tomorrow. He said it would be an honor to act as valet to any member of your family."

Thinking to rid herself of any prying eyes in the event that the sea captain did decide to be difficult, she hurriedly voiced her appreciation to Mr. Randsome and personally saw him out the door of the drawing room. He seemed flattered and pleased that she would attend him so courteously, and appeared not to notice her impatience, which she made every effort to hide.

When the door closed behind him, the silence in the room seemed as heavy as lead. Victoria found herself wishing she did not have to turn around and face Jedidiah. She knew she must, so, taking a deep breath, she swung around with a purposefully bright smile. "Well, I for one feel as if we have accomplished a great deal this afternoon. I'm sure Mr. Randsome will have some things ready for you by tomorrow." She moved across the room to reach for a tasseled gold cord that hung from the wall. "Would you care to take some tea now?"

Jedidiah came to stand before her in three long, purposeful strides. Victoria looked up at him, swallowing. Who could have thought anyone could move so far so quickly, and with such grace? She tried to smile politely, but the look of disapproval on his face halted her.

He spoke slowly, and with an obvious effort to control himself. "Have I completely mistaken what that man was talking about, or have you really had the audacity to send for a valet for me?" He eyed her with wariness and long-suffering exasperation. "Do, please, tell me that I am wrong."

She raised herself up to her full height although she still was no taller than his shoulder. Victoria refused to allow that realization to quell her. "No, I am afraid I cannot tell you that. I have sent for a valet."

His lips thinned to a straight, disapproving line. "And why would you do that?"

She raised her brows. "Because all gentlemen require a manservant."

He bent low over her, the sardonic expression that came into his eyes giving her pause as his gaze traveled over her. "I am no gentleman. Haven't you figured that out yet... Cousin?"

For some reason, it had suddenly become difficult for her to breathe as her attention had settled on his mouth. Victoria realized that she should not try to push this man too far. Some of the very qualities that made him of use to her were things that also made him dangerous, such as his bravery and his disregard for social convention.

The other members of the nobility whom they must meet and socialize with over the course of their stay in London would most likely not agree with her assessment of Jedidiah McBride. They had their own ideas of what a gentleman should be, and neither she nor Jedidiah was going to change that.

Not for any reason did she wish to have Jedidiah think that she found him lacking. She also felt a sense of discomfort at knowing just how pleasing she did find him, and that brought on a certain irritation with herself. That irritation made itself known in the slight edge in her voice. "Mr. McBride, may I please explain myself, before you decide that you will not allow me to hire a valet?"

His expression remained cynical, but he nodded.

She bowed her head slightly in thanks. "I did not mention the matter to you because it did not occur to me. You see, every gentleman I know has a valet, and I did not realize that it would appear strange to you. Sergeant Winter was in fact the valet in training for my own father before his death. Hart, who had been with Father from the time he was a boy, was getting on and thinking of retiring. Hart recommended Sergeant Winter, who was a distant relative of his." She met Jedidiah's skeptical gaze levelly. "The reason I thought you might get on well with him is that he was a soldier. I hoped you would not find him, shall I say, too fussy for your taste? Nonetheless, let me assure you that in spite of that, he will know how to tie a proper neckcloth and will be able to look after your clothing appropriately. He will know which coat to wear in the afternoon, and which one to don for a morning ride." She drew herself up, and the pride in her voice was evident. "My father was the duke of Carlisle, and he was not too proud to accept the direction of his valet. He was the consummate gentleman at all times, and perfectly attired for every occasion." She went on, "There is no need for you to feel any insult. If it weren't for their gentlemen's gentlemen, few noblemen would be garbed as they should be, their cravats straight, their boots polished. It is no insult to you to admit that you are no better than they."

She came to halt, looking at him closely, to see if he could find some fault in this logic. To her relief, he seemed to be mulling over what she had said. That at least meant he had not rejected it outright.

As he watched her, that distinct gleam came into his green eyes, which made her think that Jedidiah McBride might not continue to be so amenable to her desires. A slight uneasiness rolled in her belly.

"Oh," he began, a cynical laugh escaping him, "you are very good, *Lady* Victoria. It all makes perfect sense when you put it that way. But the crux of the matter is that you get your own way, and I think—" he took a step, bending so close over her that she could clearly make out the gold flecks in his eyes, feel the warm brush of his breath on her forehead "—that you are very accustomed to getting your own way."

Her breath caught as a strange, tingling awareness grew in her breast. He was so tall, so self-assured, so male.

She did not know how, but suddenly he was very close, so close, in fact, that she could feel the heat of his body through the bodice of her gown. He leaned over her, his breath now brushing her mouth, as her lids fluttered down. He whispered. "Is that it, Victoria?"

She could hardly think, indeed could not focus on what he was saying as her heart thudded in her chest. "What . . . ?" she murmured.

His voice was low, and carried an undertone of something that she did not understand, but that made her shiver nonetheless. "Are you just too used to getting your own way? Do you need a man who'll push back, show you when he's had enough? Give you what you really need?"

She had the feeling that she should be angry, should be defending herself, though she wasn't sure from what. "Jedidiah, I don't know what you—"

She sensed his withdrawal as he went on. "No. I don't believe you do. And it's not my place to explain." She looked up at him, confused by her own feelings and his indecipherable remarks. A moment ago he'd seemed so... And now he seemed to almost resent her.

It took her a moment to focus on what he was saying as he continued. "Again I will do as you ask, but make no mistake in that you will not always get your own way with me."

With that, he turned on his heel and left the drawing room. Victoria could only stare after him, working to recover her scattered wits. As she went over what he'd actually said, she knew a growing indignation.

Always got her own way. He was completely mistaken. Or was he? And what did he mean when he said she would not always get her own way with him?

The arrogance of the man! She mollified herself by remembering that there was little likelihood of her ever putting that threat to the test. After she found herself a husband, she would never see Jedidiah McBride again.

Unexpectedly, the thought did not bring her the satisfaction it should.

Sergeant Winter arrived the very next morning. He presented himself at Jed's bedroom door as he was getting dressed for the day.

The moment the sturdy ex-soldier held out his hand, Jed knew Victoria had been correct in thinking he would like him. His blue eyes were direct, and there was not a hint of a fussy nature evident in him. Oh, he was well-groomed, all right, from the top of his carefully combed graying brown head to the creases in his dark brown trousers. His hands, though hardened by physical activity, were clean down to the nails.

He did not blink an eye when he mentioned that he was happy to be serving Lady Victoria's cousin. Nor did he look upon Jed's clothes with any hint of censure. In fact, Jed could find no fault with the man in either manner or dress.

If he had to have such a thing as a valet, this one would do well enough. When the boxes began to arrive from Mr. Randsome's shop that very afternoon, Winter, as he had asked Jed to call him, took them over with quiet efficiency.

With nothing else to do, Jed made an unobtrusive tour of the surrounding countryside on horseback. The house lay at the center of lush and beautiful parkland. All the outbuildings, the stables, the storage sheds and various other buildings lay out of sight to the left of the house. There were rolling hills and patches of forest aplenty. It was a place designed to bring tranquillity to any man's soul. That is, unless the man was dealing with the lovely but aggravating Victoria Thorn.

He had no wish to run into her before he had to. His reticence might be due, in part, to his having no idea what had moved him to talk to her the way he had the previous day. There was no denying to himself that there had been a definite sexual context beneath the surface of what he'd said. Any woman less innocent would certainly have understood him.

Again he could only think that his aggressiveness was due to his not having been with a woman in weeks. But the idea of finding one to relieve himself upon did not appeal.

Before he returned to the manor house, Jed ended in expelling some of his excess energy in helping to clean up an overturned wagon full of hay. Yet even the hard physical activity did not rid his mind of the vision of how Victoria had looked as he leaned over her. Her lids had dipped down low over those smoky eyes, and he knew that she would not have stopped him if he kissed her.

The knowledge was not welcome.

Jed cursed himself for agreeing to act as her protector. At the time, he'd had a mere hint of the awareness that existed between them, and the hope of possibly locating his son had overridden any other consideration. Never would he have stayed if he had known. Getting involved with the daughter of a duke was the last thing he wanted. And he meant to keep that from happening. No matter what.

When it was time to ready himself for the evening meal Jed found himself dressed in a pair of gray pants, a matching vest and a darker gray jacket. Looking at himself, he realized that Victoria had chosen well in the tailor. Though Jed was certainly dressed more elegantly than he had been, the cut and fabrics were of a style that he could feel comfortable in.

Victoria was in the dining room when he arrived. She turned from her contemplation of a bowl of fresh-cut roses to look at him. In what seemed almost a self-conscious gesture, she brushed a dark curl from her forehead as her eyes met his across the space that separated them. She was dressed in a hooped gown of dark rose pink that was cut low in the bodice, just showing a hint of delectable cleavage. When his gaze lingered there for a moment, her cheeks suddenly rivaled her dress for depth of color. She was beautiful and vibrant and full of life.

Jed felt a tightening in his body as her own gaze traveled the length of him, then came back to his face with an expression of approval and something else, something he did not want to see or acknowledge. It could only bring disaster to notice the longing that darkened her eyes to smoke. When her tongue flicked out to dampen her supple mouth, he felt his own go dry.

As she came toward him, it was all Jed could do to keep himself from reacting, from holding out his arms. He forced himself to recall the decision he'd made to quell his interest in her. He reminded himself of how obstinate she was, how accustomed to ordering everything around her to suit herself. It seemed the only way to get his wildly rising desire under control.

When she continued to look at him that way, it was extremely difficult to remember that he did not want to be controlled by this beautiful, beguiling aristocrat, who appeared in this moment to be all soft and vulnerable. Jed looked away. He had to stop himself from thinking this way.

Clearing his throat with determination, he spoke coolly. "I have met your Sergeant Winter."

Her suddenly closed gaze swept over him again. "I knew that he had arrived," she told him, and he wondered at the slightly husky sound of her voice. When she continued, her words were like a cold wave rolling over his heated senses. "But if I hadn't, the drastic change in your appearance would be a clear indicator."

His lips tightened when he heard that. He scowled down at his hands which were scratched and rough from forking hay. The very sight of them was a further reminder of the differences between them. He answered brusquely. "It's all on the surface, Victoria. The valet has not changed me into a gentleman, no matter how much the idea might appeal to you."

She paused for a long moment, drawing his attention to her averted profile. When she spoke, he saw that she had chosen to ignore his remark. "I trust he meets with your approval."

The witch, he swore silently. He had been a fool to think even for a moment that Victoria Thorn would be attracted to him. She was the daughter of a duke. He was the son of a drunken Irishman whose only remarkable quality had been his ability to handle horses.

Whatever had happened between them the day before, she now had it completely under control. Victoria's interest in him was not personal. It would save him a great deal of trouble if he remembered that.

Before he could even form a suitable reply, the serving woman arrived with the first course. Jedidiah took his place across from her without another word, remaining quiet throughout the rest of the meal.

If Victoria took any notice of his reticence, she made no comment. She, too, seemed lost in her own thoughts. He would have thought her completely oblivious of his presence if it had not been for the fact that as he was reaching for his wineglass, he glanced at her for perhaps the hundredth time since sitting down, and paused.

She was watching him, and in her eyes was an expression he could not quite understand. It seemed somewhat wary and, if he was not completely crazy, sad. As on the first night he had met her, Jedidiah sensed a well-guarded vulnerability inside her.

But that made no sense whatsoever. What reason did Victoria have to be saddened because of him?

She hurriedly looked away, and only moments later excused herself, saying she had business to attend to in her father's office. Rising politely, he stared after her straight back with a frown of self-castigation.

Victoria Thorn had not been hurt by anything he had said or done. In order for that to happen, she would have to care what he thought. And certainly she did not.

Chapter Five

Victoria Thorn rose and rubbed the back of her neck with a weary hand. She had been very busy over the past few days. There was always much work to be done in seeing to her estate, but with the trip to London coming in the next week, she was even more occupied than usual.

It did not help that her thoughts were too often centered on a certain sea captain. This was especially maddening considering the way he felt about her. The situation was only made worse by the fact that the manor folk seemed to have taken him to their bosoms gladly.

More than one of the servants had informed her of how much they enjoyed having Mr. McBride there. She'd been told how he'd helped to right an overturned wagon and guided the farmer in distributing his load more evenly so that it wouldn't happen again. He'd shown one of the grooms how to mix a balm for the injured foreleg of her favorite stallion. He'd organized a game of what he called stickball with the estate children.

When Victoria tried to show her appreciation for his efforts on her people's behalf, he'd only arched a lofty brow and told her he needed something to do. On every possible occasion, Jedidiah had made his disdain for her and her way of life clear. But never more so than on the night when she'd first seen him dressed in his new garments. His sarcastic assurances that he had no wish to be turned into a gentleman had hurt.

It had been doubly painful because of the way she reacted to him. She'd been struck hard by the sight of Jedidiah McBride dressed as a gentleman. He'd worn the new clothing with the same easy grace as he had his seaman's apparel. Victoria had not known what to say when she looked up and saw him standing there in the doorway of the dining room that evening, looking so very like the noblemen he so professed to dislike, looking as if he...belonged there.

It was becoming increasingly clear to her that there was more to Jedidiah McBride than he was willing to reveal. Even the revelations about his being a successful man of business gave little help. They did not explain why he was so bitter toward the upper classes.

Irritated that she was dwelling upon the matter, Victoria told herself she should instead be devoting her time to considering just what qualities she was looking for in a husband. The man she married would have to do more than wear fashionable garments with aplomb. He must, of course, understand that her responsibilities came first. Her own personal interests must always be secondary.

He would of necessity be a man who would willingly turn his loyalty and attention to the people and things she cared about. He must be her equal in more than social position. He must be so in values.

She knew that Jedidiah McBride viewed the nobility as snobs who thought themselves better than those who labored for a living. And to a great extent he was right, but not all were that way. Her father had not been. He had taught her that with her position came an obligation to work for the good of others.

How difficult it might prove to find such a mate who would feel the same, Victoria could not even hazard a guess. She knew only that she must do so. She looked at the open estate books on the desk with a sigh, and made to go back to her seat.

But just as she did so, a shrill scream rent the air.

Jedidiah McBride was just reaching for the packet of letters that had been delivered by messenger from West-acre. He halted as a high screech pierced the peaceful morning.

Realizing that the sound was coming from somewhere at the rear of the main section of the house, Jed turned and hurried across the marble foyer to the archway at the far end. Just as he was passing the doorway to the library, Victoria emerged, her face creased with concern.

Seeing him there, she said, "It's coming from the kitch-ens. I'll show you the way." Jed stepped aside, allowing her to take the lead down the long hallway.

The noise came again, and Jed hastened his step when he heard the pain and terror it contained. Victoria seemed to be fired by the same sense of urgency, for she, too, quick-ened her pace.

Soon they passed through a wide doorway that opened into a spacious and brightly lit chamber that Jed knew immediately was the main kitchen. An enormous cooking stove and oven stood directly across from them. On the other wall was an equally impressive open-faced hearth. It was in front of this fireplace that several servants had gathered.

Another shriek erupted from the center of the huddled group. A woman was sobbing somewhere in the midst of this jumble of bodies, and at the scream the sobs became louder and more hysterical. As for the rest of them, they were all talking at once.

"Put some butter on it."

"No, lard, definitely lard."

"Why was the child allowed to get so close to the pot?" This remark elicited even more hysterical sobbing.

None of them even noticed the arrival of Jed and their mistress.

Victoria left Jed's side to hurry over to them, sidestepping just in time to avoid being hit on the head by one of the heavy iron pots that hung over the butcher-block counter in the center of the room.

Jed followed her.

"What has happened?" The lady of Briarwood spoke calmly but forcefully over the din.

A robust woman with iron-gray hair that was covered by a mobcap turned to face them. "My lady." She nodded respectfully. "I told Millie she should not bring the child in to work with her. I told her that you had expressly forbidden children being in the kitchens. She said her mother was too sick to care for the little one today. I did need Millie's help with the baking."

Jed saw the worry on Victoria's face. "Let me see what has happened," she said, still in that controlled, even tone, despite the obvious fearfulness in her eyes. The servants moved out of her way, and Jed could now see a small child of perhaps four or five clasped in the arms of a crying woman. The child let out another shriek, and Victoria made a soft sound of sympathy, moving to take her.

The young woman, her face streaked with tears, her eyes dark with torment, looked up at her mistress. "I'm so... sorry, my lady. I had to bring her... and now look what's happened. It's all... my own... fault." She clung desperately to the child, making her cry out anew, even as Victoria tried to look around her grip to see the damage.

With what Jed could see was deliberate patience, Victoria met the watery blue gaze with her own. "There is nothing to be gained by belaboring the point now, Millie. Give her to me and let us see what has to be done.'' Still the woman did not loosen her grip on the little girl.

Jed knew this had gone far enough. He stepped forward. Speaking as he would to his own crew, he ordered, "Give the child to your lady." The woman reacted without hesitation, only looking for the source of the authoritative voice when she had done what he said. As soon as she realized that she no longer held her child in her arms, she began to cry again, sobbing so hard her whole body quivered. She put her hands to her face, but they did not deaden the sound.

Jed turned to one of the footmen. "Take care of...Millie." The lad hurried to lead the hysterical woman to the other side of the room.

Jed then moved to Victoria's side as she examined the burn on the child's arm. His lips thinned to a grim line as he saw the extent of the injury. The skin was peeling back from the dark red scald she bore along her left arm.

Victoria looked up at Jed, her eyes dark as charcoal. She held the little one carefully, tenderly soothing her. Her gentle touch seemed to break through some of the child's pain and terror, for she began to quiet somewhat, burying her face in the striped lavender silk of the lady's bodice.

More touched by this new maternal side of Victoria than he cared to admit, Jed forced himself to concentrate on what needed to be done next. Swinging around, he pointed to one of the housemaids. "Fetch a bucket of cold water. And you—" he addressed another of the footmen "—get the doctor and bring him here. Now! Someone else fetch a clean cloth." All jumped to do as he said.

Having seen the burn, Jed knew they could not wait for the doctor to begin treating it. He wasn't sure what was the best way to handle the situation but he could only think of the time his own ship's cook had been burned by a vat of boiling grease. The man had been in such pain from the horrendous heat of the injury that he had immersed his hand in a tub of cold sea water to try and soothe it. To everyone's amazement, the burn had not blistered and had seemed to heal much more quickly than any had ever heard of.

When the maid returned with the water, Jed took it and moved to kneel at Victoria's side. She looked at him curiously as he reached for the clean cloth.

"What are you going to do?" she asked.

He dipped the cloth in the bucket of cool water. "I am going to try something I've seen help in a situation like this." He met her uncertain gaze with his own. For a long moment, they sat like that, and then she nodded, her expression trusting.

For some reason that he could not even begin to understand, her complete faith in him was more moving than anything in his memory. He felt that because of her belief in him he could indeed do anything. That together they could do anything. He spoke softly. "She will not like this, but you must hold her until it begins to help the pain subside."

She nodded again. "I will."

For the next few minutes, Jed and Victoria worked together, each of them seeming to anticipate the wishes of the other without speaking. The room had fallen into complete silence, except for the little girl's reactions to what they were doing to her. The servants looked on in awe. Millie rejoined the group, for she now seemed to have regained some measure of composure and looked on with interest, though her expression did not lose its fearfulness.

When at last the doctor arrived, he took careful note of the procedure that was being carried out. He also saw the way the little one sighed each time the cloth was rewet in the cool water and placed back on her arm.

Only when the doctor moved to take his place did Jed back away. As he did so, he motioned to one of the more mature-looking housemaids to take the now settled child from Victoria's arms. She looked as if she had the presence of mind to control one small child, with her direct brown eyes and self-assured expression. The maid laid the child across her comfortable lap, hushing her gently but confidently when she began to fuss, and Jed knew he had chosen well.

Victoria moved to stand beside him, her eyes unreadable as she faced him. "I . . . Thank you for your help."

He was infinitely aware of the many eyes that observed them. "There is no need to thank me. Anyone would have done the same."

She looked up at him for a long moment, then shook her head. "No, I do not think so. Not for an unknown servant's child. I believe, Jedidiah McBride, that you do not know what a rare man you are."

His mouth turned down as she spoke. "Then perhaps you are spending time with the wrong people, Lady Victoria. That this was a servant's child makes no difference to me, would not to anyone who has the least amount of common decency."

Victoria bit her lip. Again he had misunderstood her. She had meant only to compliment him, to say that few men would have cared for any strange child. She had not intended to say that it was a greater deed because the little one was the offspring of a servant.

She'd been so glad to have him there, to have him lend his strength in taking care of the situation. Victoria had not known of the method he used to soothe the burn, but something had told her Jedidiah would not use that process on a child unless he was very certain of its benefits.

For the first time in the years since her parents died, she'd felt that she had someone to help her in a time of trouble.

For once, the burden of knowing what to do had not rested entirely on her shoulders.

But Jedidiah McBride always seemed prepared to look for the worst in her. Raising her head, she spoke in a voice barely above a whisper as she answered him. "I was simply trying to thank you, and meant nothing more than that. But you may, of course, think what you will."

With that, she turned on her heel and left the room, uncaring as to what might be made of it.

Victoria sat dressed in a riding habit of royal blue as her hair was done.

Her maid, Betty, stepped back for a moment to view the effect of her handiwork. She nodded in satisfaction. "That color is most becoming on Your Ladyship," she said as she pinned the matching bonnet atop her head. The black tulle trim that reflected the color of the braiding on the jacket front slanted across one pale cheek.

Barely glancing at her reflection in the dressing table mirror, Victoria muttered, "Yes, yes, but it won't matter in the least to him." Her mind was on the one person who had served to drive all other thoughts away. Namely one Jedidiah McBride.

"My lady?" the maid questioned in confusion. Betty's gaze burned into Victoria's back.

Victoria scowled as a deep flush stained her cheeks, feeling obligated to explain her odd remark in some way. "I mean there's no one to notice.... No, that is not what I... Oh, good gracious." The lady halted, realizing she had said far too much. Grabbing up her riding crop, Victoria left her chambers, knowing she had drawn the girl's speculation with her uncharacteristic agitation. She was determined to expel some of the pent-up energy she felt on horseback.

In the foyer, she met the very man who so plagued her. Jedidiah McBride was handing a sealed envelope to one of the footmen. Victoria hesitated, not wishing to speak to him at this particular moment, not having done so since the scene in the kitchen yesterday. She told herself not to be ridiculous. She was a fool to allow the man to unsettle her so completely.

What he thought of her mattered not in the least.

Then, in spite of her resolve, she found herself taking a deep breath as she went on toward him. At the sound of her booted feet clicking across the marble floor, Jedidiah turned and, seeing her said, "I have heard that little Sarah is doing very well."

"Yes," Victoria replied. She had insisted that the little one be kept at Briarwood overnight, and had already been up to see her this morning where she lay, ensconced in one of the smaller guest rooms. She seemed to be doing very well indeed, and had shown off her white bandage with pride. The doctor had told Victoria he was sure Jedidiah's treatment had made a great difference in how well the burn was doing. Though she was grateful, Victoria had absolutely no intention of trying to thank the intractable captain again.

When she made no further comment, Jedidiah ran an assessing gaze over her. He scowled. "You should have told me you wish to go riding this morning. I'll come with you."

Victoria ran her tongue over her upper lip as her gaze wandered to where his strong hands rode low over those slender hips. "No, thank you, Mr...." She felt the footman's gaze upon her. "Cousin. I see that you are busy, and I really do not require your assistance. I have been riding alone since I was quite small." She attempted a polite smile, even as her mind whirled. The last thing she wanted was for this maddening, all-too-attractive man to accompany her this morning. In spite of his prickly nature, her dreams were filled with images of him that she had no wish to even contemplate.

He moved to stand closer to her, his expression commanding. "I am not busy." He motioned toward the letter in the footman's hand. "I was simply sending instructions to my first mate as to the disposal of the cargo we brought with us to England. I am more than available."

Victoria looked at her hands as she fought back a blush. Heavens above! He was available. This was not what her fruitful imagination should be hearing. For she knew from his own lips that Jedidiah McBride was certainly not available to her, or anyone like her. He had nothing but contempt for her and her kind, and that she would do well to remember. "Really, I have no need of your services this morning." She waved an airy hand and made for the front door. "And I'm sure you would much rather attend to your business."

His words halted her, as he replied with growing impatience, "I have said that all is under control. The letters are written and are now being sent. Wait here while I get my coat."

Abashed, she glanced around, to see him stride across the floor and up the stairs. Why, the nerve of the man, she thought. She had no intention of leaving her own parklands, and felt completely safe there.

Swinging around toward the front door, she caught the amazed gaze of one of the footmen. She knew he had never heard anyone speak to her in that manner, and meant that he should never do so again. His expression was quickly schooled to one of proper blandness as she arched a regal brow. He raced to open the portal for her.

Once outside, Victoria made her way to the stables with as much haste as decorum would allow. Although she did not wish to show her hurry, she hoped to be gone from the stables before Jedidiah could reach them. Even though she assured herself that she was quite capable of matching her will to that of the obstinate man, she had a great reluctance to put it to the test.

Once Victoria was securely mounted atop her favorite mare, Queenie, and racing out across the greensward, she made no effort to silence her sigh of relief. Firmly she told herself that it was only because she wished to avoid a scene, and nothing more.

Jed made his way down the stairs with impatience evident in his every step. He'd been delayed by some minutes on finding out that Winters had taken the initiative to remove his riding coat to the kitchens to have it cleaned and pressed. The manservant had rushed to retrieve the coat, apologizing most profusely.

Jed had felt obliged to respond with civility, especially considering his own philosophy about being waited on. The only thing was, Jed had told himself silently as he paced his room, he would have worn the coat as it was. When it arrived, he had had to admit that the garment looked better than it had after he wore it the previous day. Jed had given no thought to his appearance when he took his mount jumping over streams the evening before. Only his irritation with himself and Victoria had mattered at the time. He had been angry with himself for reacting to her words about the child being a servant, and with her for making him feel guilty when she acted hurt.

As he shrugged into the garment, he'd known Victoria would not thank him for keeping her waiting.

There was no sign of her when he reached the foyer. This came as no great surprise, yet Jed could not stop the rush of annoyance this brought. He told himself it was due to his concern for her.

It seemed to him that the woman was somewhat mad. She had entered into an agreement with him because she was afraid for her safety, but she did not want him to keep her safe.

Jed could see no sense in this whatsoever.

For some reason, it had become very important in his mind that he carry out his duty as the lady's protector with complete dedication. It helped to keep him centered on the fact that their's was a business relationship. He need not feel any personal insult when she showed, by word or deed, just how much of an aristocrat she was, in spite of any appearances to the contrary.

He went out to the stables, hoping but not really expecting to find her there, either. She was not.

Soon Jed had saddled a horse. He headed off in the direction the stable boy pointed out to him. He was not sure why he was making this attempt to follow her. Having thoroughly explored the rolling hills and verdant forests himself over the past days, he knew it was unlikely that he would locate the lady of Briarwood in this vast area of parklands.

Yet as he cantered along, he told himself that he had great need of the exercise himself. Perhaps, if he spent enough time in the saddle, he would sleep better.

But he was not sure that any amount of exertion could erase the sort of images that had kept him tossing and turning until well after dawn. He could not stop thinking about the way Victoria had looked at him the previous day, her eyes full of trust and confidence in him. Of how tenderly she had held little Sarah, soothing her as he bathed her burned arm. In spite of the worry that creased her brow, she'd been radiantly beautiful, as only a woman who is not afraid to show kindness toward others can be.

Even earlier this very morning, when he turned and saw her coming toward him, Jed had been hard-pressed not to tell her how beautiful she looked in that pert blue riding hat. And the habit, Lord, the royal blue velvet had hugged the curves of her breasts and shapely hips like a lover's sigh.

What was he doing, he asked himself, following her now? Was he completely crazy?

No, he insisted silently, kicking his horse to a quicker pace. He was only doing what he had promised to do. When Jedidiah McBride made a bargain, he stuck with it. There was no way he was going to let his attraction to an English aristocrat keep him from keeping his word—no matter how distracting she might be.

Jed began to take note of the beauty of the countryside, through which he passed. The grass was a bright emerald green that nearly hurt the eyes with its intensity, and the oak and birch trees that lay scattered on the gently rolling hillsides were eagerly offering their new leaves to the soft breeze. As he took all this in, he couldn't help thinking that Victoria was a very fortunate woman to be able to live in such surroundings.

If not for the very idea that he would soon be mixing with members of the society he had such little regard for, Jed would have had to admit that he was not unhappy here. The house and lands were beautiful. He liked and admired the people he had met. Victoria's servants, though well trained and dressed in fine livery, treated her with no more than the respect due any employer, and did in fact seem to show a marked affection for their lady.

Since his care of little Sarah yesterday, their affection seemed to have transferred itself, at least in part, to him. His coffee tray this morning had been bright with fresh lilies from the garden. The maid who brought it had smiled with open admiration and told him the cook was making steak-and-kidney pie for breakfast in his honor.

Yes, he did indeed appreciate being at Briarwood. His dilemma was that he could not allow himself to relax and enjoy the life of a country gentleman without feeling he had betrayed his own values in some way.

He could not help knowing, though, that this place, these people, were becoming more real to him than the ones back in America. He knew he was welcome at Peter's home in Bridgeport, but he spent little time there, preferring to be at sea. As for Bar Harbor, he'd not been back there since his mother's death. The town had few happy memories for him other than those of his mother, and even they were tainted by the recollections of how badly his father had treated her, of how out of place he had felt growing up.

He suddenly realized that when he found his child he would not be so free to roam the seas. That did not worry him. Jed wanted to be with his son, had not known until he learned of the child how very much he missed having someone of his own, as he had not since his mother died.

Perhaps he and his son would build a home in Bridgeport, perhaps not. The world was a big and amazing place, a lot of which Jed had been fortunate enough to see. He was free to live wherever he wished. Where he chose did not even matter. What did was that he would have someone to help him find a place to call home. Someone who belonged to him.

For some reason, Jed had a momentary image of Victoria's face. With a grunt of frustration, he prodded his mount on, determined to banish the aggravating lady of Briarwood manor from his thoughts.

It was because of his own irritation with himself for thinking of her that Jed was slow to understand what he was seeing a moment later, as he topped a gentle rise. There was, some distance from him, a woman in a royal blue riding habit mounted atop a striking white mare. But that was not what captured his attention. It was the two mounted men who had come to a halt on either side of her.

Victoria. And, if he did not mistake them, Reginald Cox
and his cohort, Lloyd.

Even as he watched, one of the men reached out to pull
the woman up before him onto his gray. The act galva-
nized Jed into action. He drove his heels into the horse's
flanks, and the animal reared up, then hit the ground at a
gallop.

Down an incline and up the hillside, Jed was on them
before either man noticed his approach. As he came near,
Jed could see why.

Victoria was not accepting this new assault with ladylike
forbearance. She had just jammed her heel into Reginald's
shin. That sorry excuse for a man was calling out for a
flustered Lloyd to help him subdue her. When Lloyd
reached over from his own horse to do that, he received an
obviously stunning blow to the eye from her right fist.

Then, just when Jed was upon them, Victoria planted an
elbow in Reginald's ribs. He let go of her and rocked back
in the saddle, crying out in pain. Victoria teetered precari-
ously in front of her captor, nearly losing her perilous position. Then it was she who gasped in hurt surprise as
Reginald Cox inadvertently kicked her in his attempts to
keep his seat.

Damn the bastard, damn them both, Jed thought. If she
sustained even one more slight injury or fell, he would kill
Reginald Cox and Lloyd Jenkins.

Having righted himself quickly, Reginald reached for
Victoria, then fell back when Jed's fist connected with his
jaw. When she slid sideways as Cox jerked away, Jed managed to reach out and pull her onto his own horse.

She didn't even hesitate, and threw her arms around his
neck. Jed held her tightly to him, not stopping to analyze
the amount of relief he felt at having her safely before him.
It was nearly overshadowed by the rage he felt at this new
threat to her.

He turned his attention to her attackers. Jed saw that he was not going to get any relief from the rolling anger inside him in that direction.

As soon as Reginald realized what was happening, his eyes became as round as barnacles and he struck the reins against the gray's backside. It gave a start of surprise and thundered off across the grounds. Jed swung around to look where Lloyd had been, to find that he was long gone from the scene, his back just disappearing into the woodland up ahead.

He must have seen Jed coming and abandoned Reginald before the sea captain arrived on the scene.

For a moment, Jed considered putting Victoria down so that he could go after them and throttle the two inept kidnappers. But as he focused his attention on Victoria again, he realized she was trembling.

His heart turned over in his breast at this evidence of her fright. He'd watched how bravely she fought the two men, and he sensed how much it would pain her to be reduced to this reaction. His lips thinned to a straight line of fury. Damn them both to hell.

Yet as he held her, his reaction changed, his rage seeping away, being totally eclipsed by his concern for the woman in his arms. It became more important to comfort Victoria than to beat the tar out of the two men. With a last glance in the direction they had gone, Jed promised himself that their time would come.

Then he slipped to the ground with the lady in his arms.

Victoria looked up at him, her eyes damp with tears she clearly refused to shed, and he was struck again by her pride and courage. Then, as if even her will could not contain it, one lone tear slipped from the corner of her eye to glide over the smooth perfection of her cheek.

God, but she was so beautiful, he thought, with her dark hair tumbling wildly down her back and curling about her face, which was flushed a delicate peach. Without pausing to think, Jed reached up to gently wipe the tear away with the back of his forefinger. "It's all right to cry," he told her softly.

Victoria shook her head stubbornly. "No, it isn't. I haven't cried since the day my parents were buried. Tears are not to be shed for little things."

He could only stare down at her, his heart slamming against his chest in reaction to the pain revealed by her statement. He whispered, "You are so brave. So beautiful."

She caught her breath, those gray eyes growing dark with an emotion he did not want to acknowledge, even as he felt an answering reaction stir in himself. It was the same emotion he had seen that day in the sitting room, the one he had tried with all his might to drive from his mind. Tried and failed.

He could no longer pretend to deny the desire she felt for him. That he felt for her.

"Jedidiah," she whispered, his name a husky caress coming from her lips. His gaze focused on her mouth, so sweetly rounded and full. So inviting.

Jed could not stop himself, could not think past this moment and the feel of her so yielding and womanly in his arms.

He dipped his head to claim her lips with his.

Victoria could hardly believe what was happening. When Jedidiah's mouth touched hers she was lost, swimming in a sea of heady sensation. His lips were firm, yet supple, and they played over hers, making them part of their own accord.

Her breasts felt heavy and full, the tight bodice of her habit serving only to increase the feelings of neediness inside her. She squirmed closer in his arms, gladdened when he tightened his hold on her, molding her to the hard contours of his body.

Jed grasped the firm curves of her bottom and felt his heart race. He'd known she would feel like this from that first time he saw her, her skirts thrown over her head.

His eyes flew open. The first time he saw her.

God help him, what was he doing? He had no right to touch her like this, to kiss her. For heaven's sake, he was supposed to be protecting her.

He pulled away, taking her hands to hold them against her sides when she reached for him. She looked up at him clearly dazed. "What...what are you...?"

Her gaze cleared when she saw the grim determination on his own face. "Jedidiah, what is wrong?" she asked, her tone rife with exasperation.

"This is wrong," he told her. "You and I. We can't do this."

"Why?"

Because we come from different worlds, and even if you think that doesn't matter right now, it will later. He shook his head. "Believe me, I know. I've been through something like this many years ago."

She looked at him, her eyes dark with pain. "Nina?"

He nodded.

Without another word, she got on her horse and left him standing there. Jed made no move to follow her. There was nothing more he could say.

Chapter Six

Victoria relinquished the care of her horse to the groom who had accompanied her to the vicarage in Carlisle. She had no idea if Jedidiah McBride knew of her visit to see her friend, and she did not care. What she did know and was grateful for was that she had managed to go without seeing him; thus, there had been no embarrassing offers to attend her. Although she now understood that she could not take a solitary ride at this time, she was not ready to be alone with the sea captain after the way he had rebuffed her.

Her face flamed every time she recalled the way she had reacted to his touch, his kiss. She had been so overcome by the burgeoning emotions and feelings springing to joyous life inside her that nothing else mattered. Even now, as her face flushed with shame at the memory, her traitorous body was flooded with tingling awareness.

She closed her eyes, trying to suppress the sensations, the images. It was simply too much to bear, and yet she could not escape the fact that the incident had happened.

Even the fact that she had managed to avoid Jedidiah completely yesterday by working through meals, had done little to help. This morning she had awakened knowing that she could not continue in this vein indefinitely.

Victoria had felt an overwhelming urge to see Mary, to speak with her. As to what she would say, well . . . she was not sure what she had planned to say.

When she was with her friend, saw her worry for her father, Victoria could tell the other woman nothing of her own troubles. It was clear that Mary had sensed something was wrong. But Victoria had refused to be drawn, and the golden-eyed beauty had accepted this.

Victoria was just crossing the courtyard when the man she least wished to meet came out the door. She smoothed her hand over the white velvet of her riding skirt, fingered the black frogging that complemented her little black hat, then stopped herself. It was obvious from the expression on his face that he was not pleased with her.

The first words from his lips confirmed her suspicions. "I thought we had come to an agreement about my accompanying you when you went riding. I would think that the reason for this precaution would be doubly apparent after yesterday."

She flushed from the roots of her hair to the tips of her toes, avoiding contact with his gaze as she allowed self-righteous anger to become her armor. "Mr. McBride, you have no right to speak to me that way. I'll have you know that I did not go riding alone. I was attended by one of the grooms." She looked at him then, her brows arched. "And, as you can see, I am perfectly well."

He scowled at her. "At least you had the good sense to do that much."

A blinding wall of outrage rose up to block her vision, making her inhibitions about speaking of what had happened between them evaporate like dew. "You...you have gone too far. How can you possibly have the gall to tell me that I am safer with you than anyone else?"

She made to go around him.

But she was halted when his hand closed around her arm. "Victoria...I..."

The subdued, remorseful tone of his voice penetrated the fog of her ire, and she looked up into his green eyes, and was lost. Never could she stay angry with him, when he appeared so clearly tormented by what had happened himself.

He went on softly. "I did not mean for that to happen. I can only think we were both overcome by our relief that you were safe. And you are absolutely correct to reproach me. I had no right to speak to you as I did. I reacted badly to my own guilt."

She did not know what to say. She wanted to believe that he was right, that she had felt those stirrings of desire only out of her relief at being saved a second time. Somehow there remained a trace of doubt that she could not quite dismiss.

Firmly she brushed it aside. They had to find some way to go on from here. Because of their agreement, they must remain in close proximity to one another over the next while. Squaring her shoulders, she nodded. "Yes, I believe you must be right. And I accept your apology."

He looked at his hand on her arm, as if only just realizing that he held her. He let go and stepped back. "Thank you. It will not happen again. Especially not after we have those two arrested."

Victoria's eyes grew round with amazement. "Arrested? I do not see how anything would be solved by that."

He stared at her in shock. "You can't mean to let them go a second time."

She frowned. Arresting Reginald and Lloyd would serve no purpose. They were cowards, the both of them. Because they were aristocrats, there was little likelihood either of them would be suitably punished, for what, in truth, had they done? She had come away safely each time they accosted her. It was not worth the scandal that would be brought on the name of Thorn.

She didn't even wish to discuss the situation, but Jedidiah McBride continued to stare at her in amazement.

Why did he have to be so obstinate? As soon as they settled their differences on one matter, he was on to the next. With deliberate politeness, she said, "I thank you for your concern, but I have no wish to make any of this public. Neither Reginald nor Lloyd is very brave, nor indeed very bright. They had no idea that you were still with me, and so thought I would be an easy mark for their schemes. Finding out that I have someone to protect me will have completely changed their thinking." She paused for a moment, then shrugged. "After I am married, they will no longer feel they might gain by taking me."

Jed looked down at her in consternation. Could she not see that she was as beautiful and desirable as a summer morning? He knew she believed Reginald was only after her money, but the man would have to be even more of a fool than he seemed to not see Victoria for what she was. Intelligent, kind, courageous—and, God help him, passionate.

But he knew she would not listen to him now that she really felt that the threat was past. Why she did not want to see the two men punished for what they had done was lost on him. But this time he would bow to her wishes.

After what he had done the previous day, he felt he had little right to press her about this.

Without meeting her gaze, he nodded. "Very well, Victoria. It will be as you wish." But even as he acquiesced, he made a mental vow not to relax his guard until she was safely married.

Then he realized that thinking of her safely married made him even more uncomfortable than he felt about any possible danger from the two would-be kidnappers. He was saved from having to contemplate just what this might mean by the arrival of one of the footmen.

He approached them hesitantly. "My lady?"

Victoria looked to him in question. "Yes."

He flushed, looking decidedly uncomfortable about disturbing her. "We are having some difficulty in repairing the eaves that were broken in the recent thunderstorm."

Jed watched as she immediately became the mistress of Briarwood, putting her personal concerns aside. Victoria motioned for the man to lead the way. "We'll come and see what can be done, John."

Having been included, Jed followed them around the side of the huge sandstone mansion. They came to a halt at the rear of the right wing. Looking high above them to where John the footman pointed, Jed saw two of the other male servants standing on the slate roof.

John addressed his mistress. "See there, right above the third-floor window. It's that piece of the eaves. We can't get to it from above, and it's too far for any of the ladders to reach from below."

Jed took in the situation with a frown of concentration.

He then turned to Victoria, who was tapping her lips with a fingertip.

She said, "I see. Well, it appears that we will have to call in someone who can repair the damage."

Jed spoke up. "Not necessarily."

She looked at him in surprise, and he said, "If they were to rig up a bosun's chair, the house servants could easily reach the damaged section, and in perfect safety."

Victoria smiled at him with dazzling brilliance, and Jed felt his heart contract. She was so very lovely with her gray eyes shining up at him like that. He forced himself to think about where they were and who they were, even as she answered him. "Can you tell them how to go about this?"

He shrugged, looking up toward the roof at the footman, at the sky, at anything but her. "Of course."

He addressed John directly, telling him exactly what would be required. In minutes, the servants had done as he instructed and one of them was soon lowered over the side in the bosun's chair.

Once they had seen that the contraption would indeed work, the men waved down cheerily, then went about fixing the eaves. Jed could see their smiles from the ground.

Victoria then turned to him again. "Thank you so much. Never would I have thought of such an ingenious idea."

He felt uncomfortable with her praise. "It is a common enough sight on a ship, used for repairing sails and rigging. Not a great invention of my own, by any means."

She would not be put off. "No, really, it may seem so to you, but I am grateful for your help. It is sometimes difficult to look on a situation in a new way. You bring a fresh perspective to the problems of running an estate because of your many experiences at sea. Twice now you have come to my aid in this way. I shall certainly miss your assistance when you have gone."

She suddenly became very quiet, and Jed would not allow himself to wonder why. It could do neither of them any good.

With a shake of his head, he swung around, just walking, doing anything to keep from thinking about her. What Victoria might make of his abrupt departure, he did not know. Firmly he told himself he did not care what she believed. He was using her for no other reason than to find his son.

To his surprise, he realized that Victoria was with him. Glancing over at her, he could tell she was preoccupied with something, her expression faraway as she walked along at his side.

Even as he watched, she turned to him with a thoughtful expression. Her face was also undeniably weary, despite her beauty, as she wiped a stray curl from her forehead. "I really don't think you understand how good it is to have someone to take even a small amount of the responsibility of taking care of all this." Her hand swept the air around her. "There is always so much to do, especially at this time of year." A harried laugh escaped her. "At any time of year. Old stores have to be sold or transferred to make way for new crops in the spring. Everything must be nursed along in summer. Then comes the harvest in the fall. The problems of cold and hunger in winter. And that is making no mention of the estate's other business interests, the mills, the mines, the potteries."

"Don't you have people to manage such things?"

"Oh, yes," she replied, "but my father preferred to have a close hand in everything that happened on his estates. It is the way our family has done things for generations. The best way to make sure everything is done as you wish, is to do it yourself."

He could see the sense in this. It was the way he had made his own not-inconsiderable fortune. He realized his assets were probably meager in proportion to what Victoria was responsible for, yet the principle was the same. Jed felt an almost unwilling admiration for her. Unwilling because he didn't want to feel any such emotion toward her. The physical desire that drew him to her with nearly irresistible strength was enough.

At the same time, he couldn't help thinking that fate had dealt a cruel hand to Victoria, in spite of her obvious advantages. It seemed she had little time for any activities other than work. No wonder she wasn't married. He only hoped that she would find a husband who would take some of this burden from her.

She deserved the things that other women took for granted, such as having children. Jed knew that, given an opportunity, Victoria would make a good mother. She was gentle and patient with children, as he had seen in her treatment of little Sarah. A dedicated and loving husband would free her to have that.

But Jed did not want to think of Victoria as a mother. Especially not as the mother of another man's children.

To his surprise, he heard himself saying, "If you need anything else while I am here..."

She looked up in astonishment, her gray eyes studying him closely.

He went on quickly, feeling inexplicably uncomfortable. "I mean, if there is anything I can do to help with things..." Jed motioned around them absently, all the while wondering what was going on inside that head of hers as she continued to watch him.

Victoria smiled then, and he felt his heart come to a halt, then start again. Good Lord, he found himself wondering, how could she do that to him so easily, even as he made an attempt to focus on her words. "Thank you so very much, Jedidiah. You have already helped me more than you know just by making such a kind offer." Her smile faded, and she looked down at her riding crop as she tapped it with seeming absentmindedness against the toe of her white leather boot. "But I could not trouble you further. My problems are not yours, and I would not dream of taking any more advantage of your good nature than I already have."

Jed wanted to tell her that she hadn't taken advantage of anything, that he wanted to help her, to take some of her burdens from her. He held his tongue. He had been hired to protect her from harm, not to offer advice about her affairs.

Jed looked up to see that they had come to the patio at the back of the main section of the house. From inside, it was accessed by going through the French doors that lead from one of the formal sitting rooms. The patio itself curved around the back of the house and was edged by a series of wide steps that lead down to the formal gardens, which now lay in glorious splendor before them.

They continued on without speaking, seeming to anyone else, he was sure, to be taking a pleasant stroll together. The truth was that Victoria appeared to be lost in her own thoughts again, and Jed was somewhat reluctant to break into them. He was feeling things he did not want to feel toward the woman at his side, feelings of protectiveness and sympathy that he wished would simply go away.

They did not. He passed through the perfectly maintained rows of roses, lilacs, lilies, various ground covers and hedges without really appreciating them.

They reached the end of the gardens without having exchanged another word, halted only by the simple fact that they had reached the edge of a large ornamental pond. As he stood there Jed heard her sigh as she gazed out over the water. Damn, for some reason he was suddenly overwhelmed by the wish that he could in some way lighten the burden that had been placed on Victoria's slight shoulders.

To his complete amazement, he found himself reaching toward her, placing his hand on her arm. "What do you do to relax, to forget your troubles?"

Victoria looked at Jedidiah in astonishment. She had been lost in her own thoughts, wondering if she would ever find someone to share her life with. Trying with all her might not to picture the man beside her in that role.

Then he touched her. All her efforts to forget how attractive and strong he was, to forget how much she liked having him to lean on, dissolved.

Collecting herself with difficulty, Victoria shook her head, unable to ignore the warmth of his fingers through the thin fabric of her sleeve. "I...do not know." She tried to think, to answer him, anything to get him to take his hand away. "It has been some time since I even thought of such a thing."

"Think back, then," he insisted. "When was the last time you remember doing something just for amusement?"

Prodded by his obvious determination, she cast her mind back. The image that entered it was the memory of the day her father had taken both her and her mother rowing on the pond. She pointed out over the water. "My father took my mother and me out in the rowboat one afternoon. I haven't thought of it in years, but that was a wonderful day." In spite of the fact that the memory was poignantly sad, considering that the incident had taken place not long before her parents died, she felt herself smiling in fond remembrance.

"Then let's get moving," he told her. "I believe I can find my way around a rowboat."

Before she could form a reply, or even question why Jedidiah McBride would care about her lack of diversion, he led her toward the small dock that jutted out over the water. The next thing Victoria knew, she was climbing into the rowboat that was moored at the end of the dock.

Jedidiah removed his coat and slung it across the seat for her to sit on. Without even understanding why she was going along with this foolishness, she sat down on it. It was impossible for her to relax. There was so much she had to do. Already she'd spent too much time walking with Jedidiah. Mr. Jameson, the overseer at Riverview Farm, was coming to see her later this very afternoon.

More than that, this small craft was just too intimate a space to contain both herself and the handsome American. She allowed herself a brief glance at Jedidiah as he undid the rope that held the boat to its mooring.

Why was he doing this?

Jed seemed completely unaware of her tension as he settled in and reached for the oars with an expression of determination. Only moments later, they were off, gliding across the small lake.

Neither of them broke the silence that had fallen between them. Looking over at Jedidiah from beneath her long dark lashes, Victoria was amazed anew at just how attractive he was. He stopped rowing for a moment, rolling up the sleeves of his white shirt to expose strong forearms. He then reached up to unbutton the gray waistcoat he wore, and she found her gaze drawn to the wide expanse of his chest beneath his white cotton shirt as he began to exert himself again. His long legs were stretched out before him, and she realized that the tip of his black shoe was touching the tip of her own small boot. There was something unsettlingly intimate about the contact, and Victoria knew she must think of something, anything, other than the man seated across from her.

It was a hazy day, with a hint of dampness in the air, but for the piercing sweetness in her heart it might have been sunny. Victoria leaned back, telling herself that it was completely foolish of her to take so much pleasure in being with him, in the fact that he was being so nice to her. But she could not totally expel the swell of pleasure inside her.

Trailing her fingers in the cool water to distract herself, she focused her thoughts on a family of swans as they glided past them. The pair were busily attending a group of small, unattractive offspring, and she watched their antics for a moment.

Unexpectedly her mind drifted back to that day with her family. The swans had just hatched their young then, too.

Mother had brought a book of poetry, and she and Victoria had taken turns reading from it in their most theatrical voices. Her father had teasingly told them that if he should ever lose his fortune he would place them on the stage and they would earn his keep.

The memory was deeply poignant, and her eyes glittered with unshed tears. She did miss them so.

Jedidiah's voice interrupted her thoughts. "What is wrong, Victoria? Are you so conscientious that it distresses you to leave your work for an hour?"

She looked at him in surprise, at first not comprehending the question, because of her own distraction. Then she saw the teasing glint in his eyes, and could not prevent herself smiling, in spite of her sadness. "No. I'm afraid I was thinking of nothing so noble as that." She looked around her, waving a hand to indicate the idyllic scene. "I was simply thinking of the last day my parents and I spent some time here. It was shortly before their deaths."

He stopped rowing, his eyes growing dark with compassion. "I'm sorry. I didn't mean to upset you by reminding you of something painful. I'll take you back in."

Victoria found herself drowning in the warmth of his gentle concern, unable to look away. It was the very thing that had attracted her to him on the night they met, that and his strength. She had responded to it the same way every time she really needed someone since, such as when Sarah had been burned. He showed her just how kind and gentle a man lay beneath the tough and overconfident exterior. Just as she had been those other times, Victoria was drawn to the sea captain, in spite of the fact that she knew it was sheer madness.

She held out her hand to him. "No, don't go back. I'm not upset. I was only remembering. And the memory is a happy one, for all that I miss them terribly."

He hesitated, watching her closely. "Are you sure? Don't try to spare me."

She looked down. "I am not trying to do that." If only he knew how much she liked being with him, how much she wished to stay here on the lake with him. "Let me assure you," she told him firmly, even as she tried to keep her voice coolly polite, in direct opposition to all the feelings churning inside her, "that I do wish to stay." Keeping things on as impersonal a level as possible was the only way she could allow herself this time with him. She gave a self-conscious laugh. "Although it is quite irresponsible of me to do so."

He gazed out over the lake. "You are the most responsible individual I have ever known." He made a sweeping gesture with his hand. "All of this means more to you than your own happiness."

She felt warmed by the comment, because something told her he was not trying to flatter her. There was a trace of something that almost sounded like regret in his tone. Yet she knew that could not be, for what would cause it?

Unwittingly Jedidiah allowed his eyes to move over Victoria's lovely features, those dark lashes, that luscious mouth. It dipped lower, to trace the curve of her breasts in her high-necked gown of white. He dragged his gaze away, then found himself looking down at her slender ankle, which was stretched toward him. It was a trim ankle in white laced boots. For a moment, all sound ceased, and he found his attention focusing on that one small point, Victoria's delicate, narrow foot in that white boot. He saw himself reaching forward, to undo the ribbon laces, gently slipping it off. He had never kissed a woman's ankles, and for the first time in his life he found himself wondering why.

A sound intruded, the sound of Victoria's voice saying his name. "Cousin Jedidiah?"

He gave a start, swallowing hard, then licked his unbelievably dry lips. "Yes." What in the hell was wrong with him? He'd been with his share of women in the years since Nina had left. Not once had he been so stirred up over the sight of a booted foot.

In fact, he couldn't remember being so worked up over the sight of a completely naked female. He gave himself a mental shake. Obviously he had been without a woman for far too long.

"Perhaps we should go in."

Looking over the space between them, Jed found her watching him with an oddly wistful expression in her gray eyes, an expression that brought an unexpected sense of yearning. She glanced away as soon as he met her gaze. Perhaps they should.

Then, just as he was about to reply, he felt a drop of rain hit the back of his hand. Victoria seemed to notice at the same moment, for she looked up just as he did.

Somehow the cloud had moved in even as they sat there. Jed realized he must have been too occupied with thinking inappropriate things about Victoria's ankles to notice. He heard her gasp as the rain began to pour down more forcefully, and felt very much the fool for having failed to see it coming.

Now they were stuck out here, far from shore, in a downpour. He had certainly managed to help her enjoy her afternoon.

Then, to his complete amazement, he heard a noise that sounded like laughter erupt from Victoria. Knowing that he had to be mistaken, Jed swung around to face her.

She was smiling widely, holding out her hand to catch the fall. She laughed aloud again, making his heart turn over in response. At that moment she looked up at him, her eyes growing round as their gazes met, then darted apart. Suddenly she scowled, making him wonder at her mercurial change of mood. Even as he watched, she glanced around them in perturbation and said, "Row us over to the back side of the lake, please." She pointed to the opposite side of the lake. "That shore is closer, and there is a place where we can take shelter at the top of the hill."

With sure, quick strokes, Jed moved the boat in the direction she pointed. He couldn't see any reason for her sudden change of attitude, and decided against trying to find one. This woman would drive him to drink if he allowed himself to get upset every time he didn't understand her.

Concentrating on getting them over to the bank gave Jed something less aggravating to think about. He couldn't see any shelter on the hill behind the lake, but he trusted in her assertion that there was.

Victoria watched surreptitiously as Jed rowed them close against the bank, unable to keep from noting the way the rain had turned his white shirt transparent. That was what had brought on her abrupt change of mood. Seeing Jedidiah that way made her think of things she had best stay away from.

Yet her appreciative gaze dwelled on the muscles in his shoulders as they rippled with each stroke. When he stood and held out his hand to help her up, it was a long moment before Victoria could put her own unexplainably cold fingers in his warm ones. She swallowed hard as she rose, not looking at him. As soon as her boot touched the ground, she withdrew her hand from his and started up the steep bank.

When they reached the top of the rise, Jedidiah finally understood where she was taking them. All his attention was now centered on the ruins of the old castle before them. It looked to be of ancient design, and he moved after her with a thoughtful expression.

Once they were on level ground, she hurried ahead. If he hadn't been watching closely, Jed would not have seen where she went as she disappeared through a hole in the once formidable stone wall. He went after her and found himself beneath a wide archway that led to what must have been some sort of hall. At the opposite end from where they had entered there stood the remnants of an enormous fireplace. The roof and portions of the walls had crumbled away along either side, and the floor had grown up with bright green grass. But at this end a part of the roof remained attached to the arch and provided an effective shelter from the downpour.

Victoria stood looking out over the ruin of the hall, her arms wrapped around herself. Though it was not a cold day, in spite of the rain, she appeared chilled.

He looked out over the ruins. "What is this place?"

Her gaze followed his. When she turned back to him, she smiled with pride and a kind of nostalgic affection. "This is the ruins of the first castle on this site. It was built by my Norman ancestor, Gaston de Thorn, and his Saxon bride, Rose."

"You speak of them almost as if you know them."

She touched the cold stone wall lovingly. "I do know them, in a way. The legend of their love story has lived long after them. Rose was a Saxon maid who had been given as a prize of war to none other than Gaston's own older brother, Hubert. But Rose fell in love with Gaston, as he did her, in spite of the fact that he was her enemy. They had a difficult time of it, yet in the end managed to come together, and in so doing founded the Thorn family dynasty.

They have been held up to Thorns throughout the ages as the model of what can be accomplished by two people through love and dedication.''

He frowned at her last words, unaccountably disturbed by hearing Victoria talk about what two people in love could accomplish. "You believe in love, then? You, who would marry the first suitable man you meet?"

She stiffened, obviously stung by his ill-considered remark. The sharp retort she uttered reminded him anew of her inner strength. "And what would you have me do, Mr. McBride? I have to marry someone. It is not my right to remain unwed." She waved a hand to indicate the ruins. "Do you see this? Where I come from? It is my responsibility to carry on, to continue the line. My husband must be willing to have our children take the name of Thorn and wear it proudly." She paused, then went on. "As the legend is told, my ancestor Rose was alone and afraid, the last of her line, but she did what she had to do. In the end, she knew true happiness."

This time she paused longer, and when she spoke again, her tone was regretful but firm. "I do not expect to find that kind of happiness, but I will do what I have to. It is my duty to see that there is a legacy for the others who come after me."

He watched her closely, saw the regret in her faraway expression. And realized anew that, in spite of her brave words, Victoria was lonely, and feared that she might always be so. Unexpectedly Jed felt a swell of sympathy for her. He was deeply sympathetic to her need for someone to care about, because he, too, felt it. Even though he did his best to hide the fact, even from himself, it was there inside him.

This made him more drawn to her, for he, too, had resolved to live without love. His reasons were not hers, having risen out of his own resolve that he would not be hurt again, but they were just as binding.

He moved silently to stand behind her. Was it fair for such a lovely and fascinating woman to live her life for duty alone? For she was both, as Jed had come to know over the few days he had spent with Victoria Thorn.

Jed didn't understand what drove him to whisper what he did, but the words could not be stopped. "And what about passion, Victoria? Is it your duty to live without that, too?"

Victoria could hardly give credence to her own ears. After what he had said to her yesterday, she would never have expected such a thing to come from those lips that had brought her such pleasure and pain.

When she turned to see if she had indeed imagined what Jedidiah had said, he was so near that she could feel his warm breath on her face. She gazed up into his eyes, eyes as dark as a stormy sea, and felt as if she were being pulled under by a powerful wave of emotion. Far from being unpleasant, the sensation was terrifyingly pleasurable.

Her heart began to pound and, judging from the tightness in her chest, she wasn't sure if she would ever be able to take a whole breath again. Oh, heaven help me, she thought, even as she unconsciously leaned closer to the warmth and strength of him.

To her great horror—and greater satisfaction—Jedidiah's arms closed around her. Victoria could no longer stem the tide of longing she had felt since the first time she saw him. The tide that had swept over her the first time he kissed her and could not be held back now. She gave herself up to the overwhelming need to be held close against him. As she melted into the embrace, she lifted her face to him.

Jedidiah's head dipped, and he placed his own lips over hers. Victoria felt the pliant but firm press of his mouth on hers with a sigh of pleasure. Her own lips opened to him, and as his tongue flicked out to test hers, she gave herself completely to the ripples of sweet desire that radiated out from the core of her, reaching up to hold his head still closer to hers.

Jed traced the contours of Victoria's mouth with his tongue, understanding as he did so that he had known she would taste like fresh dew, her lips damp from the rain. He sucked in the sigh that escaped her, taking her breath inside him, filling his lungs with the sweet essence of Victoria.

She tightened her arms on his neck, raising up on tiptoe to press her mouth more fully to his, giving him measure for measure. Jed knew a pulse of piercingly erotic pleasure. He drew her more fully against him, feeling the firm swell of her breasts against his chest.

Victoria nearly cried out with the sheer sweetness of it when Jedidiah placed his hand over her breast. It seemed to take on a life of its own as it grew heavy and aching against his palm. When he circled a thumb over the delicate peak, it grew turgid, even as a ripple of desire undulated though her to settle in her lower belly. His other hand came up to close over the other breast, and she could no longer hold back a gasp of rapture.

She sagged against him, her hands falling to his hard chest. Even as he continued to caress her, she was overcome by the need to explore his body as he was hers. Her eager fingers traced the contours of firm muscle beneath smooth golden skin, with only the wet cotton shirt to hinder them.

She looked up at him, and a fresh wave of longing swept through her. He was so incredibly beautiful, his head thrown back, his handsome face damp from the rain, his eyes closed with the power of the sensations he was experiencing. Victoria felt a wash of exhilaration at the knowledge that she could arouse him. She put her lips to the strong column of his throat, tasting the rain on his skin.

Jed groaned aloud, drowning in the need that rose up inside him. Her cool hands scorched his heated flesh, and he knew an overwhelming desire to get closer to her, to feel her skin beneath his hands.

His arms slipped down her slender back, molding her hips to the burgeoning length of his arousal. When his hands moved lower and he drew up the back of her riding skirt, she made no demurral, simply pressing herself more fully to him. There was too much cloth between himself and her, and he was maddeningly thwarted, first by her skirt, then by her bloomers. At last Jed found his way past the waistband of her undergarment to the deliciously silken skin of her firm bottom. He could not prevent himself shaping those delectable mounds, and he heard her hoarse cry of reaction. He reveled in the sound, remembering how she had sighed earlier, when he kissed her. Judging by her reaction to his touch now, Jed knew that that sigh had been brought on by desire—the same desire that had gripped him.

The desire he had fought so hard to resist.

As the thought came to him, Jed stiffened, his eyes opening in shock. Good God, what was he doing? Victoria was not for him. Everything he knew about her, including what she had said to him only minutes ago about lineage, tradition and adherence to duty, told him how far apart their worlds were. He would not be bound by such rules, the very rules that had made his mother an outcast from her own family.

He was behaving like a madman to kiss and hold her like this.

His only connection to Victoria Thorn was to make sure she was safe until she married. That was all. He certainly was not supposed to be seducing her. Yet he knew that that was exactly what he was doing. Though her responses were all that he could have wished for, Victoria was an innocent. He looked down at her, her lovely face flushed from his kiss, her lids heavy and nearly closed. Even as he was drawn to her, he was disgusted by his own actions.

Some of his distress must have transferred itself to her, for she opened her eyes to look at him in confusion. What she saw in his expression must have given her some clue as to his thoughts, for she put her hand to her lips, pulling away from him with dawning dismay.

She backed away from him without saying a word. Her smoke-dark eyes were filled with the very condemnation he felt toward himself.

He reached out, but she jerked away before he touched her. Jed felt as if she had slapped him. He rasped out. "I . . . I'm sorry. I didn't mean to."

She shook her head, her hands going to her breast. "How could you do this to me again?" She closed her eyes. "Please, don't say anything. I can't bear any more."

He drew himself up. "Maybe I should get my things and go."

She looked at him, her eyes round with some emotion he could not identify. "No. I . . . I don't want you to go. You have rescued me twice, and I owe you something for that."

He opened his mouth to tell her that she owed him nothing, then shut it when he realized what he was seeing in her gaze. Surely it was fear. How could he leave her like this, with no one to protect her? He was obligated to do what he had said he would. And besides, he reminded himself, there was little hope of his finding his son without her. Stiffly he replied, "I will do what I have agreed to. Only when the debts are settled between us will I leave you."

She nodded, without facing him. "I will do what I can to see that your son is found." With that, she turned and ran from him.

Jed made no move to follow her. He felt a wave of self-castigation and bitterness rise up to engulf him. Clearly Victoria would be glad to see the end of him, in spite of her fear. It was obvious that she was disgusted by the fact that she had responded to him.

It seemed that the lady was not so very different from the others of her type. She was ashamed of any feeling she might have for a man like him, a simple sea captain, with no long family lineage to make him acceptable. Again he recalled the story she had told him about her ancestors and her pride in their accomplishments. It reminded Jed that Victoria was very aware of herself and who she was.

His jaw hardened, and he hit the stone wall next to him with his fist. The pain of the contact did nothing to bring him out of his torment. What had he been thinking of, to kiss her, to put his hands on her—?

He hadn't been thinking, only feeling the loneliness inside her, a loneliness that answered an equal need in himself. What Jed had to remember was that Victoria, no matter how vulnerable she might seem, was the mistress of this vast and noble estate.

She could not forget who she was. And he, if he was not as big a fool as he had just acted, could not forget again, either.

Chapter Seven

Victoria tried to occupy herself with looking out the open window of the carriage. But she was infinitely aware of the man who sat so silent and seemingly unaware of her across the narrow aisle.

He lounged back against the comfortably padded seat, his eyes closed, as if he were sleeping. Her gaze went to his hands, where they lay folded across the tops of his muscular thighs. She glanced quickly away as she had a vivid flash of memory, a memory of what it had been like to feel them close around the bare flesh of her bottom.

Heat rippled through her body with an intensity that shocked her. Heavens, what was there about this man that so compelled and enticed her?

Whatever it was, she was determined to put it aside.

She forced herself to focus on the passing scene outside once more, but couldn't stop the perspiration beading on her forehead. Victoria refused to reach up and wipe it away. Perhaps ignoring her reactions would make her unreasonable attraction to Jedidiah McBride go away.

Yet moments later her attention had strayed back to him, to the strong line of his jaw, the masculine angle of his nose, the thick fringe of his lashes against his tanned cheekbone. She gave a guilty start when he reached up to brush at his cheek. Almost as if he had sensed her regard.

What was the matter with her? Never had she been so helpless against any problem or obstacle. Her feelings for this man were such that it was more than she could do to even examine them. And he had made his disregard of her all too obvious. An exhaustion such as she had not experienced in her life swept over her in a formidable wave.

Victoria leaned back and closed her own eyes. Despite her near-sleepless night, she did not expect to actually succumb, but the gentle swaying of the carriage and her own fatigue did overcome her.

Jedidiah was not sleeping.

There was no way on God's green earth that he could settle down enough to rest in the presence of the misty-eyed siren seated across from him. What he had done yesterday had been a mistake—a terrible mistake.

Somewhere during one of his many recollections of what had taken place, Jed had realized that he had not been completely honest with himself about his reaction to the story she told him about the legendary Rose and Gaston. He had been moved by the tale of her ancestors and how they had fought against opposition to make a life together. It was possible that he had somehow, unconsciously, compared them to the lady of Briarwood manor and himself. He understood that the young maid, Rose, had felt the same sense of duty and responsibility that Victoria did, that she had needed someone to care for her as Victoria did.

None of this had anything to do with himself and Victoria. Her ancestors might have been able to overcome their differences and find true love. That had been hundreds of years ago. Victoria was not some Saxon maid desperate to make peace with her enemy for the good of her people.

Victoria was an aristocrat, a product of hundreds of years of privilege and wealth. No matter how yielding she'd felt in his arms, she could only, in the end, be what she was. That was not something Jed needed or wanted in his life.

More importantly, Jed did not care for her. Even if she would have him, which he knew was impossible, he felt nothing beyond desire for her. As intense and overwhelming as it might be, it was still only that—desire.

He was certain she felt the same. Victoria had allowed him to kiss her, but she'd been upset, and he already understood that she was lonely. To think that she would want him for more than that was sheer insanity.

She had in fact been as horrified as he when she realized what they were doing. Her final words to him were proof of that.

He opened his lids just enough to take a careful peek at the woman who so plagued him. He was surprised to find her asleep, her head tilted back on the plush seat. Lord, but she was beautiful—there was no denying that. Her dark hair had been pulled up into a respectable chignon beneath her bonnet, which was tied beneath her chin with a big bow of pale pink satin. The dark tresses had already begun to curl in soft ringlets about her forehead and cheeks. Her delicate lips were slightly parted—inviting.

He wrenched his gaze away. Inviting what, he asked himself? Nothing he could give, came his angry reply.

Again he reminded himself that he was with her for one reason only, to help her find a husband. A man of her own social position. Something Jed was not and would not wish to be.

He was brought out of his reverie by the jarring of the carriage as it hit a rut. The motion was unexpected, and his long leg was cast into contact with hers. The pitch of another rut kept him off balance enough that he could not move to break the contact. Even through her pink-and-gray-striped skirts, the touch was disturbing, for Jed knew the shape and loveliness of those long legs from having inadvertently seen them the first night he met her. A flash of intense heat raced through him and settled in his lower belly.

Victoria was wrenched instantly from sleeping by a jolt from the carriage. She nearly gasped aloud as her eyes flew open and she realized that her leg was touching his, and that it was from that contact from which a pleasurable sensation emanated.

Her horrified gaze found Jedidiah's face. That devil of a man was watching her with the same mockingly distant expression with which he had viewed her since yesterday.

A feeling of intense irritation gripped her. Oh, what she would give to see him lose that ever-present control of his. Yet she knew that was not likely to happen. Jedidiah McBride was not about to allow anyone to get close enough to him to make that possible.

The rocking of the vehicle hindered her efforts to sit up straight. Finally, they seemed to have made their way over the worst of the ruts, and she was able to resettle herself. Leaning back, Victoria made every effort to match his indifferent expression with one of her own.

He eyed her coolly, almost as if he were aware of her discomfort. "Excuse me."

"Of course," she replied with equal civility, glad that he could in fact not know her thoughts. Then Victoria scowled as he turned to stare out the window. She would certainly be glad when they reached London and the end of this journey.

They arrived in London on the evening of the next day. The night had been spent at an inn along the way. During that time, Jedidiah had been dedicated and courteous in seeing to her comfort. She had not been surprised to see the way the innkeeper and his staff hastened to do everything he bade them. Jedidiah's proud stance, his air of command and, of course, the fact that he was dressed as a gentleman made them treat him as they would a peer of the realm.

Yet, in spite of his care of her, Victoria could not help being aware of the distance he kept between them. An example that she felt she must follow, and that began to wear on her terribly. By the time they reached her London home, Victoria was exhausted from being so careful of everything she did and said. She looked upon the immense Georgian mansion in Grosvenor Square with a feeling of relief.

Jedidiah was his own imperturbable self as they alit from the carriage. He followed her without comment as she climbed the steps and the door opened. The housekeeper, Mrs. Dunn, emerged in a flurry of black silk skirts, her cheeks flushed with pleasure at seeing her mistress.

She dropped down in a deep curtsy. "My lady, we are so glad you have come."

Victoria nodded as she came to a halt before her. She wondered what Jedidiah would make of the more formal atmosphere of the London house. She squared her shoulders. Let him think what he would. She would not be ashamed of who and what she was. "I am glad to be back. I trust all is well?"

The woman rose. "Oh, yes, my lady. All is in readiness for your stay." She moved back to motion Victoria forward. Her gaze barely brushed Jedidiah, where he stood behind Victoria. The housekeeper's face remained impassive.

Victoria followed after her, wondering, with some amount of amusement, at the woman's self-control. She was certain that her arrival with a strange man would cause Mrs. Dunn a certain amount of curiosity. The London staff could not already know the story they had told the others at Briarwood, namely that her cousin was visiting her. Both

Sergeant Winter and her own maid, Betty, were following behind in another conveyance with most of the baggage.

Thinking to get the matter over with as quickly as possible, Victoria turned to the sea captain with what she hoped was gracious warmth. "Cousin Jedidiah, this is the housekeeper, Mrs. Dunn."

Jedidiah nodded. "Mrs. Dunn."

Victoria went on. "Mrs. Dunn, my cousin Jedidiah McBride. He will be staying with us."

Now the housekeeper could not retain her pose of formality. "Your cousin?" It was clear that she was working very hard to keep the incredulity from her voice.

"Yes, from America." She kept her expression carefully neutral as she faced the other woman, but she could feel Jedidiah's attention on her back. Drat him, she knew he was amused by her discomfort. Victoria told herself not to care what he thought, and to remember that the lie was necessary. It was the only way to keep the blackguard with her. Under no circumstances would an unchaperoned woman be allowed to reside with a man who was not even a relation. After what had already passed between herself and the man behind her, Victoria was beginning to understand why this was so. If she had not needed him to act as a protector, had not agreed to help him locate his son, she well knew, he should not be in such intimate contact with her.

Flashing memories of Jedidiah's lips meeting hers, his hands on her body, entered her mind and were quickly pushed aside. She would forget that those things had ever happened.

Jed was awakened the next morning by a dainty little maid with a spill of dark hair and shy green eyes. Hurriedly she set the tray she carried on the table beside the window and opened the drapes. Without looking at him, she asked, "Will there be anything else, my lord?"

He still did not care for all this "my lord" business, but had come to understand that he would only confuse her if he said so. With resignation, Jed shook his head. "No, that will be everything, thank you."

With a swift curtsy, she departed.

Jed looked around the room as he made his way over to the tray. The heady aroma of coffee greeted him, and he nearly smiled, knowing that Victoria had remembered to tell the servants he preferred the beverage. But he did not smile. He did not want to think about the lady in any but the most impersonal of terms.

To do otherwise was to court disaster. As he had learned.

He stepped into the buff trousers he had been wearing the previous day and buttoned on the clean shirt in the one case he had brought in the carriage. As he did so, Jed looked around with assessing eyes. The bedroom he had been given was nearly as large as the one at Briarwood, and was decorated in the best of taste, with heavy cherrywood furnishings and sumptuous materials of green and gold. But it did not have the homey feel of Briarwood manor. Embroidered pillows, samplers done by less-than-expert hands and various other simple touches made the enormous mansion feel a little more like a home. But, as he had observed last night and this morning, the "London house," as Victoria called it, was not so comfortable as Briarwood.

For some reason he could not quite define, Jed was uneasy with the realization that he thought of Briarwood as comfortable, as being homey. Anyway, he told himself, it didn't matter what he thought; neither house was his concern, and that was just the way he wanted it.

He was just adding sugar and cream to his coffee when there was a rap at the door. Having come to recognize the distinct signs of Winter's presence over the last few days,

Jed was not surprised that it was the gray-haired sergeant who entered at his call.

"Ah, Mr. McBride, Doreen said you were awake. I trust you slept well."

"Yes," Jed replied, though it was a lie. He'd not had a decent night's sleep since meeting Victoria Thorn. "And yourself?"

The squarely built soldier came into the room and stopped with his hands folded before him. "Fine, just fine. We arrived some time after you had retired, and I decided to leave the delivery of your things until this morning."

"That was very nice of you," Jed told him, taking a sip of the strong, hot coffee. Just the way he liked it, just the way it was served at Briarwood. When he was aboard the *Summerwind,* he was fortunate to get a lukewarm cup that was half-full of grounds.

He was almost beginning to like being looked after this way. As soon as that thought entered his mind, he pushed it away. He would not allow himself to get accustomed to being pampered.

Winter interrupted his disturbing thoughts. "May I have the cases brought in now, sir?"

"Oh, yes, of course," Jed answered quickly.

The older man turned and beckoned to someone out in the hallway. "You can bring them in now."

Two liveried footmen, wearing the same blue as those at Briarwood, entered with their arms laden. They set down their burdens, and the sergeant ushered them from the room.

He turned to Jed with raised craggy brows. "Do you mind, sir?"

"No, go right ahead." Jed waved him on. He was now secretly glad that Victoria had insisted on sending for the manservant. Jed would not have cared to spend even one moment fussing with his new wardrobe.

As the sergeant went about his duties, Jed marveled anew that the man was able to go about such a persnickety task with such masculinity. Even when he was hanging a pair of trousers so that the crease in the legs was razor-perfect, he managed to do so with a quiet sort of dignity.

Not for the first time, Jed found himself wondering about the man, and why he had chosen to take up this profession. He spoke hesitantly, not wishing to intrude where he might not be welcome, especially given how little he cared for prying. "Winter?"

The servant halted in the act of brushing imaginary flecks of dust from a coat sleeve, preparatory to placing it in the deep cherry wardrobe. "Yes, sir?"

"Do you mind if I ask you a question?"

"No, not at all. Go right ahead, sir." His openly surprised expression told Jed that he was genuine in what he said.

"How did you come to work for the Thorns, for the duke?" Jed poured himself another cup of the delicious coffee.

"My uncle Walter was the duke's man at the time, sir. He was getting on in years, and I was injured in the shoulder fighting against Boney's army in France. The army had pensioned me off, and I was looking for a position. You see, I was supporting my widowed sister and her sons at the time, and the pension would not really cover." This was all said matter-of-factly and without a hint of self-pity.

Nonetheless, Jed felt as if he should not have asked. "I'm sorry," he said. "This is your own business. Not mine."

Winter shook his head, smiling. "Oh, my, no. I'm happy to talk of it. The Thorns have been very good to me and mine. When the duke died, only some months after I had completely taken on the position, Lady Victoria made sure that everything would be all right for us." His pale blue eyes grew damp, and he made no effort to hide it. "My sister's oldest boy was studying to be a doctor, and she made sure there was the money to send him on. He now looks after that orphanage of hers along with his practice. The other isn't quite finished yet, but he'll be a solicitor." He nodded fondly. "I'm sure she has something in mind for him, as well. Likes to see them give back, if you understand what I mean."

Jed could only look at him for a long moment, wondering why this information made him feel so odd, so displaced, as if he did not know what was real and what wasn't. Why should it matter to him that Victoria was so thoughtful, that she had the intelligence and good sense to expect her good deeds to be passed on to others?

Then he drew himself up quickly, thinking that it was time he went for a ride. Victoria had informed him the night before that the stable here was amply stocked.

He was not likely to run into the woman in question, as she had told him she would be spending the day ordering new gowns for herself. When he questioned her as to her safety, she had assured him that she would be attended at home. It seemed Mr. Worth himself was willing to make his person available to the daughter of a duke.

As he finished dressing and made his way out of the house to the stable in back, he told himself that with her vast wealth Victoria could well afford to be generous. There was no denying that it certainly made her look better.

Though the words did not quite ring true, even in his own mind, Jed refused to examine them any further. He did not want to see Victoria as a kind, generous and unpretentious woman. Somewhere in the back of his mind was the understanding that to do so would be to risk all he believed in.

That he was not prepared to do.

* * *

Victoria went down to the dining room in one of the new gowns that she had purchased from Worth's. Only two of the ones already made had proved suitable. The rest of what she required would be made up as soon as possible. This one was a lovely confection of dark green silk and ivory lace that trimmed the sleeves and the scooped neckline. Her hair had been swept up, with only a few tendrils left loose to curl about her brow and neck. One final glance in the mirror had shown her an attractive young woman—despite, or possibly because of, the anxious excitement in her gray eyes.

Jedidiah McBride arrived only moments behind her. He barely glanced in her direction as he took his place opposite her, in one of the striped blue silk chairs. Dinner was served immediately, and he seemed to be eating the roast partridge, cucumber soup, potatoes and various other dishes with avid concentration.

In the face of his continued disregard, Victoria barely touched her own meal, simply pushing the food around on her plate. She had not thought Jedidiah would actually compliment her on her appearance, but she had hoped, in the deepest reaches of her heart, that he might at least take notice of her. Anything would be better than this total lack of awareness.

As the minutes passed, Victoria realized she might just as well excuse herself and go to her room. As she moved to take her napkin from her lap, she felt the edge of the invitation in her pocket. Oh, yes, she thought. She had brought it to show Jedidiah. A messenger had delivered the envelope in the late afternoon. In it, her presence was requested at Lady Worthington's ball the very next evening.

Victoria had been a bit nervous about accepting, knowing how very seriously the lady took herself and her social position. In the end, that was what had made her decide to say yes. If Lady Worthington gave Jedidiah the stamp of her approval, it was not very likely that anyone else would even think to question him.

She hoped Jedidiah would agree to go to such a large event so soon. Considering the way he had been treating her, she also found herself hoping he could bring himself to pretend they were getting along. Any hint that they were on the outs would cause speculation they could not afford.

Reaching into her pocket, she removed the missive. "Cousin Jedidiah," she said, her voice sounding surprisingly hoarse to her own ears. She cleared her throat as he looked over at her, his brows raised in question, though there was no real interest in his green eyes.

Squaring her shoulders, she went on. "This came today. I have taken the liberty of sending our acceptance." She held the invitation toward him.

He simply stood there staring at her. Suddenly she'd had enough. She drew herself up. "Mr. McBride. I understand this situation is unpleasant for you. Yet I really must tell you that you cannot continue to treat me this way. I have not done anything to upset you, nor do I mean to. I am trying to get on with things, so that our association might come to a speedy end, as you so clearly desire."

He scowled at her darkly. "Victoria..."

She interrupted. "No, spare me. I just want you to give me your assurance that you will try to behave as if we are not enemies when we attend this function or any other. It is absolutely necessary to do so. If you treat me as you have been, it will certainly cause comment."

"I have not—"

"Again, I say, please spare me. Now, are you willing to make some effort to hide your true feelings for me while we are in public? If not, we may as well put an end to this charade now."

His expression did not soften, but obviously he had realized there was no point in denying the truth of the matter any further. He looked away from her, the muscles in his jaw flexing. "As difficult as this situation has become, I agreed to help you, and I will do so. I have no more liking for the way things have turned out than you. But you don't need to worry about my behavior, *Cousin Victoria*. I will play the fond relation as well as you."

Victoria knew she should be glad of this, that the truth was at last out in the open. For some reason, her heart swelled until it was hard and aching in her chest. She rose with as much poise as possible. "I thank you for that. Now, if you will excuse me."

She turned her back to him, walking slowly from the room, though she had an overwhelming desire to run from Jedidiah McBride, and the wound of his rejection. Not for any reason would she allow him to see how very much he had hurt her by his admission. It was one thing to know he did not have any fondness for her, and quite another to hear him say the words.

Pride was her only ally at this moment, and she would hold it close about her like a heavy cloak.

Chapter Eight

The footman's voice resonated when they paused at the top of the stairs and Jedidiah handed him their invitation. "Lady Victoria Thorn and Mr. Jedidiah McBride."

The ballroom was filled to overflowing, and Victoria felt hundreds of eyes come to rest upon first her, then the man at her side, as their names were announced. She raised her head high on her slender neck. In no way would she give any sign that there was anything untoward about her being here with Jedidiah McBride.

From the corner of her eye, she cast the man in question an assessing glance. If Jedidiah was the least bit ill at ease in this situation, he certainly gave nothing away. He wore his black evening attire with perfect aplomb, and the arm beneath her fingers was steady.

He had been preoccupied during the carriage ride here. Now she watched as, before her very eyes, he took on a decidedly protective air. His gloved hand closed over her fingers as if in reassurance, or affection. His lips curved in a pleasant smile as he looked down at her. Obviously, Jedidiah meant to stand by his word.

Victoria felt her heart lurch in reaction. Although she knew he was only acting, she could not stop her response. Nor could she help wishing it was not an act.

Immediately she told herself that she was a fool. Not for any reason could she allow this intractable man to know how very much he affected her.

As they began their descent of the formal staircase, she watched surreptitiously as his indolent gaze swept the room. It made no sense, given what she knew of him, but it was as if he had been born to these surroundings and was bored by them. A strange bit of pique swept through her, and her fingers tightened momentarily on his arm. Did nothing ever unsettle the blackguard?

As if sensing her displeasure, Jedidiah graced her with a glance of amusement, before turning his attention back to the assemblage before them. She had the feeling he was reminding her of her own assertions that they must appear amicable. Victoria elevated her chin just fractionally, determined not to let the man know he had disturbed her.

At the foot of the stairs, they were met by Lady Worthington. The lady was dressed in a ruffled gown of pale lilac that little served her portly frame. Her pale blue eyes rested on Jedidiah with open curiosity as she reached out a hand to Victoria in greeting.

Victoria steeled herself as she took that plump hand in hers. The moment had come to see how willingly society would accept their charade. "Lady Worthington," she said, surprised at the even timbre of her own voice. She nodded toward the man at her side. "I don't believe you have met my cousin Jedidiah. As he is visiting me, I took the liberty of adding his name to your invitation."

Lady Worthington gaped, her Cupid's-bow mouth making an O. "Your cousin? Why, I did not even know..."

Victoria inserted smoothly. "Oh, but surely you must recall that my grandfather's brother went away to make his fortune in America."

The lady frowned pensively. "Why, yes, I do remember..." Her brows rose in a perfect arch. "An American, you say?"

Jedidiah spoke up then. "Yes, Lady Worthington, an American, and very pleased to be here in England, absorbing some of your culture. Not to mention the pleasure of meeting such a lovely lady as yourself." He smiled with those even white teeth, his green eyes the color of a summer sea. Victoria's stomach tightened, and her lips went dry.

She watched as Lady Penelope Worthington, known to be one of society's most snobbish and class-conscious matrons, beamed up at the handsome sea captain like some besotted parlormaid. For a man who claimed to have so small an opinion of aristocrats, he was doing quite a good job of ingratiating himself. She could not help casting Jedidiah a scathing glance.

They moved on, Victoria barely attending to what was said as she was greeted by the others in the receiving line. She knew even less of what Jedidiah said, though she noted that he managed to have both of the young ladies present blushing and giggling.

He did not even appear to be aware of her until they were finally moving away from the receiving line. They walked through a high arch that opened onto the ballroom floor. It was lit by the bright glow of a thousand candles. Jedidiah leaned close over her with a hiss of annoyance. "And what are you looking so angry about?"

She stiffened at his censure, as they paused just inside the archway. She barely noted the women in silks and satins gliding about the polished marble floor on delicately heeled slippers. The men, in dark evening dress and spotless white gloves, held their dancing partners at a respectable distance at all times. Victoria continued to be no more than peripherally aware of the throng of guests as she glared up at the tall blond man. "For one who professes to think so very little of society, you have made a good effort at putting yourself forward."

His hand tightened on her arm, making her pull away abruptly as his dark eyes met hers. "Isn't that the reason I'm here with you? Did you not remind me yourself that I was to abide by my end of our bargain? Are you now telling me, *Cousin* Victoria—" his meaningful gaze drifted to the throng around them "—that you do not want me to behave as if I belong here? Are you further telling me you want everyone to suspect I am not your cousin, as you have said? It seems you are having some problem with making up your mind." He gave her a long, indecipherable look. "I am not. My mind is set. I must appear to be what you say I am in order to have any hope of finding my son. And that, my dear *Lady Thorn,* is more important to me than my pride or my dislike of your class."

A deep flush stained her cheeks as she unconsciously rubbed her arm where he had held it so tightly. "Forgive me... I...do not know what got into me. I simply had not expected you to be quite so adept at acting your part. It seems there are things about you that I do not know."

At that, she saw his jaw harden. Hurriedly she continued, not having meant to anger him by the remark. But even as she went on, she wondered at his reaction. "Of course you would be willing to go to any lengths in your search for your child. It is understandably of the utmost importance to you." Victoria realized that she was babbling most uncharacteristically, but she could not stop herself. "And of course you are following through with our agreement, no matter how distasteful it may be, in order to locate him."

Jedidiah made no reply.

A long, heavy silence fell between the two of them as they stood there alongside the ballroom floor. Victoria looked away, forcing herself to concentrate on the scene before her. She saw the mature women, in bright splashes of color, and the debutantes, like Easter lilies planted among more exotic flowers, in their demure white gowns. She vividly recalled the night of her own debut, how proud her parents had been, how they had stood arm in arm as she met and was welcomed by society. How long ago that now seemed.

Tonight she wore a new gown of silvery satin. It was trimmed with the most delicate lace in a matching shade, as were her slippers. The only other adornment was a large rose of palest pink that rested just below the scooped neckline of the gown and matched the one Betty had pinned in her upswept hair. There was no one to care how she looked, no one to smile with, no one to share a secret. Her sigh was more wistful than she would have liked.

Some inner sense made her aware of Jedidiah's attention on her, and she turned to him, her eyes questioning. He was watching her with a mixture of curiosity and sympathy.

He leaned close, even as she wondered what could have brought on his abrupt change of mood. For a long, breathless moment, she stared at him, her heart thudding in reaction to his gentleness.

He shook his head, and when he spoke, his tone was softly questioning. "What is it?"

She held her head high, and forced a smile. "There is no need for concern. It is simply the first time since Mother and Father..."

He grimaced. "Of course, this would be very difficult for you, Victoria. Is there something I...?" But even as he began to speak, his gaze fell on some spot behind her and he muttered, "What the—?"

Jed started across the rim of the ballroom floor with obvious determination, though where he might be going she had no idea. Victoria went after him, her brow creased with confusion. Jedidiah stopped at the door leading into the dining room, where refreshments had been set out. His eyes searched the throng.

She put her hand on his arm. "What . . . Jedidiah, what is it?"

His worried gaze went to hers. "Cox," he told her. "I'm sure I saw him in the ballroom. He was coming this way."

Victoria studied the crowd closely, though she did not believe Reginald would act against her, even if he was present. It was possible that she might at some time see him again. Even though she had expected he would make himself scarce for some time to come, they did move in the same circles. Despite this understanding, she felt a sense of anxiety at the thought of his being near.

Seeing no sign of the would-be kidnapper, Victoria forced herself to relax. She turned to her escort. "Really, I believe we are becoming overanxious. Surely he must be ashamed of what he has done and would not show his face in polite society. And even if it was Reginald you saw," she reasoned, "he obviously does not have the courage to face you. Thus, he is no longer a threat to me."

She squared her shoulders. "We should go back to the ballroom. I do not wish for his foolishness to spoil this night for us, or any other, for that matter."

As Jedidiah allowed her to lead him back the way they had come, he looked down at her with doubt still clouding his dark eyes. "I do not have the same faith in Cox's desire to do the proper thing that you do. The man is scum, and would not have tried to kidnap you if he had the least amount of decency in him."

Inside her, Victoria knew that what Jedidiah was saying might well be true, but she had known Reginald most of her life and could not believe that two such respectable people as his parents had raised a child completely without morals. She still hoped that once Reginald realized just how despicably he had behaved, the young nobleman would come to his senses. She did not bother to say any of this to Jedidiah. It would do no good. She was well aware of his feelings toward the other man.

She gazed up at the handsome sea captain for a moment, nearly overcome by the sheer masculine force of him. For he was never more formidable or more autocratic—or more attractive—than when he was disturbed over her safety. When she answered him at last, her voice was unexpectedly husky, giving away more than she would have in her agitation. "I fear you are right. I do not mean to defend him in the least. I only wish to forget what happened and not live in dread. I could easily do so, you know. My fear of being forced to do something against my will is strong. It is the reason that drove me to ask for your protection." She glanced down at her gloved hands, then back to his face. "I can think of no other man I would trust to do so, which leaves me to wonder if Reginald and his kind are really so very rare. It seems that there are few men of your caliber, Je—Cousin Jedidiah."

His eyes locked on hers, and Victoria felt a strange current pass between them. With that current came a vivid flash of memory, a memory of the feel of Jedidiah's lips on hers. The strength of his arms around her, his hands on her back, her waist, her buttocks.

A liquid warmth settled in her lower belly. Her chest ached with the effort it cost her to breathe. The sensations were only heightened when his own gaze darkened with an emotion she was afraid to name.

The next instant, she was drawn firmly back to an awareness of her surroundings as a deep male voice spoke from her other side. "Lady Victoria."

Still somewhat dazed, she looked up to see Sir Roger Kasey standing beside her. The pleasant-featured young man looked toward Jedidiah with a polite expression in his dark gray eyes, then turned back to Victoria. "May I claim the privilege of the next dance?"

She glanced up at Jedidiah, who merely nodded, his gaze not meeting hers. His expression was as remote as ever it had been. She swallowed down the lump that rose up to block her throat and addressed Kasey. "Yes, of course."

Unable to bring herself to look at Jedidiah again, she took the arm Roger Kasey held out to her. As they moved out onto the floor, she wondered desperately why she could not begin to control her reactions to the American. She seemed to have no sense whatever as far as he was concerned.

Her lack of sensibility could only be blamed on her reaction to his obvious care for her safety. Jedidiah McBride took his responsibilities very seriously, and protecting her was one of them. Victoria would do well to remember that his feelings for her went no deeper than that.

She looked up at Roger with a falsely bright smile. He did not appear to even notice her forced animation as he beamed down at her. It was well known that Roger was in search of a wealthy wife, and had no illusions that the young fortune hunter would do for her own purposes. But she was indeed grateful that he had rescued her from again making a fool of herself in front of Jedidiah McBride.

Jed watched from the sidelines, trying hard to convince himself that the displeasure he felt toward the man was brought on by the nobleman's lack of respect for Jedidiah. Why, Victoria might very well have promised the dance to him already.

Just like the rest of his fellows, Jedidiah thought, totally lacking in any consideration for anyone other than himself. Well, if that was what Victoria was looking for in a husband, it wouldn't take long to find her one.

As he watched her leave the dining room, Jed had had the feeling that Victoria was hurt. The urge to comfort her had been great. But he could not do that. It had been more than his battered willpower could withstand. He'd known that he could not touch her and control himself.

If she only knew that he was so very careful of her safety because it near drove him mad to think of anyone touching her against her will—of touching her at all. How could he explain that to her, even if he wanted to, especially when he did not understand it himself?

His thoughts left him feeling decidedly uncomfortable. Unwilling to examine the reason for this, he watched the couple as they circled the floor, keeping Victoria ever in his sight. When she smiled and gazed up at her partner with rapt attention, Jed's lips thinned.

The only thing that held him back was a certainty that Victoria would not take the young buck seriously. He was round-cheeked, and slightly clumsy in the steps, seeming somewhat in awe of the dark-haired beauty. Not at all the sort the lady had described as her future mate.

He was relieved when that dance ended, and was just thinking that he should retrieve his charge when she was immediately approached by another man in evening dress, who led her out onto the floor again. That this fellow was not of the same ilk as the other Jed could immediately see. He was tall, very slender, and walked with a confident grace that bespoke a certain physical strength. His hand slid around her slim back with practiced ease as he moved her into the steps. This was no easily controlled boy, but an experienced man.

Jed's scowl deepened.

Victoria could feel Jedidiah watching her, and wondered at his continued concern. She had barely taken note of her new partner as he took her in his arms, so occupied was she in thinking about what had just happened between them.

Thus preoccupied, she was surprised to hear her partner speak. "What could bring a frown to such a lovely lady's face?"

She looked up into a pair of arrestingly dark eyes. Good heavens, she was dancing with none other than Lord Ian Sinclair, known throughout the social world as Lord Sin. Victoria had never actually met the man before, but his reputation had preceded him. It was well-known that he had a penchant for women, gambling and racing.

As she studied him, Victoria could not help noticing that the man looking down at her was decidedly handsome, with his aquiline nose, regal features and air of sensuality. But, to her surprise, the realization left her quite cold. It was a pair of sea-green eyes that rose to fill her thoughts. Impatient with herself, she pushed the image aside.

Jedidiah McBride was not available to her. Even if he was, she would not have the disagreeable man. He was far too commanding and sure of himself.

She concentrated on the man who held her in his arms, answering his question as directly as it had been asked. "And why do you have the audacity to inquire about my frown, sir? A gentleman would be too polite to ask."

He studied her closely, assessingly, then shrugged and glanced around the room as if he viewed little of interest. "Because it is the first genuine expression I have encountered all evening. I did not feel you were wearing the thing so as to affect any kind of response on my part, but because you might actually be vexed about something."

Victoria could not withhold a laugh. "My, but you are indeed direct."

He looked at her with some show of surprise, his dark brows arched over those compelling dark eyes. "A trait that many find displeasing. What of you, Lady Victoria? Do you find it displeasing?''

She could not conjure up a coy reply. ''No, sir, I do not. I fear I am amused by it. But I can see why others might not be. Do you always begin a conversation with a stranger so unconventionally?''

He grinned, showing a streak of boyishness that she was sure had caused many a heart to turn. ''Not always, but I often do with the young debs. It quite unsettles them, you know.''

''You are a devil, just as they say you are,'' she told him.

He looked away, an expression of pain passing quickly over his handsome features before it was replaced by that look of studied boredom. Suddenly Victoria realized that this man had hurts of his own. As they all did.

It made her warm even further toward him, and she smiled with more sweetness than she realized. ''Tell me about yourself, Lord Sinclair.''

He looked down at her, his eyes darkening with appreciation. ''For you, dear lady, anything. What would you care to know?''

She understood that he was flirting with her. ''Whatever you wish to tell me.''

He gazed at her for a long moment, and then a wicked gleam came into his eyes. ''The first thing I would do is admit that the reason I am attending this tedious affair is that I do enjoy shocking the young debs. Dear Lady Penelope would not have sent around an invitation at all, except for the fact that she is afraid of offending my esteemed father, the earl. He believes if I continue to come to these affairs I will eventually find some suitable female and marry.''

Her brows rose in an incredulous arch. ''Marry? You, Lord Sinclair?''

Again she saw that sad expression run fleetingly across his face before he was able to successfully mask it. "My father does insist that the line must be made secure. He does so hate to be thwarted." She could not have mistaken the bitterness in his tone.

Victoria gazed up at him, realizing that whatever pain was between father and son had deeply scarred this man. Could that have something to do with his wild reputation? Was he simply defying his father in all he did? She could not prevent herself asking, "Is that why you have become Lord Sin, to displease your father?"

He looked at her even more closely than before. "I think, Lady Victoria, that you see too much."

Victoria realized she had indeed overstepped herself. This man was a stranger to her, and she had no right to interfere in his affairs. "I... Forgive me, my lord. I had no right."

His dark eyes swept over her, and she felt herself flush from the heat in his gaze. Even though she was not attracted to the handsome nobleman, she, being neither dead nor unconscious, could not help being aware of his charm.

Thus, his next words left her momentarily speechless with shock. "If I ever did marry, Lady Victoria, I should think it would be someone not unlike yourself."

Jedidiah watched Victoria dancing with the tall slender man with growing displeasure. They were far too engrossed in whatever conversation they seemed to be having. Neither had appeared to even notice the end of one set and the beginning of another.

When Victoria tipped back her head and laughed with what he considered far too much abandon, Jed felt his stomach clench. What was she thinking, to carry on like this? It was the lady who seemed so very preoccupied with her reputation. He glanced around and saw that more than one person seemed to have taken note of the couple. More than one delicately patterned fan was raised to shield the topic of conversation. But the direction of their gazes gave the gossipers away.

Jed was wondering if he should, in all consideration for his responsibility in looking after the lady, cut in, when a female voice sounded directly behind him. "Mr. Mc-Bride."

He turned to see their hostess, Lady Worthington, bearing down upon him. She had in tow a rather shy-looking young blond woman dressed from head to foot in debutante white. As Lady Worthington dragged this obviously reluctant female to a halt before him, she said, "My dear Mr. McBride, I must introduce you to my niece, Felicia Tidesdale. She is just come out this season, and one only wants her to meet the best people, you know."

Jed barely restrained a mocking grimace. As the "cousin" of the duke of Thorn's daughter, he was among "the best people." If this woman knew him for whom he truly was, a lowborn sea captain, she would not be introducing him to her niece, the innocuous Felicia Tidesdale.

Being ever aware that he must not do anything to bring censure on Victoria, he asked the young woman to dance, as was clearly expected of him. While a beaming Lady Worthington stood looking on, he swept the girl out onto the floor. He was now completely sorry he had allowed himself to be manipulated, but there was no way out.

Determined to get this done, then find some quiet corner to have a few minutes to himself, Jed was careful not to make eye contact with the girl. He clenched his jaw and went through the motions of the dance.

It came as a surprise to him some moments later to hear her speak, however hesitantly. "I must apologize for the way my aunt forced you to dance with me. It would be quite all right for you to take me back now. I'll say I don't feel well."

Jed looked into a pair of brown eyes that, while still filled with shyness, also held a glint of intelligence. Unexpectedly he found himself feeling sympathetic toward her. It really was not Felicia's fault her aunt had appropriated him, and he could be a bit more compassionate toward her own embarrassment. She might, after all, have been as unwilling as he. He smiled down at her. "I'll be happy to comply, Miss Tidesdale, if that is what you want. But I would very much like to finish our dance." Unexpectedly he realized it was true. His mother had taught him many years ago, and he hadn't had many opportunities to dance since.

Her gaze searched his face for a time, and then she smiled in return. "I, too, would like to complete our dance."

Felicia grew unusually quiet again, and Jed wondered at the cause of her preoccupation until his gaze followed hers, to light on a young man who stood at the sidelines. He was of medium height and build, there was nothing to set the fellow apart but the openly desirous look in his eyes as they rested upon the young lady. Her own expression was equally yearning.

"So that is how it is," Jed interjected. "Why aren't you dancing with him?"

She blushed scarlet, glancing up anxiously. "He is not quite what my aunt would wish for me. Henry is only an honorable." As he looked into her eyes, he realized there was something fresh and unspoiled about her that reminded him of his friend Peter's young sister, Leanne. For some reason, that surprised him and made him feel somewhat protective of the girl. He would not have thought to find himself thinking such thoughts about a young debutante.

Jed's expression was indulgent as his dark brows rose. "Only an honorable?"

"Yes." He watched as she scowled with determination. "My aunt has sponsored me for my coming out, and so I must do as she says while I am in London. But as soon as the season ends, Henry is going to call on Papa. Papa is the younger son of a baron, but has no care for titles himself. He only agreed to have me come to Aunt Worthington because I begged him so. He will accept Henry's suit."

Jed studied her closely. It had not occurred to him that there were those among the nobility with varying opinions on the wisdom of their ridiculous rules. Obviously Felicia had grown up in such a household.

They went on for a moment in silence. Then she said, "My, Lady Victoria is quite brave to dance so many dances with *him.*"

Jed looked across the room, to where Victoria was still gliding in the arms of the tall stranger, and looking too entertained for his taste. He turned back to Felicia, asking more gruffly than he intended. "What do you mean, *him?*"

Her brown eyes went round with uncertainty. "Why, I did not mean to criticize. I admire your cousin greatly, and wish that I could be so bold as to do as I wished."

Taking care to keep his tone even, Jed said. "I understand. Now tell me, who is he?"

She glanced over at the couple in question. "Why, that is Lord Ian Sinclair." She lowered her voice to a whisper. "He is a notorious rake, though I am not supposed to know that, nor can I elaborate on all his nefarious deeds. Suffice it to say that he is known by all and sundry as Lord Sin."

Lord Sin, Jed scowled. He glanced over to the couple and saw the way the man was looking down at Victoria. Now there was no mistaking the avid interest in the man's attention.

The music ended at just that moment, and Jed lost sight of the woman who so occupied his mind as he returned his charge to her aunt. Quickly he extricated himself from

Lady Worthington's clutches and went in search of Victoria. He had an overwhelming need to rescue her from this new threat.

She seemed ever to be in need of his assistance. A fact that gave him an unexplainable sense of gratification.

Searching the ballroom for her, Jed began to feel a strange sense of uneasiness. Which, he told himself, was absurd. Nothing could happen to her in the midst of all these people, yet he still made his way to the wide archway at the other end of the room with purpose.

A moment later, he saw the man she had been dancing with lounging indolently in one of the chairs against the wall, a drink in one hand, a cheroot in the other. There was no sign of Victoria.

He turned about in frustration. The man was not with her, but Jed could not shake his sense of unease.

Again he recalled that momentary glimpse he'd had earlier of a man who looked very much like Reginald Cox. At the time, Victoria had been convincing in her assertions that it could not be him. The doubt he had felt then began to nag at the back of his mind.

He did not see the lady in the crowd of well-dressed people gathered around the buffet table, and his trepidation grew. Going back into the ballroom, he made his way to the French doors that led out onto a wide flagstone patio with steps that went down into a darkened garden. The area was vacant of anything besides some decorative shrubs in flagstone planters.

He was just turning to go back inside when he glimpsed a furtive movement below. Acting purely on instinct, Jed bounded down the steps. "Victoria!" he called.

Another noise came to him. He could not actually have said what had made it, but the sound was enough to direct him to where he wished to go. When he dived into the brush at the side of the path, Jed discovered none other than Reginald Cox lurking there in the darkness.

He sprang forward, barely noting the abject terror in the other man's eyes. Jed's voice was harsh with anxiety. "Where is she?"

Reginald backed away from him, coming up against a shrub. "I don't know." He waved his arms wide. "As you can see, she is not here."

Watching him closely, Jed asked, "Why did you run from me?"

"Why, indeed?" the dark haired man replied. "I saw you come out onto the patio, and did not want a confrontation."

Jed scowled as the other man rubbed his jaw, where he had taken a blow the last time they met. Ignoring the gesture, Jed said, "Why should I believe you? I could not find Victoria, and I have reason to think that if you had the opportunity you would do her harm."

Reginald gestured broadly again, his lips twisting in derision. "Then where is she? Have I hidden her in my pocket?"

Jed started toward him with a muttered curse.

He was halted by a voice behind him. "I am here."

He turned to see Victoria standing on the path behind him. Sweet relief flooded through him like a fresh brush of wind in limp sails. "Victoria."

She looked from him to Reginald. "What is going on here?"

Taking a step toward her, Reginald held out his hand. "Victoria, this man was accosting me. Tell him I have done nothing."

As he moved in her direction, Victoria flinched toward Jed, who instinctively placed himself between her and the other man. This seemed to completely incense Cox, for he stamped his foot like a petulant child. "Victoria, how could you do this? How could you allow this oaf to threaten me? Why, he's not even a gentleman!''

Jed moved toward him, the very nerve of the bastard making him want to throttle him. He certainly did not think of himself as a gentleman, but neither, in his opinion, was Reginald Cox. "Where I come from, Cox, gentlemen do not try to kidnap ladies.''

Reginald turned to Victoria with an expression of superiority that could not quite disguise his fear. Yet his words were brave enough. "You will call off your hound, Victoria, if you are wise. I know enough to make trouble for the two of you that you don't want."

Again Jed started toward him, but Victoria's hand on his arm held him back. He turned to look into her worried gaze as she asked Cox, "What do you mean, you know enough to make trouble for us?''

Cox laughed now. "I mean, Lady Victoria, that I know you are going about town with the story that this man is your cousin. Having been there when you met, I very much doubt that this is the truth. A little investigating would surely prove me right and you both as liars.''

Jed growled. "If you tell people how we met, then you'll have to admit to everyone what you were doing in her coach that night.''

Reginald blanched, then shook his head, his expression becoming determined. "So I would." He looked to Victoria. "But I believe I have the least to lose here. Your reputation would be ruined if the truth got out. Not even your position as the daughter of the duke of Carlisle would be enough to protect you from the scandal. You would drag your family's name through the muck.''

"Don't listen to him," Jed told her angrily. "We should call the authorities, at the very least. The man has twice tried to abduct you, and now he's resorting to blackmail to keep himself out of trouble.''

Reginald made a soft scoffing sound, interrupting them. "Victoria, if you would but see reason and marry me, all would be well. Your family and mine were friends. Why can you not see that it would be a sensible answer to my devotion to you and your lack of a husband?"

Jed looked at the other man with disbelief. His absolute conceit really seemed to have left him with no understanding of the reality of the situation. He ignored Cox, addressing Victoria directly. "Turn him over to the police. As you can see, he is crazy."

"I cannot," Victoria answered, her voice filled with regret, but also with determination. "It matters little for myself, but I cannot risk the Thorn name in such a scandal. To have him tell that we have concocted the story of your being my cousin would bring shame to my children. Their very parentage might be questioned. They would not be welcome in polite society."

"He can't just be allowed to get away with this." Jed was incredulous. "It is obvious he means to continue to be a threat to you."

"I have you to protect me until I marry," she replied, her eyes dark. "After that, Reginald will see me settled and it will no longer be an issue." When he continued to frown, she said, "Please, Jedidiah, for the sake of the children I will bear someday, I cannot allow the truth to be known. I was foolish to believe we could carry this out without being discovered by anyone. I was also foolish to believe Reginald was a man of some honor and would come to his senses. He obviously means to harass me at will, but he has guessed the truth, and now we have no choice but to let him go in order to keep others from finding out."

Reginald chuckled with unholy satisfaction, making Jed want to break some of those teeth for him. In spite of what Victoria had just said, he was not going to let the other man think he could harm her without fear. He turned to Cox with an expression of absolute resolution. "Let me tell you, little worm, that I will abide by Victoria's wishes in not telling the authorities. But if I so much as see you touch her or speak to her, I will, and with pleasure, beat you within an inch of death. Is that clear?"

Reginald said not a word, trying to stare the sea captain down. But when Jed took a threatening step toward him, Cox obviously realized he had pushed the other man too far. With a grunt that could have been of either fear or rage, he swung around and ran into the recesses of the garden.

Jed turned to Victoria, who stood at his side. She said not a word. Finally he could take it no longer. "Why are you willing to live with the threat of that man simply to please society?"

She looked up at him then, her expression becoming regretful and perhaps a little sad. "You will not try to understand." She tapped her chest. "I am more than myself. I am Thorn, all that there is left of my family. I must act for the good of that, more than for my own good. You profess to care little what others think of you but I do not believe this is completely true. You live by your own set of principles, some as foolish as any aristocracy might have made. You hold your hatred of society to you like a shield, not allowing that they—we—are like anyone else, some good, some bad. I do not know what has made you this way, but there is something, and it is every bit as jealous a ruler as any dictum I might follow."

He could only stare at her in amazement, surprised by this attack, however gentle. He had a momentary recollection of Felicia Tidesdale and his realization that she reminded him of Leanne. Felicia was a child, and not yet hardened in her beliefs. His voice was bitter as he spoke of it. "Felicia Tidesdale just regaled me with an unbelievable tale of how her father is going to allow her to marry the young man she loves, even though he's not her social equal.

What I think, Victoria, is that she is living in a fantasy, as you are. She will find out soon enough how her father welcomes her 'honorable' Henry."

Victoria shook her head. "There you are wrong, Jedidiah McBride. Her father is a good man whom I have known well because of his work with the poor. His elder daughter is married to a simple country parson. I'm sure he will allow Felicia her choice."

Jed scowled. He could not dispute her words, but neither would he let himself accept them.

She took a step closer to him, her face soft with compassion. "What is it, Jedidiah? Why do you hate us so? And do not tell me it is Nina, for I think it goes beyond that, to something deeper and more painful."

Jed shook his head, calling on all his will to reject the sensitivity in her eyes. He was not going to let Victoria Thorn get inside him.

Something told him that if he did, he would never get her out again. And that was something that could not be allowed. They came from different worlds, and that was the way it would stay. Because there was no other choice.

Was there?

He looked down into her eyes, so dark in the shimmering light of the moon, so deep and fathomless. What did she want from him?

"Tell me, Jedidiah," she whispered. "I want to understand."

For a moment, he felt something rise up inside him, a long-buried sense of hope, the hope that anything was possible. That it didn't matter who you were or where you came from. As soon as the feelings rose, he felt the hard lessons of truth rise up to shout them down.

Victoria was wrong. He had not chosen his system of beliefs. It had been drummed into him by experience.

With a groan of frustration, Jed swung around and headed back toward the house, the lights, the distant strangers. He had to get away from Victoria and the false promise of hope she raised inside him.

Chapter Nine

Victoria tried her very best to concentrate on what Mr. Fuller was saying to her. He had come up from the country to bring some paperwork that would not wait for her return.

Unfortunately, her efforts to focus her attention were meeting with little success. As had become her habit, she was thinking of Jedidiah. She knew he was not happy about the things she had said to him the night of the ball. In the past two days he had, if it was possible, become even more remote than before. There was very little conversation between them, and he was rarely in her company.

She knew she had gone too far in confronting him so directly. His view of the world was not her affair.

But even when she was angry with him and frustrated at his lack of understanding, she was still attracted to him. His strength and sense of personal honor drew her as the sun drew the roses from their buds.

If only, she told herself, things could be different.

Unconsciously she sighed.

Mr. Fuller coughed, drawing her attention. "Forgive me, Lady Victoria, I have kept you too long."

She looked to him in surprise, and some embarrassment. "No, forgive me. I became distracted for a moment. You came all this way, and we must finish."

He stood, gathering his papers together. "With all due respect, my lady, I find I, too, am tired. Might we please finish in the morning, before I return to Briarwood?"

Knowing the man's sudden exhaustion stemmed from a concern for her, Victoria nodded. "Thank you, Mr. Fuller."

He bowed, and she rose to see him to the door. As they left the library, she said, "Mrs. Dunn has prepared a room for you. I hope you will be comfortable."

"I'm sure I will, my lady," he replied, seeming pleased at her solicitude.

Just as they moved out into the hallway, a sheet of paper fell from the stack in the estate manager's hands. He bent to retrieve it. As he did so, he paused, looking at it with a frown. He then turned to Victoria, indicating the sheet. "If you don't mind, my lady, there is one thing that I have kept neglecting to mention to you."

She nodded. "Of course. What is it?"

"It's the boilers, madam, the ones that were meant for shipment to Germany. With the advent of the Crimean War last year, they were not sent. There are still a number of them in your warehouse. Surely we should find another buyer?"

A male voice spoke from behind them. "Boilers?"

Victoria turned to see Jedidiah McBride standing behind them. It was apparent from his attire that he had been out riding. He was taking off a pair of kidskin gloves even as he spoke. "Did I hear this man say you have some boilers for sale?"

She answered as evenly as possible, for he was so very handsome with his dark blond hair tousled by the wind and the quickening scent of spring all around him. "Yes, he did say that."

He barely looked at her as he turned to the other man. "If they are in good working order I would be very interested in buying them. I have been looking for a return cargo for my ship, and this one seems perfect. My partner and I have recently gotten into the business of steamship building.''

Mr. Fuller assured him quickly. ''They are in perfect working order, sir.''

Only then did Jedidiah look to Victoria, his tone as impersonal as if he had been addressing a stranger. ''Do you have any objection to my purchasing these boilers?''

Victoria felt her heart ache at the way he was treating her. Only with the help of her pride was she able to rally herself quickly. ''Of course I have no objection. Why don't I leave you two to discuss the details?'' Without waiting for a reply, she turned and made her way toward the stairs without a backward glance.

Later that evening, Victoria looked up from her seat in front of the Louis XIV dressing table as the door opened behind her. It was Betty, and she carried the gown of ivory silk Victoria would wear to tonight's ball.

As the maid moved to lay the elegant confection across the bottom of the bed, which was draped in pale blue and white brocade, Victoria lowered her gaze to her hands. In a deliberately casual tone, she asked, ''Has my cousin returned?'' She looked up to study Betty's reflection in the mirror. Jedidiah had gone out for another ride before the evening meal, and she had not seen him since.

The maid's eyes took on a dreamy expression. ''Oh, yes, Mr. McBride returned from his ride some time ago. I believe he is even now bathing.'' The girl's blue gaze took on a yearning expression that told Victoria quite clearly that she would not be averse to seeing such a sight.

Unable to stop the wash of memory that filled her own mind of a vivid view of Jedidiah's appealing form, Victoria stood abruptly. No matter how she told herself to put such thoughts behind her forever, they continued to surface when she least expected them. The most disturbing times being when the man in question was present.

Going to where her hoops and petticoat awaited donning, the lady turned to her maid. "I am ready to dress now."

Betty gazed at her with a puzzled frown. "Don't you want me to finish your hair first?"

With an embarrassed start, Victoria laughed, trying to appear unconcerned. "Oh, of course."

She went back to the dressing table and sat quietly while the emerald-tipped pins that were to be her only adornment were placed in her hair. Though she did not meet the maid's eyes, Victoria could feel her speculative gaze upon her. It was not the first time since Jedidiah McBride came into her life that she had behaved in an unusual fashion.

Heaven only knew that it was not likely to be the last.

It was some time later that Victoria arrived in the hallway downstairs. She needn't have worried that Jedidiah's late-afternoon ride would delay him. He was waiting there for her, chafing to be off, as always.

She tried not to notice how very handsome he looked in a tight-fitting black jacket, cut away to show a paisley vest, and buff-colored pants. In spite of that air of impatience, which in truth was one of the things she found intriguing about him, he looked elegant and at ease in evening dress.

Did any man have a right to be so handsome and so very self-assured at the same time? For he was self-assured, completely so. It was obvious in the proud angle of his head, the restless stance and squared shoulders.

When he glanced up and saw her approach, he stilled for one long moment, and Victoria felt her heart throb in answer to the naked appreciation in his eyes. But in the time it took to take a breath the expression was gone, and Victoria thought she must surely have imagined it. Not since the day he kissed her in the ruins of the old castle at Briarwood had Jedidiah so much as hinted that he might be attracted to her. Though it was no more than a week ago, it might have been years, for it seemed that any inclination toward her had been completely wiped from him.

Victoria knew she should be grateful for this, for anything that occurred between them could only be a mistake. Yet telling herself this and feeling it were not one and the same.

His days were spent in riding, and who knew what else. All she had been able to glean from his stilted conversation at meals was that he was making further inquiries about Nina Fairfield. In their public appearances, he had been politely attentive. She knew that this was only out of necessity, in fulfilling the terms of their bargain.

She turned her gaze to the marble floor, not looking at the man as he wrapped her green satin evening cloak around her shoulders. Moments later they were in the carriage and headed through the warm spring night. Jedidiah seemed no more eager to make conversation than she, and they rode in heavy silence. The coach lantern had not been lit, and she was grateful for the darkness, which hid the sadness she could not have explained even to herself.

The mansion was brightly lit, and the conversation was cheery as they entered the foyer and were greeted by their hostess, Lady Bainbridge. Victoria moved stiffly through the receiving line, ahead of her escort. She barely noted what was said to her, as she was paying close attention to the way young Miss Bainbridge, who was in her second season, giggled and fawned over the innocuous remarks Jedidiah made to her. She held on to his hand for such an extended period that her mama, who was next in line, gave a nervous titter and told her that the line was becoming quite long.

What a silly goose Susanna Bainbridge was, Victoria thought as she heard the girl openly invite Jedidiah to ask her to dance. Then she found herself smiling unexpectedly as he extricated himself from having to do so with smooth charm. He told the girl that he would not dream of taking unfair advantage of the other young men who would be eager to enter their names on her card. Susanna was so gratified that she actually flushed with pleasure.

As ever, Victoria was amazed at the way Jedidiah, who professed such disdain for society, managed to move through every situation as if born to this life. He had bested Susanna at her own flirtatious game, and made her feel flattered while doing so.

Victoria couldn't help glancing back with raised brows. As she did so, her gaze met Jedidiah's, and a strange current of amused understanding passed between them.

Victoria had to look away to hide the rush of happiness that sharing such a moment, however insignificant, brought. Whatever was wrong with her, she thought, that everything occurring between herself and this man seemed so much more interesting and exciting than anything else in her life?

With these thoughts riding hard on her mind, Victoria hurried through the rest of the receiving line. She then made her own way to the ballroom.

Victoria was immediately approached by none other than Lord Ian Sinclair. He had been in attendance at nearly every function she attended thus far, and seemed always to seek her company. She knew that despite his reputation, Ian was much sought-after as an eligible bachelor. His interest should flatter her, but though she had grown to like the attractive man, she really felt nothing beyond that.

Unaware of her thoughts, the seductive heir to an earldom smiled with obvious appreciation as he bowed before her. "May I have the honor?"

As Victoria accepted the proffered arm, she wondered why it could not be this man who drew her. It was not as if he were unattractive—quite the opposite—but there was none of that breathless internal commotion she felt when Jedidiah looked at her.

"It is good to see you again, Lady Victoria," Sinclair told her, his eyes holding hers.

Victoria looked up at him from beneath her lashes, wishing again that she could feel something for him. He made no effort to hide his interest in her.

His hand tightened on hers. "It really is so very good to see you again. I find that you are the one bright spot in these dull affairs."

Perhaps, she told herself with determination, she should try to think of him in that vein. There was no denying that she was here in London looking for a suitable husband, in spite of the fact that she had so little enthusiasm for doing it.

So thinking, she smiled with forced brightness as he swept her out onto the floor so capably. "How very kind of you, Lord Sinclair. And perhaps I am just a little bit pleased to see you, as well." To her amazement, she gave a flirtatious laugh.

He laughed in return, a sensuous, husky sound that unfortunately did nothing to her whatsoever. No breathlessness, no thrill of awareness. Drat. Jedidiah's merest glance could bring more of a reaction.

At that moment, Victoria felt a tingling along her spine and glanced over across the floor. Jedidiah McBride was standing in the archway that led to the ballroom, his attentive gaze turned upon them, a scowl marring his brow. For one brief second, their eyes clashed, and she felt that very same sensation that was missing when she was in the arms of Ian Sinclair. Her heart pulsed and her chest tightened.

Then she was swept around by the steps of the dance and his face was no longer within her sight. The devil take him, she thought with irritation.

Jed watched the dancing couple with ill-concealed disapproval. This was the man who had seemed so taken with Victoria the night they had encountered Reginald Cox. The events since had kept Jed from dwelling too much on the fellow's behavior. He had managed to make himself available to Victoria at the other occasions since, but Jed had been determinedly occupied with making inquiries about Nina. He had felt ashamed on realizing that he had completely forgotten to do so on the first night they went out into society. It was, after all, the reason he was in London.

Even after Jed began to pursue his objective, he'd had no luck at all in discovering anything over the course of the past few days. The one family he had found by the name of Fairfield had turned out to be an innkeeper and his wife. When he questioned the wife while having a tankard of ale, she had clearly borne no knowledge of any well-placed family members.

Now, as he watched Victoria and the stranger begin their second dance, he knew a sense of misgiving he was not prepared to question. He told himself it was because of the unfavorable things Felicia Tidesdale had said about the man.

Also, Victoria had not before now seemed overly interested in him or any of the other young men who claimed her for dance after dance. Tonight, there was a difference in the lady. She was smiling at the man—flirting.

His stomach twisted painfully. If any of what Felicia had said about the man was true, he was not a suitable companion for Victoria. Jed thought it would be a good time to find out something more about the man.

He did not think there would be any questions about his wanting to know everything he could about the too-attentive, too-attractive fellow. He was, after all, posing as Victoria's cousin, and could openly make inquiries about any man who might pursue her.

Purposefully he approached his hostess, who was standing with her daughter at the front of the sumptuous ballroom. Jed soon learned that young Miss Bainbridge did indeed still have this dance open and would be happy to attend him. Carefully hiding his true annoyance at the way she simpered up at him, Jed led her out onto the floor beneath the beaming gaze of Lady Bainbridge.

How differently, he thought once again, they would all behave if they knew who he truly was.

The young lady seemed willing to answer his questions about Victoria's partner.

"Oh, that is Lord Ian Sinclair," she replied eagerly to his inquiry. "Mama has forbidden me to dance with him, though he is quite handsome, and the son of an earl." Her voice dropped for a moment as she whispered, "He has a dastardly reputation with the ladies. There was some rumor of a duel between him and the Honorable Norman Humphreys only a short while ago. It is also rumored that he is an incurable gambler, that being the way he is said to make his living. He is called—" she paused dramatically "—Lord Sin. Mamma did worry about asking him tonight, but she could not quite cut him dead when he said he would like an invitation to the ball. You see, he is the earl's heir, though some say he may not inherit for many years to come. His father, though an older man, is in excellent health. It is bandied about that the earl is quite tight with the purse strings, if you know what I mean." She ended with big-eyed innuendo. "That is why he must gamble, you know."

With every word spoken by the little featherbrain in his arms, Jed's disapproval deepened. He looked over and saw Victoria throw her head back and laugh at something the bastard had said to her.

Lord Sin, indeed.

Trust Victoria to involve herself with a man like that. She was, after all, the same woman who had kept trying to convince him that Reginald Cox was harmless.

Miss Bainbridge leaned her head forward, as if she were about to share a secret, drawing his attention back to her. "Of course, Lady Victoria might do as she pleases, with little fear of damaging her reputation. She is, after all, the daughter of a duke, and well thought of among our set. Her father was a great philanthropist and spoke in the House of Commons about the conditions of the poor. You know the sort of thing I mean." She prattled on. "He had a great concern for those living in the poorhouses and the children working in the mines. Lady Victoria has continued to support such causes, though as a woman she cannot do so as publicly." She paused, fluttering her long lashes at Jed. "That is all well and good, and she is much to be admired. But I believe a man wants a woman who will look after her husband and children. Do you not agree, Mr. McBride?"

Jed could only stare at her for a brief moment. Did she really expect him to make some reply to this ridiculous statement? What man would choose such vapid silliness over kindness and intelligence? Especially when it came in a package as delectably lovely as Victoria Thorn.

Jed did not want to think about that right now. He was more concerned with making sure the lady in question was not putting herself in harm's way by being with this "Lord Sin."

It was entirely true that the longer Jed knew Victoria, the more he was forced to respect her. It was also true that he felt she was somewhat naive and must be protected.

As soon as the set was over, Jed took his charge back to her mother and bade her adieu with polite purpose. He then turned and made his way across the floor to where the notorious Lord Sinclair was just drawing the lady of Briarwood back into his arms.

Jed met the other man's dark eyes with absolute confidence and a hint of warning. "The lady has already done me the honor of agreeing to dance this one with me."

Sinclair eyed him levelly. The cool appraisal brought no discomfort to Jed, but he did feel a certain amount of respect for the other's self-assurance. Here, finally, among all these fops, was a man of some substance. Too bad he did not use that strength of character for some better purpose than womanizing and gambling. He could not be allowed to attach himself to Victoria.

Without waiting for either of them to reply, Jed drew Victoria into his arms and away from the other man. Only after they had moved some feet distant did Jed become aware of the resistance of the woman before him.

She held herself so stiffly that she felt like a wooden masthead in his arms. He scowled down at her with irritation. "What is wrong with you?"

She stared up at him, her gray eyes round with incredulity. "What is wrong with me?" she sputtered. "You come along and whisk me away from my partner without even asking. I did not promise this dance to you." She looked away, taking a deep breath. "You never asked for this one, or any other."

Against his will, he was made achingly aware of the beauty of her profile as she refused to look at him. He also became aware of the feel of her in his arms. Though propriety dictated that he hold her some inches away from his own body, his hand rode low on her slender back. One of her delicate hands was clasped in his, the other rested, tense as a bird poised for flight, on his shoulder. Contrary to all his good judgment and sense, Jedidiah found himself re-acting to her nearness as he always did.

He had an almost overwhelming urge to pull her close, to press his mouth to the tantalizing curve of her breast above the low neckline of the ivory silk gown. The very thought made his body tighten in reaction.

This caused him to speak more harshly than he in-tended. "Victoria, what were you doing dancing with that man? Do you know who he is?"

If it was possible, she became even stiffer. "I wanted to dance with him. And yes, I do know who he is—whatever that has to do with anything." Her gray eyes glared her de-fiance, and he found himself caught by their spirited beauty. He forced himself to pay attention as she went on. "And what business of yours it is, I do not know."

His jaw hardened at her words. But he spoke with cool reason, in spite of the heady rose scent of her, in spite of the rise and fall of her full breasts above the deep circle of her décolletage, in spite of his arousal. "You made it my busi-ness when you asked me to protect you."

That seemed to silence her, but only for a moment. She answered him through thinned lips. "We are looking for a husband for me, are we not? Lord Sinclair is the most likely candidate thus far."

Agitated by her statement, Jed nearly tripped in his smooth gliding circle around the room. It was bad enough that she should remind him of their purpose in finding her a mate. But to say that that rake was a likely candidate was nothing short of madness. Hadn't she told him she wanted someone dependable, someone to help her, someone to count on? According to what Jed had learned of him, Sin-clair would fit none of these needs. His tone was rife with sarcasm as he spoke. "And you believe that 'Lord Sin' would actually suit your purpose? Really, Victoria, I had thought you more discriminating."

When she gasped aloud, Jed realized he had gone too far this time. He was quick to rush in. "I... I apologize. I should not have said that. But I can't help wondering if the man has been honest with you about his reputation."

His apology seemed to mollify her—somewhat. When he looked down into her gray eyes, he saw that they were dark with stubborn determination. "He has told me of his reputation, and some of the reasons for it. No matter what you might think, Jedidiah, I do like Ian. I find his honesty refreshing."

Jed grimaced. Already the fellow was "Ian." How long had it taken him to get her to call him by his given name? Still she insisted on Jedidiah, though it irritated him no end. He had to think of some way to make Victoria see that she might be making an error in judgment here, that she should not simply trust people because they appeared to be honest with her. Why, he himself might have been some opportunist, bent on taking advantage of her.

Glancing down at her averted profile once more, Jed knew he had to find some way to convince her to at least go carefully. The truth was that, no matter how he had tried not to see it, Victoria was not like other women of her social circle. In all honesty, he had to admit, at least to himself, that she was special, uniquely herself.

She needed someone of her own kind. Her generosity, her openness, the naiveté that cloaked her in spite of her wealth and position, these were the reasons he could not bear to see her with a man who would not make her happy. What Victoria deserved was a man with many of the same noble qualities she possessed.

Even as the thought that perhaps no man would answer his criteria passed through his mind, Jed pushed it aside. He would help her find just such a mate. And not just because of their bargain.

"Victoria . . ." he began, his tone made softer, more caring, by his desire to assist her. She looked at him now, her eyes wide with surprise and a sudden uncertainty. This uncertainty grew as he went on. "I only wish you would see the situation for what it is. All these men—not just Sinclair, but others, at every function we attend—fawn on you and vie for your attention. You attract them as honey does bees, but none of them has been worthy of you."

She interrupted him, even as a deep blush stole over her pale cheeks. "They care nothing for me, these men. They want only what I can bring them by way of wealth and social position. I am nothing to them."

Jed looked at her, appalled that she might actually believe this, for her pained expression told him she did. He shook his head. "Victoria Thorn, there may be some among them who answer to that description. The majority, while they are aware of those things, want you for your beauty and intelligence. You far outshine any other female who has graced the ballrooms, parlors, and dining rooms we've visited in the past days. You, Lady Victoria, are a desirable woman in a vast sea of simpering girls. That is not the problem."

His tone deepened with sincerity as he went on. "The problem is, as I have said, that none of those men, so far, have even come close to being good enough for you."

Victoria could only stare up at him, her heart swelling in her chest at his words. Jedidiah seemed totally oblivious of the havoc he had wreaked on that wayward organ. That Jedidiah should say this to her was astounding.

And it meant more than she would ever admit to anyone, least of all herself. She had seen the way the women of the ton had treated him, thrown their daughters at his head, fawned over him. For his part, the sea captain had given them no more than cursory attention in return. A fact that she had believed was caused less by their lack of charm than by the simple fact that he was very single-minded in his determination to find his son and return home, to the life he knew and preferred.

Somewhere in the deepest recesses of her womanhood Victoria felt a thrill of pleasure that Jedidiah compared her so favorably with the other women he had met. But she was, as yet, unwilling to ask herself why.

She knew how he felt about her world, the way she lived. Victoria was bound by time, tradition and responsibility to carry on her birthright. There was no choice in her future.

Jedidiah's acknowledgment of the very attributes that kept her from being able to act as did other young women her age was a heady thing indeed. How could she tell him that, far from attracting other men to her, her strengths repelled them? Only Jedidiah seemed not to completely disapprove of these qualities.

She glanced up at him from beneath her long, dark lashes, her heart beating in triple time as she realized that they were actually dancing. Dancing together for the first time. Despite the seriousness of their conversation, she couldn't help noting that their steps matched perfectly. He held her with complete assurance, in a light but secure grip that left her in no doubt as to who was leading.

Not for the first time, she wondered where he had learned to dance, to speak so well, to present himself with such polished ease amid the society he so disdained. Puzzled, she ran her gaze over his handsome face. So many things about this stubborn, honorable, fascinating man were a mystery to her.

At that moment, the music ended and Jedidiah stopped, looking around them at the crowd of finely dressed guests. When he turned back to her, his expression had become unreadable.

Clearly he had withdrawn from her again. Her heart sank with disappointment, and she opened her mouth to ask him why.

At that very same moment, a young man appeared at her side. She recognized Leon Cranshaw without enthusiasm.

"May I have the privilege of claiming this next dance with Lady Victoria?" His clipped British tones lent an impression of superiority to his words. Victoria realized this was not in the least appealing to her. She found a slightly drawling English rested more pleasantly on her ears.

She looked up at Jedidiah, wishing in some far corner of her being that he would send young Lord Cranshaw packing. He did not.

Jedidiah glanced over to the fellow, his eyes taking in the man's noble bearing, his air of hauteur and his perfectly tailored evening dress. He turned to Victoria with a mocking bow, and stepped back. "Well, then, *Lady* Victoria, I will leave you in better hands than mine."

With that, he walked away without a backward glance, and Victoria felt regret rise up to constrict her throat. Even though she knew there could never be anything between them, his dismissal hurt.

His pointed emphasis on her title said it all. They came from different worlds. She could not leave hers, and Jedidiah would never allow himself to become part of it.

Chapter Ten

When they returned to her home some hours later, Victoria was still reeling from Jedidiah's most recent rejection. His attitude was even more difficult to accept than before, now that he had made the disclosure that he actually admired her.

Looking up at his averted profile as he stepped aside for her to enter first, she could hardly credit her own remembrance of what had been said. It seemed utterly impossible to believe that this cool, distant man had said she was lovely and intelligent, not to mention all the other wonderful things that had emerged from those tightly held lips.

Not bothering with the pretense of wishing him a pleasant good-night, she hurried up the stairs to her room.

Some two hours later, Victoria found that she still could not sleep. The stirrings she had felt at being held in Jedidiah's arms kept coming back to haunt her.

Rising from her bed, she pulled a lace-trimmed white velvet robe over her gossamer-thin white night rail. Victoria then made her way downstairs to the library. Perhaps if she read for a time, sleep might come to her.

Victoria was just crossing the hall to go to the library when she took note of a light coming from the sitting room. With a puzzled frown, she changed direction, wondering who else might be awake at this hour.

She entered and saw Jedidiah sitting in one of the wing-back chairs. When she saw that the chair had been pulled up next to a table that bore a single lit candle and a whiskey decanter, she made to back out of the room. But her entrance, however quiet, did not go unnoticed by the man.

He looked up from the glass he held in his hand with a mocking smile. "Ah, Victoria, just the woman I was thinking of." He gestured toward her with the nearly empty glass. "Come and join me."

Her heart thudded in response to this invitation as she took in the reduced level in the bottle on the table next to him. Jedidiah had been drinking, and possibly more than a little. She knew that alcohol caused men to lose their inhibitions. A strange, but not unpleasant, turbulence spread through her abdomen, but whether it was due to a fear of what he might do, or a fear of her own reaction, Victoria did not know.

When she spoke, she was disturbed to hear the breathlessness in her own voice. "Are you drunk?"

He laughed derisively. "Drunk? No, I wouldn't say so, though I have been drinking."

Though his words were meant to be reassuring, Victoria did not feel so. There was a strange reckless quality to his tone and words that she had never heard before. And heaven help her, she found this new side of him dangerously appealing.

The candlelight shed a delicate golden glow over a small circle that surrounded him. The rest of the room was cast in long, dark shadows that made the area where he sat seem to beckon her toward him.

He gestured with the glass again. "Would you care for a drink? I'll get you a glass—I believe there is another one over there." He moved to rise and go to the darkened end of the room, where she knew glasses were always kept on a silver tray.

Victoria halted him hurriedly. "No, please. I could not, really."

He subsided, giving her a long, enigmatic look that made her run her hand self-consciously over the long, dark braid that hung over her shoulder. "Come, sit with me, even if you won't have a drink," he directed.

Victoria's stomach quivered, and she knew she should refuse, should turn and run to the safety of her room. Yet something, some mystical force, held her immobile. She knew it came from somewhere inside Jedidiah McBride. Even shadowed as they were, his eyes held the power to compel her.

Almost against her will, Victoria found herself going forward. As she stopped beside him and his dark gaze raked over her, she pulled her robe more closely about her neck. Seeing the sardonic smile that stole over his mobile lips as he took in her action, Victoria stiffened. She had the uncomfortable feeling that he sensed the painful struggle inside her, the fear of remaining here in the seductive darkness with him—and the overwhelming compulsion to stay.

Calling on her pride in desperation, she raised her chin and took the seat across from him. Trying her very best to pretend that there was nothing at all out of the ordinary about their being here in the middle of the night, she asked, "Was there something that you wanted to speak to me about in particular?" Victoria was surprised and pleased when her voice did not give away her agitation.

He sat back in his seat, and the change in position effectively shadowed his face. The candlelight now cast his features in sharp angles, so that his eyes were two dark wells that she could not begin to read. He raised his glass and sipped from it before he said, "Is there something in particular? I'm not sure what you mean by that. Perhaps everything in particular. Now that you ask, I don't know where to begin, or even if I should. Nothing in my life has prepared me for you, Lady Victoria."

She leaned forward, her innate curiosity about this man driving her unease to the back of her mind. "What has your life prepared you for, Jedidiah? Where do you come from? How do you know all the ways to behave among society, when you hate them so?"

For a long moment, he said nothing, and she feared she had gone too far once again, that he would never reply to her prying. At last, however, he spoke. "I take it that what you are asking me is how I learned to behave myself in good company."

His tone was rife with sarcasm, and Victoria blanched, not knowing what to say. It became obvious that he did not expect a reply when he said, "Well, *Lady* Victoria, you are right. There is an explanation for what you would call my 'good manners.'" He paused, his gaze focusing on something only he could see, and she listened with bated breath as he went on. "My mother came from one of the 'better' families in Boston society. I think that even here on this side of the ocean you might have heard of Malone Shipping and Ironworks."

Victoria took a quick breath. Of course she had; anyone who read the papers knew of the American shipping magnate Patrick Malone. He was reported to have made a fortune in his various American ventures, and had holdings in Britain, as well.

The sound drew his gaze, and he grimaced as he looked into her face. "I see you have. Well, my mother was his youngest daughter. I say was, because even before she died, she was dead to him, and the rest of her family. She had committed the unforgivable sin of running away with my father. He had been brought directly from Ireland to work in my grandfather's stables. He had quite a good reputation as a horse breeder and handler, but he was a drinker."

Jedidiah looked down at his glass with a wry expression, then set it very carefully on the edge of the table before going on. "I don't know if he ever really loved my mother, or if he was only interested in her because of who she was." He shrugged. "When her father refused to take them in after they eloped, he took her to Bar Harbor, Maine. Why there, of all places, I don't know. Possibly because he couldn't get a job looking after horses when Patrick Malone put the word around not to hire him. He took to fishing for a while, though he was a poor hand at it, and finally ended up abandoning us. Mostly what he did, even when he was around, was drink."

Jedidiah's expression now hardened to the point of hatred, and Victoria shivered as he said, "My grandfather never forgave my mother. She tried, after the old man deserted her, to contact Patrick Malone, to tell him he had a grandson, but he sent the letter back unopened."

Victoria swallowed hard to hold back the tears that sprung to her eyes at the harshness of this. Such callousness seemed unbelievably cruel. But she knew Jedidiah would not thank her for her pity.

He turned to her then, his face achingly bare with the pain and sad yearning of speaking of his mother. "It was my mother who taught me how to speak, to read, to dance, to behave politely. She didn't realize how it would set me apart from most of the people around us. The two of us were so isolated, though she was a woman of rare kindness and generosity, often sharing the little we had from the sewing and laundry she did with those who had less. People admired and respected her, but they did not come too close. Everyone knew she was different, that she was a lady."

He looked into the candle flame, the softness with which he had spoken of his mother gone from his voice. "That was why meeting Nina and feeling she loved me made such an impression. I was seventeen, and didn't know then how much position and wealth matter to people. You see, my mother had given up everything in order to be with my father, because she loved him. Although he was a miserable excuse for a man, I didn't know that money and social position could make others behave even more despicably. My father, after all, was an ignorant drunkard. One would think that those who professed to be his betters would act with more honor."

Victoria couldn't help asking. "Did you ever tell Nina about your mother's family?"

He cast a hard glance in her direction. "Never. And I'm glad of that. If knowing I was related to that coldhearted bastard would have made a difference, I wouldn't have wanted her anyway. Why don't any of you see it's what is inside a person that really matters, not whether they were fed with a silver spoon? The friends I've made, Peter Cook and his family, those are the people I value. When my mother died, only a few months after Nina left Bar Harbor, not a soul in the world cared for me until I met them. They took me in when I developed a fever during a voyage down the coast to Virginia. The ship's captain put me off without compunction in a small rowboat at night, saying he couldn't afford the chance that I might be contagious to the rest of the crew. Peter's father found me floating there the next day, out of my head with fever, and took me home. They were just ordinary people, struggling to keep their shipbuilding firm afloat, and didn't have to live up to anyone's expectations of how to behave but their own. It was knowing they were there, that someone cared if I lived or died, that kept me going in the years of struggle before I began to make something of myself."

She looked at him then, saw the way his jaw worked with emotion on admitting this, on showing her some of his grief. Carefully, she whispered, "I'm sure they are very fine people. I wish it were possible for me to meet them someday. I think that I should like them very much, if they would show such kindness to a stranger.''

He turned to study her closely, then said, ''Somehow, I believe you.''

Victoria met that dark gaze, and found that she could not look away. Never had she expected Jedidiah McBride to share so much of himself with her. It was as if his doing so had shattered a barrier that could never come between them again. There was a naked sort of longing in those stormy eyes. Her breath caught as a strangely potent current passed between them and held her firmly in its grip.

He looked away from her, shaking his head slowly. ''Victoria Thorn, what am I to do about you? You occupy too much of my time and attention.'' He laughed in self-derision. ''I am here to find my son, and I have made no headway whatsoever. I go out to search for information and find myself thinking about you instead. Thinking things I have no right to think.'' His hot gaze raked her, taking in her tousled dark hair, her wide, unconsciously yearning eyes, the erratic pulse that beat at the base of her neck.

She raised her hand to her throat, instinctively covering that pulse. But her voice gave her away as she spoke his name. ''Jedidiah.'' The sound was filled with longing, uncertainty and soft, breathless anticipation. Unaware that she had even moved, Victoria leaned toward him.

It was only by the merest fraction of an inch. But Jed was unable to ignore the tentative invitation.

Almost before she knew what was going to happen, they were in each other's arms and his lips were descending to take hers in a fiery kiss. Victoria tasted whiskey, the faintest trace of mint and the hot muskiness of desire as her mouth opened beneath the demanding onslaught of his.

Far from being shocked or dismayed by his eagerness, Victoria was emboldened by it. She reached up, holding his head to hers, as a radiant hunger transferred from his mouth to hers. It spiraled down to ripple through her body in rays of sweet longing, making Victoria arch more fully into his embrace.

Jedidiah's hand splayed over her back, sliding down to mold her hips, and she sighed against his kiss. When his hands moved lower to cup and knead her bottom, Victoria whimpered as she felt a pooling of honeyed warmth in that most secret place between her thighs.

This gasping response was more than Jed could resist, and the truth was that he'd lost the will to try. He lifted her into his arms, never taking his mouth from hers.

She simply wrapped her arms more fully around his neck as she continued to return his kisses in equal measure. Unerringly Jed found the stairs that led to the upper floors.

Now he was forced to take his mouth from hers as he made his way up them, but she made no demurral, only burying her face against his throat. He took her to the closed door of her room.

To his surprise, before he could even move to open it, Victoria reached out and turned the knob herself, then settled back against him to press her warm lips against his throat. Hot desire spiked through him, and he wanted to take her right then and there, against the door. Nothing mattered beyond salving this aching need that drove him.

Victoria sensed that some intense emotion held Jedidiah in its grip. The very fervor of his reaction transmitted itself to her, and she was aroused to an even greater pitch. When at last he was able to move toward the bed, she nearly cried aloud with relief. She was not sure what was going to happen, she only knew it must occur, that he must carry her to her bed and follow the path that had been set on the night they met.

With an infinite tenderness that surprised and moved her, Jedidiah laid her down on the bed. Only the candles she'd left burning beside the bed lit the chamber. Standing as he was, with the glow to his back, Jedidiah's face was in shadow, and her own was illuminated. He stood looking down at her, and even though she could not read his expression, the heat of his perusal was scorching.

Then, as if by a great force of will, he took a deep breath and moved one step backward, so that the light was on his own features. His expression was tight with control, giving very little away, but he could not hide the desire in his gaze as he said, "Victoria, are you sure this is what you really want?"

Without hesitation, she held out her hands, reaching toward him, her heart in her eyes. "It is what I want." She knew it was true with every part of her.

That seemed to break the superhuman force of his control. The next thing Victoria knew, she was in his arms, his mouth seeking hers with unerring purpose.

She opened to him immediately, offering him all the passion that had been building inside her from the moment they met. His tongue tangled with hers in a union of heated flesh.

She reached to hold him down to her, but Jedidiah resisted her, pushing back onto his side. Victoria whispered, "Don't go."

He leaned over to kiss her quickly, then met her eyes with a look that would have melted iron. "I'm not going anywhere," he replied, his voice husky with promise. "Not for a very long time."

Her chest tightened at that look, for it was rife with the promise of pleasures as yet not understood by her. Oh, but she was so very willing to learn.

With his gaze still locked on hers, Jed reached out and traced one finger along the parting of her robe. Victoria closed her eyes and sighed, inviting him to go further with her reaction to his touch.

Jed did not disappoint her.

Slowly, allowing himself to savor every moment, he pushed the rich velvet back to expose the full curves of her breasts, which were covered by nothing more substantial than a transparent sheath of white lawn. Jed swallowed hard, his own eyes closing for a moment, as he was forced to block out the sight of her perfection in order to control himself.

When he opened them, she was still lying there before him, her head thrown back, her breath coming quickly from her parted lips, as if in anticipation. Her full, rounded breasts seemed eager for his attention, the delicate dusky pink tips hardened and beckoning.

His own body surged in reaction, and he dipped his head to take the delectable offering into his mouth. As Victoria gasped and arched upward, he laid his hand over the other breast, feeling it swell satisfyingly beneath his touch. Urged on by her response, he began to suckle her, teasingly, tauntingly, even as his thumb played deliberately over the opposite peak.

"Oh, help me," she gasped out, holding his head to her with both hands. Never could she have foreseen the rush of hot pleasure that weakened her limbs and added to that liquid warmth between her thighs.

He rose up then, his breathing fast, his body aching with the need to take her, to make her his own. His eyes not leaving hers, Jed removed his shirt. There was no demurral in the fervent gaze that ran over his naked chest. And still none when he stood briefly to remove his trousers.

If anything, the expression in her eyes became even more eager as her smoky gaze came to rest upon him, stirring him to even greater passion. His manhood reared, holding her heated gaze, making Jed wonder if he could restrain himself long enough to see to her pleasure. She fired him so, with her abandoned response. He was not wholly surprised. Jed had sensed the latent passion in this proper English beauty from the start.

Even as he watched, she leaned up and shrugged out of her own robe, tossing it to the floor. She held up her arms to him. "Come to me."

He knelt beside her, holding her close to him, for a moment overcome by his exhilaration at having this woman want him. Never in all his twenty-nine years had any woman ever been so open in her desire.

But soon the moment, and her near nakedness, drove him to forget everything but his need for her. He leaned over Victoria, pressing her back into the bed as he once more moved up to suckle at her bosom.

Seeming frustrated by even the covering of her thin shift, Victoria herself reached up to pull the fabric down. When it tangled, resisting her efforts, she felt no compunction about tearing the fragile garment down the front to the hem.

Laughing at her impatience, but also further heated by it, Jed helped her to discard the filmy shreds. Then he turned to her again, the soft glow of her creamy skin now fully exposed to his appreciative eyes. God help him, but he had never seen such beauty, he thought as he ran a reverent hand over the smooth perfection of her flat stomach.

Jedidiah's hand on her flesh was like a mark of ownership. His fingers traced her skin, skin touched by no man before him, and she reveled in his possession.

His mouth on hers was magic, his kisses heating her, making her want more. What she wanted, Victoria was not sure. Only the certainty that Jedidiah did know kept her from completely losing her tenuous hold on her scattered emotions.

Then, as his fingers trailed lower, to tangle in the hair at the joining of her thighs, her breath caught. When they dipped to explore the delicate folds of her, she cried out, arching in an unwitting invitation, as a wave of over-whelming pleasure surged through her.

She tore her lips from his. Her voice emerged, husky and breathless. "Oh, Jedidiah, I want... Oh, I don't know. How can I stand any more?"

His breath was hot against her ear as he replied, his fingers continuing to search her secret recesses. "You will stand more, sweet, and with pleasure."

Her only answer was an incoherent whimper as she clung to him in growing desperation. His fingers were driving her near mad, making her understand that the center of all these erotic sensations was there where he was touching her. The salving of the ache inside her would come from there. Unconsciously she opened her legs wider, inviting him to go on.

Jed knew that the moment had come. He need wait no longer, had known she was ready for him when he felt her so dewy and scorching to his touch. Still he knew he must go carefully, must remember this was her first time, how-ever heated her responses. He had no wish to hurt her. Somewhere inside him he was aware that his own pleasure could only be lessened by any unpleasantness for her.

Raising up above her, he moved between her unresisting thighs.

Victoria's gaze locked on his, her eyes hooded and as dark as flint. Not a hint of hesitancy clouded her gaze, yet he paused above her, not wanting to proceed even now, if this was not what she desired as much as he did.

Victoria saw the indecision on Jedidiah's face. She wanted to say something to reassure him. He needed to understand that she was not some young, callow girl, in spite of her physical innocence. How could she convey that she was a confident woman, fully able to appreciate the importance of this moment?

She wanted what was about to happen more than she had ever wanted anything in her life. Yet she knew there were no words that could ever tell how she felt about him and the way he made her feel.

She could only show him with her body. So thinking, she rose up, impaling herself on the hard length of him. She trembled and gasped aloud at the indescribable delight that rippled through her. Any pain that she might have felt was completely overshadowed by the sheer pleasure of having him sheathed inside her.

Jed shuddered above her, unable to retain any hint of self-possession in the ecstasy of being buried deep within her body. Instinct took sovereignty over his body, and he began to move in a rhythm that brought him a pleasure that was agonizing in its intensity.

Victoria felt the sweetness continue to build, driving her higher and higher along a knife edge of agonizing joy. Then, suddenly, it burst around her in a cascade of shimmering, glittering completion that made her cry out in rapture.

Jed watched as she arched under him, giving of herself completely and without restraint. When the moment of her fulfillment came, he met her passion-darkened eyes as he was carried to his own peak by the power of hers.

He gasped her name. "Victoria." Then the enjoyment took him in that moment beyond himself to a bright place where he was at one with this delightful siren.

She lay beneath him, holding him tightly to her, knowing that this moment, this event, had forever changed her. Never again would she be able to see this man, speak to him, without thinking of this incredible experience. Jedidiah had made her feel like a woman in every sense of the word.

He lifted his head, looking at her with a strange sort of uncertainty. "Victoria."

She put her hand to his lips. "Ssh... Not now. Later, later..." She did not want to think about anything right now, not what would happen next, not anything but how good she felt just being here in his arms.

He nodded, rolling over onto his back and pulling her with him.

Victoria snuggled against his side, burying her face against him. Breathing in the warm, pleasantly salty scent of his sweat-dampened skin, she closed her eyes. She sighed as he pulled up the tumbled sheet to cover them.

It was only moments later that sleep claimed her.

Chapter Eleven

The next morning, when Victoria awoke, she was instantly aware of what had happened the night before, and of the implication of her actions. Last night, she had wanted nothing so much as to keep those implications from intruding on her pleasure in being with Jedidiah McBride. Now she could no longer hold the painful truths at bay.

Taking a deep breath, she opened her eyes and looked toward the other side of the bed. Jedidiah was gone.

She was not surprised. It was what she had expected. Yet, in some far corner of her heart, she knew a sinking feeling of sorrow.

Pushing her grief to the farthest corner of her subconscious, Victoria rose and went to her dressing table. It was still quite early, and Betty would not be bringing her tea for some time, but right now she could not spend another moment in that bed.

The bed in which she had given of herself so freely. Given herself to Jedidiah, and no other. She recalled, in fact, her realization last night that their making love had been preordained in some way.

Now that the deed was done, she realized that she could not continue along that path. They might, for whatever cruel reason the Fates had conjured up, have been meant to become lovers. But they could not continue to be so. It would be completely unfair, both to her and to Jedidiah. Everything she'd learned about him only served to make her see there could be nothing for them.

Jedidiah had exposed enough of his past to her to make her understand that his prejudices could not be easily overcome. He and his mother had indeed been wronged, leaving him with no desire to overcome those prejudices. His wounds effectively separated him from anyone who might hurt him as his grandfather had.

And she, who came from that distrusted world, she was to marry and produce a child who would carry on the Thorn line. It was her duty and her destiny. She had always known this, yet the ache inside her at the thought of losing him now that she knew what it was like to be held close to his hard body, to feel him moving inside her, was more painful than she could possibly have imagined.

She had been a fool to give in to her attraction to him, her sympathy at the way life had treated him. Not that what she felt for him was pity. It was impossible to attach such a weak emotion to a man as strong and resourceful as Jedidiah McBride. She had simply been overcome by the idea of his loneliness as a boy, had felt a desire to share herself with him. Not really for his sake, but because she wanted and needed to be with him. Had not she, too, known that kind of isolation, for different reasons?

But what they had done was wrong. Nothing had been solved by her giving in to her desires.

It was up to Victoria to make Jedidiah understand that she did not expect anything of him. They had made a mistake and they must put the matter behind them. It was the only way they would be able to go on.

Squaring her shoulders, Victoria knew a growing resolve to make Jedidiah see that she would not play the misused maiden here. She had been, at the very least, as eager as he.

Her face flamed as she recalled just how eager she had been. That, too, must be forgotten.

Rising abruptly, she went to her wardrobe. She wished to find just the appropriate costume for her coming encounter with Jedidiah McBride. Any small detail that might help her to get through the meeting with dignity must be utilized.

No matter what happened, she must make him believe she did not feel he had taken advantage of her. It was her only sure way to keep him from leaving. For that was what she feared would happen if she didn't do so. The man's sense of honor was one of the things she admired about him, and it just might drive him to go away.

Victoria told herself it would be wrong to deprive him of this hope of finding his son. She could not do so, not because of what they had done during one hapless moment.

She refused to allow herself to contemplate any other cause for her reluctance to say goodbye.

Jed made his way to the library with a heavy heart, knowing there was nothing he could do to rectify the damage done last night. He had awakened to find himself lying next to the lady of Briarwood, and felt a wave of self-disgust that nearly drove him to his knees.

He'd done no more than glance at her, her dark hair falling forward over the curve of her creamy breast, her cheeks still bearing the peach flush of his lovemaking. He could risk no more than that fleeting glance, for to do so would be to give strength to the unacceptable urge to kiss those delicately curved lips, to trace his hands over the perfect form that lay beneath the white linens.

As he dressed, pulling his clothes on with unsteady hands, he'd repeatedly asked himself the same question: What on earth had he done? Not only in making love to

Victoria, but in telling her so very much of what he'd kept hidden all these years?

He'd gone to his own bedchamber, being careful not to wake the sleeping Victoria. He did not want to think about how she might react to knowing his secrets. Would she think this gave her some hold over him? Or would she be too overwhelmed by shame at what they had done to care about his past?

Jed had been only slightly surprised when she sent up a note asking him to meet her in the library. Victoria would want to face this directly, as she did all things.

He clenched his hands as he strode to the appointed meeting place. God help him, what was he going to say to her? How could he explain how sorry he was for taking what did not belong to him? By saying he had been drinking? Jed only wished he had that excuse. The fact was, he had told her the truth when he said he was not drunk.

Oh, he'd been feeling the drinks he'd had when she first came into the sitting room. But as he talked, his head had cleared completely. At the moment when he took Victoria up those stairs, he had been intoxicated only by her beauty, her responsive kisses, the heady rose smell of her in his arms.

Even now his body tightened at the memory. It had never occurred to him that a man's desire for a woman could be increased by his having taken her. It had not happened to him before. Yet the experience he had shared with Victoria had left him aching to be with her again, to know those heights of passion and fulfillment.

In frustration, he hit his palm with his fist. It was over, and could not be repeated. In all honesty, Jed understood that it would be doubly hard to keep from wanting her, touching her, now. He had to resist his desire in order to protect her.

He also knew he must safeguard his own autonomy. Jed would give no more of himself away. He'd learned, the hard way, that any hint of weakness left a person vulnerable to hurt. Somehow she seemed to be able to get under his skin, and that made her dangerous to his peace of mind.

Yet this only complicated the feelings churning inside him, for he was sorry for having taken Victoria's innocence as he had. He only hoped she could forgive him. This request for his presence in the library was no doubt an indication that she had come to some conclusions of her own.

Maybe she would even ask him to leave. Jed told himself that the wave of sadness he felt at the idea was caused by his regret at the thought of not finding his son. But inside him was the distant knowledge that he would be sorry to never see Victoria again.

With a groan, he ran a hand through his already tousled hair. There would be no more thoughts like that one, no matter what happened.

Victoria replied immediately to his knock. He had expected to find her at the desk. She was not, having taken a seat in one of the two burgundy-colored leather chairs before the empty hearth. A tray laden with tea and coffee rested on the round table between them.

It was a somber room, the walnut paneling and dark shades of red and burgundy with which it had been decorated cheered little by the light from the windows. It was a formal setting, one that did not lend itself to intimate conversation. If her choice of venue was any indication, Victoria was indeed regretting what they had done.

Jed braced himself, willing to face whatever recriminations she might make. It wasn't as if he didn't deserve them.

Victoria looked up as he entered, and for a moment Jed thought he saw a hint of nervousness in her gray gaze. The impression was short-lived, and he knew he must have been mistaken, as she met his gaze directly.

With regal poise, she smiled politely. "Cousin Jedidiah. Thank you for coming." She motioned toward the tray. "Would you care for coffee?"

He stared at her for a long moment. My, but she was a cool one, he thought. This reception was not what he'd expected, and he was not sure what to make of it. Realizing that the only way to find out what she was thinking was to wait for her to tell him, Jed nodded. "Yes, thank you."

He took the other leather chair as she poured.

Victoria handed him the delicate china cup with steady hands and turned to sip her own tea. Jed sat back, his gaze running over her. Even now, it was hard to look at her delicate white hands without thinking of the way they had felt on his naked flesh. He was infinitely grateful for the plain high-necked gown of dark gray she wore. Only the narrow lace ruffle that rested just below her delicate jawline added a trace of femininity.

Yet, as his wayward gaze slid over her, he realized that even in this garb she was tantalizing beyond belief. Its severe cut did little to disguise the sweetly rounded curves of breasts and hips. He turned his attention to the cup in his hands, feeling helpless in the face of his attraction to her, and knowing it was wrong.

In spite of Victoria's apparent composure, he felt he had to say something about what had happened between them. His awareness of his own responsibility in the matter forced him to make some apology. He began as delicately as he could. "Victoria, I feel I know why you have asked me to come here. I want to say how sorry I am for what—"

She interrupted him with a raised hand. "Please, do not go on. I know what you are attempting to say and *I* want *you* to know there is no need for it. What occurred was a mistake, as much my doing as yours, and we must simply put it behind us. The only thing which has changed is that I now have more sympathy for your position. After what you revealed to me last night, I can understand that you have some cause to distrust the upper classes.''

Even though his jaw clenched at her words, Jed could not view her proudly held head, comprehend the courage and integrity it took for her to take the blame for what they had done, without experiencing an overwhelming sense of admiration. Victoria Thorn was quite a lady—quite a woman.

He pushed the thoughts aside, focusing on what must be said to make her see that he would not accept any invasion of his privacy. "You can keep your sympathy, *Cousin* Victoria. I don't need it. And I'll thank you not to mention what was said last night again."

He watched as she stiffened, and though she raised her chin high, he could hear the hurt in her voice when she answered. "I will not mention it again, sir, of that you can be assured. I do not know what could have come over me. As you've made abundantly clear on every possible occasion, your life is your own concern."

He caught the tinge of sarcasm in her tone, and again was struck by her undaunted strength. At the back of his mind, he could not help wishing that things could be different. What would it be like to have her for his own, this proud English beauty? Those moments in her arms had seemed more real, more powerful, than any he had ever known in his life.

This situation was not real. He had to fight the spell of his attraction toward her, his pleasure in the things they had shared. Even if he wanted to ask her to be a part of his life—which he did not, he assured himself—Victoria would not leave all that she was behind. And he would never be accepted into her world.

With a great force of will, Jed turned away from the lovely sight of her. He must forget her and find his son. Somehow he understood that he must do so before it was too late.

So thinking, he rose abruptly, all these thoughts having passed through his mind in the matter of a heartbeat. Carefully he put his untouched coffee on the tray. "I...I thank you for that." He looked into her smoky gray eyes then, his expression earnest. "There is something else I must say. You have attempted to ease the burden of my guilt by taking it upon yourself."

Victoria shook her dark head. "No, I but admit to my own part in what happened. Knowing you, I understood that you would place all the blame upon yourself. There is no need for that. We are both adults, and you forced me to do nothing against my will."

"But you didn't really understand what you were getting into. I did."

She raised her chin. "I will not allow you to think so poorly of me, Mr. McBride. I insist that you put aside this line of thought. Suffice it to say that both of us acted out of some unexpected and unwanted lack of judgment."

She looked away from him, and Jed was glad, because he would not have wanted her to see the surprisingly adverse reaction he had to her next words. "I require your services in protecting me until I find a husband. You hope to find your lost child by taking advantage of my easy entry into society. Those things are what we must keep sight of." She turned back to him, those lovely gray eyes remote. "You will be leaving England once our objectives have been accomplished. What occurred was completely unsuitable, and will not happen again."

In spite of the fact that her coolness left him feeling unexplainably empty, Jed was moved by her courage. He knew how hard this must be for her, knew that she had been a virgin when he took her last night. Even if she was telling him she wished they had never made love, that they should not have crossed the boundaries that separated them, she was doing it directly.

He did not want her to know that he was awed by her strength of character, drawn by all the special qualities that made her Victoria and no other. She'd been very clear in letting him know that they came from separate worlds. Yet he could not keep himself from speaking. "You are an amazing woman, Victoria Thorn."

With that, he turned and left the room, knowing he could not say more without giving away more than he dared.

Victoria became aware of the fact that she was again searching the ballroom for a sign of Jedidiah McBride with a feeling of irritation. For the third time, she turned her attention back to what her partner said.

Since their conversation in the library five mornings past, the sea captain had been judiciously polite. Whatever that last unexpected remark he had made before leaving the library might have meant, she had no idea.

Unfortunately for her, that night had proved much more difficult to forget than even she had feared. Not an hour went by that she did not relive every moment, every touch, every word, that had passed between them. The more time went by, the more certain Victoria became that no man would ever be able to replace the American. She could not imagine doing such things with any of the men she met, not even the most attractive or attentive or intelligent of them.

The thought was, in fact, abhorrent. Which did not soothe or reassure her in the least.

Once more her unconsciously yearning gaze swept the crowded chamber. She was sure he was in fact pursuing his quest to find his son even now.

Experiencing a wave of sadness, she closed her eyes. It was ridiculous of her to care. He certainly would not welcome her concern. Even as she allowed herself to be twirled around the room, her heart remained heavy.

Thus, with more enthusiasm than she might otherwise have shown, she smiled at Ian when he asked her to dance with him a short time later. She was surprised to see him at all on this particular evening, as the hour was growing quite late and he had been conspicuously absent until now.

Ian answered her question without being asked. As he led her out onto the floor, he eyed her with obvious appreciation, offering, "I was not going to come here tonight, but I hoped you would be in attendance. I am inordinately pleased to see that you are."

Victoria could smell the alcohol on his breath, and she wondered if his ebullience might have something to do with his having been drinking. She felt a deep blush steal over her face and neck as she recalled how drinking had affected Jedidiah. It had caused him to say things that created a false sense of intimacy between them. She looked up at Ian. "Lord Sinclair, you have no need to say such things to me."

His dark gaze locked on hers. "On the contrary, I have every need."

She studied him closely, sensing a certain shift in his attitude that she had not noted before. The deliberate focus of his considerable male charm was not lost on her. What kept her from feeling overwhelmed by it was a hint of something she might have described as melancholy in his tone. What, she wondered, could have brought about this change in the usually unperturbable man? Acting sheerly on impulse, she asked softly, "What is it, Ian?"

He made a great show of surprise, immediately assuming the expression of detached superiority and boredom he usually wore. "What is what, my dear Lady Victoria?"

She would not be put off. "I know we haven't known each other long, but I feel as if we are becoming friends. Am I wrong?"

He remained silent for a long moment, then shook his head. "You are not wrong."

She smiled gently. "I thought as much. That is what makes me bold enough to insist you tell me what is troubling you."

He grimaced, dropping that sardonic air. "The *earl* is after me to marry again. He has ordered me to the country to become better acquainted with the bride he has selected for me. The woman in question is a particularly disagreeable cousin. Disagreeable to myself, at any rate. She is a simpering fool who will do as instructed, fawn over me, and make babies with no complaint." His voice took on a tone of comic irony. "I'm sure my father would be very pleased with me, for a short time, at least, if I were willing to fall in with his plans. But, alas, I am not." He gave a laugh that was so bitter it exposed the hurt he was trying to hide. He seemed completely unaware of her presence for a moment, as his mind turned inward to something only he could see. "For the love of God, I am a man, fully twenty-eight years of age. Why can't he just discuss it with me, see how I feel about the woman in question? Or, better yet, understand that I wish to make the choice for myself?"

Why indeed did the elder Sinclair not allow that his son should have some say in this matter? Judging from Ian's set expression, he would not do as his father demanded, no matter what it cost him. She wondered if Ian would be a different man were his father to stop trying to interfere in his life.

Victoria could only wish her own parents were present to assist her in making the important decisions in her life. Yet she knew she would not welcome the kind of domination Ian's father seemed to display. She could not restrain a self-derisive laugh. "I, too, find myself in the position of having to marry. It is not something I relish, either."

"At least you have the privilege of choosing for yourself, without recrimination," he told her with raised brows. He seemed to have brushed away his melancholy, for that accustomed detached amusement had returned to his dark eyes.

Victoria decided to take her cue from him, for she felt she had pried far enough. "A dubious privilege," she answered lightly, "which is more torment. It would be better that I had a family to make a reasonable choice for me. I had not thought it would be so difficult to find someone who will care for my lands and the responsibilities of my position as I do."

"What of love?" he asked, his hot gaze moving over her flirtatiously. She could not help thinking, in a disinterested way, that a lesser maid would surely have been rendered faint by that look.

Victoria pointedly ignored his deliberate perusal as an image of Jedidiah's face came to her mind. Quickly she pushed it aside, yet she could not stop her heart from giving one painful throb. Love was not something she could expect to find. She glanced up at Ian. "I do not expect that particular emotion, nor do I even desire it. Respect and a willingness to care for my lands and people as I do are of greater consequence to me. The man I marry will need to have no ties that are more important to him."

His gaze caught and held hers for a long, thoughtful moment. Then he smiled. "Perhaps I am your man?"

Her eyes widened in amazement, and with some amusement. For surely he could not be serious. "Why, Lord Sinclair, are you saying what I think you are?"

His expression sobered. "Yes, Lady Victoria, I believe I am." His own voice sounded somewhat incredulous. Before Victoria knew what was happening, he had waltzed her onto the terrace, through the open doors. With practiced elegance, he brought them to a halt near a vine-covered trellis that would partially block them from the view of any others who might come out to partake of the fresh late-May night.

Victoria was shocked, not knowing what to make of all this. He could not be serious.

But as his earnest eyes searched her face, she began to wonder. He took her hand in his. "Lady Victoria Thorn, will you do me the honor of becoming my wife?"

Still Victoria wanted to believe that this was just another one of his outrageous attempts to shock her. The continued seriousness of his expression gave her pause, but she found it all very difficult to take in. "Lord Sinclair, what gives you any reason to think we would be well suited? Besides, you have just told me yourself that your father has already selected a bride for you."

He laughed then, and with unfeigned pleasure. "I have no intention of following his orders. I would, in fact, be very happy to act in direct opposition to them. Don't you see, that is the very beauty of it? My father has decided I am to marry Barbara. Just imagine how very pleased he would be if I came home with a very different sort of woman. One such as you, Victoria. You have a great independence of spirit, and make no apology for it. I cannot conceive of you allowing the old fellow to lead you about by the nose."

She scowled, not liking this reply. "I do not wish to marry simply to further exacerbate the rift between you and your father. It is poor reason for such a thing."

He shook his head, his face filled with remorse. "I have insulted you, and that was not my intent. I would be lying if I said I would not be happy to put the old fellow off his game. That is not the only reason I have asked you to marry me. I believe we would deal very well together. My father is not likely to move aside and allow me to take up the reins of my own inheritance. He very much likes being the one to call out the tune. And I..." He shrugged, gazing off into the darkness. "I am tired of living up to the reputation of being Lord Sin."

He watched her gasp of surprise. "Oh, yes, I am quite aware of what they call me, and have made every effort to live up to the appellation. I no longer wish to do so."

She studied him carefully. "How can you be certain? Perhaps you will find living as a country gentleman does not suit you at all, after being 'Lord Sin.' For that is what I would ask of any man who marries me. I have no love of parties and social engagements, and miss Briarwood more with each passing day."

He sighed. "You have no idea how much the notion appeals to me. I would gladly have left all this years ago, but I cannot be my father's lackey. At Sinclair manor, every decision must be his and his alone."

She nodded, still watching him. "Then you will understand when I say that the man I marry must also know I will be an equal partner in all decisions. I have been running my father's estates since his death. I cannot simply hand all that over to someone else blindly. It means too much to me."

He met her probing gaze without hedging. "Having been put in that very position myself, I could not do that to another, especially you, Victoria. I have come to respect and admire you in the time we have known one another." His gaze dipped lower. "And I would only be honest in telling you that I find you quite beautiful."

Suddenly Victoria found herself overcome by the realization that this was real, that Ian Sinclair had actually asked for her hand. Judging from the way he answered all her questions, he might very well be the one to fulfill her every need. Still she could not speak. For there was the one need she knew he did not meet.

He did not make her heartbeat quicken. Nor any other part of her, she told herself longingly, as once again an image of Jedidiah, his hands moving over her flesh, assaulted her senses. She was grateful for the darkness that partially hid her ensuing blush from Ian's view.

Jedidiah McBride was not for her.

But that did not mean she could say yes to Ian, she told herself hurriedly. The voice of reason was just as quick to reply that it might actually be the very reason to do so. There was nothing to be gained by putting off her marriage, by leaving herself open to the temptation of Jedidiah McBride.

In spite of this realization, she was not sure. Thinking to give herself and Ian some time to ponder, she said, "You have been drinking. I take that into consideration when I say I cannot give you a reply. I would not hold you to anything you have said here tonight."

He opened his mouth to speak, but she halted him. "I am tired now, and must think. I believe I will find my...cousin and ask him if we might go home."

He seemed to understand her need to contemplate all they had discussed, because he simply nodded. "As you wish."

Victoria did not look back as she left him, but she felt Ian's thoughtful gaze upon her.

Chapter Twelve

Victoria breakfasted the next morning alone. She had been informed by Mrs. Dunn that Jedidiah had requested coffee in his room. He'd been pointedly civil to Victoria on the drive home, but had seemed troubled by something he clearly had no wish to discuss. The only thing he had said that could be considered even remotely personal was an offhand comment about having seen her go out to the terrace with Ian Sinclair.

Giving a start, Victoria had looked at him closely, wondering if there was something specific behind the remark. She had known there was not when he failed to even listen as she muttered a hesitant reply.

Though she could not help feeling somewhat bereft at his lack of interest, she was also glad that she was not forced into thinking of something to say. For some reason, she did not want to tell him of Ian's proposal.

She was just finishing the solitary meal, which she had done no more than pick at, when her maid came to present her with Ian Sinclair's card. Surprise held her immobile for a long moment.

On reflecting back over the fact that Ian had been slightly drunk and that he was so angry with his father, Victoria had felt he would likely be sorry for the proposal he had made to her. So why then was he here at his hour?

Perhaps, she told herself, he was coming to personally explain his regret and apologize for speaking so hastily. Yes, that must be the reason.

She would soon reassure him about that.

Telling Betty to have refreshments served in the sitting room, Victoria made her way there. Ian stood as soon as she entered the room. And so did Jedidiah McBride, to her immense consternation. He was not smiling.

What, she wondered, was he doing here?

In spite of her shock and anxiety at finding the two men together, she could not help noticing that, though the young nobleman was certainly handsome, he could not compete with the sheer energy and maleness of the sea captain. Jedidiah wore a morning coat of darkest blue over matching trousers, the color contrasting devastatingly with his sun-washed hair. The white collar of his shirt only served to make his tanned throat appear more so, as did the light green of his eyes.

Ian's buff trousers and dark brown coat, though well cut, rested over shoulders that did not seem quite as large or hug so lovingly to lean hips.

Yet Victoria knew that she did not look on the two men with unbiased eyes. There was no point in denying to herself that Jedidiah's effect on her was not to be equaled, no matter how attractive another man might be. That included Ian Sinclair, who was famed for his good looks and physique.

Victoria restrained a grimace as she dragged her wayward gaze from Jedidiah. The dark-haired man could have come for one reason only, and she did not wish to discuss the proposal, however ridiculous, in front of the American.

Luckily, Lord Sinclair seemed equally reluctant to do so. He greeted her with a restrained expression and an elegant apology. "Lady Victoria, I hope I have not inconvenienced you too much by making such an early appearance.''

''Of course not,'' she replied with equal politeness. But her poise diminished as her certainty that Ian was ready to retract his proposal wavered. For the next thing he did was to reach out and take her hand. He held it for the longest moment, gazing down into her eyes with a meaningful communication that, though silent, transferred its intimacy to her.

Without conscious thought, her gaze went to Jedidiah. He was looking at their joined hands with an obvious expression of displeasure.

Hurriedly she pulled her fingers from Lord Sinclair's.

She took a step backward, infinitely aware of Jedidiah's attention on her. As if he were completely unaware of the tension exhibited by the other two, Lord Sinclair smiled at her and said, ''I have come to see if you will go riding with me this morning. It is a lovely day, and I'm sure you will enjoy yourself.''

Victoria nearly pounced on the suggestion. ''What a wonderful idea. I would certainly love to accompany you.'' It was a perfect opportunity to discuss the marriage proposal, out from beneath the other man's watchful gaze.

''Yes,'' she heard Jedidiah add from behind her. ''It is very nice of you to ask. I am sure we'll enjoy the fresh air.''

Both Ian and Victoria looked to him in surprise. Then, with the good manners that were so much a part of him, Ian responded with alacrity. ''Very well, then. What good news.''

She swung around to face Jedidiah. ''I'm sure Lord Sinclair does not expect you to disrupt your own plans in order to accompany us.'' She eyed Jedidiah with barely restrained hostility, hoping with all her might that he would respond to the hint.

He did not. "I have no other plans this morning," he countered. His expression remained bland as he stared back at her, his brows arched.

With a last murderous glance toward Jedidiah, which he regarded with feigned innocence, Victoria turned to Ian. "I shall just go up and change."

Jed rode stiffly, his thighs gripping the saddle with undue force, his fingers clenched around the reins. He knew there was something going on between the lady of Briarwood and the tall, dark nobleman. It had been apparent in the lingering possessiveness with which the man held her hand, and the decided nervousness she displayed from the moment she greeted him.

Jed had, in fact, been battling these feelings that something was wrong since the previous night. He had not been pleased when Victoria disappeared out onto the terrace with the man, and had been even less so when she returned looking so disturbed.

He had done his best to keep from reacting, even when she continued to be so rattled on the carriage ride home. Jed had resolved to keep his attraction to her from intruding between them, and he had done his utmost to live up to that decision, no matter how difficult it had been over the past few days. Yet it had been more than he could do to turn and walk away when he found Sinclair in her house the very next morning.

Feeling the curious gaze of the man in question, he looked up to see that he was riding much too close to Victoria's mare. Good God, he thought, he must be a sight, hovering over her this way. With a wave of self-derision, he let his horse fall back to trail behind theirs.

What was he thinking? Why had he invited himself along, even though he knew quite well that Victoria was the object of Lord Sinclair's interest? Jed tried to tell himself he had done so because he did not trust her to be safe in the sole company of the infamous Lord Sin, but the thought did not quite ring true.

Jed was drawn out of his reverie when Ian turned to address him. "What do you say, McBride?"

Shrugging, Jed tried to hide his chagrin at being caught daydreaming. "I'm sorry, I did not hear the question."

"Did you hear of the Great Exhibition in America? It was held right here in Hyde Park."

Jed had heard of the amazing showcase for art, science and technology. It was just the kind of thing that appealed to his interests, and he had read the accounts avidly. Today he found he could work up little enthusiasm for the topic. Doing his best to keep that lack of enthusiasm from showing in his voice, Jed nodded. "Certainly."

He continued to follow behind Ian and Victoria. In spite of his preoccupation with thoughts of Victoria, he found himself listening with interest as Sinclair went on. "The Crystal Palace was made of glass and was 1,848 feet long, 408 feet wide and sixty-six feet high. Prince Albert, who is a great supporter of science and industry, inspired the exhibition, which opened four years ago, in 1851. All nations were invited to participate. It was spectacular."

Victoria was nodding in agreement. "It was indeed. I was here at the opening with my parents. Queen Victoria seemed very proud of her husband that day."

Feeling that he should add something to the conversation, Jed said, "I read of the opening in the paper. I believe the building was designed by a Joseph Paxton."

Victoria nodded. "That is right. He was once a gardener for the duke of Devonshire. The Crystal Palace was taken down soon after the exhibition, and has been reerected at Sydenham."

Jed's gaze wandered over the park, trying to picture the event in his mind. The park would have been teeming with visitors, all of whom would have been awed by the grandeur and innovation around them. When he read the story, he'd have laughed out loud if anyone told him he'd someday be riding in the park and mixing with the English aristocracy. His voice was filled with quiet irony. "I never expected to ever come to Hyde Park."

Ian looked at him. "You hadn't ever thought of coming to England to see your family?"

Jed couldn't restrain a frown. "No." He didn't want to discuss his reasons for coming to England with Sinclair.

Sinclair clearly would have liked to ask more, but Victoria interrupted, pointing to a cluster of enormous elm trees. "Mr. Paxton altered his original design in order to keep from having the elm trees felled." The smile she turned on them seemed to Jed to be forced, but Sinclair didn't appear to notice.

Jed dropped back as they rode off to admire the towering elms. He tried to convince himself their seeming pleasure in each other's company did not bother him at all.

He looked to where they rode, side by side, ahead of him. To his surprise, he met Victoria's searching gaze. There was a strange sort of yearning in her eyes that made his own heart ache in response. Dragging his gaze away, Jed told himself he was distorting her emotions to please himself. She could only be angry with him, after the way he had insisted on accompanying them.

He forced himself to concentrate on Sinclair, who was now watching the lady, his expression quite thoughtful. Suddenly he realized that he could very well harm Victoria with his behavior, if the nobleman started to suspect there was something between them. It was this that finally brought Jed completely to his senses.

Jed scowled in self-derision. What a mess he had made of things, and all because he could not control his own feelings for Victoria.

God knew he had tried. But now that he had made love to her, it was all Jed could do to keep himself away from the lady of Briarwood. He could not even bear the thought of another man touching her, eliciting the passionate responses that had so fired his blood and mind.

The passage of days since the night they made love had not lessened his agony. His need to be with her again only appeared to increase with each hour that passed. He could not be near Victoria, speak to her, breathe in her fresh rose scent, without thinking of that night in vivid and agonizing detail.

Glancing up again and seeing Sinclair cast another appraising look his way, Jed drew himself up. He knew that it was his responsibility to rectify any damage he had done.

If Victoria found Sinclair to her liking, who was he to second-guess her? He had used her as he had feared some other man would, and he had no right to judge.

Pushing his feelings of resentment toward Ian Sinclair to the back of his mind, Jed prodded his horse forward until he was beside the dark-haired man. Calling on all the willpower within him, he smiled. "I feel I should apologize for accompanying you two this morning. I have just met my cousin, and I fear I am overprotective of her, she being my only family."

Sinclair raised his brows and glanced toward Victoria, then back to Jed. "You mean you are alone in the world, as Victoria is?"

Jed had to work hard to keep from reacting to the other man's addressing her by her first name, but he managed. "Yes, very much so. That is why I came to England. I was searching for anyone whom I might have a connection to. Imagine my surprise when I learned she was the only one left." Jed went on softly. "The scarcity of our family has made her all the more precious to me. I want to protect her and be certain she is happy." Jed could not look at Victoria as he finished, for he was afraid he would give away the effort it cost him to do this. "You understand, I'm sure."

Ian Sinclair nodded slowly, his gaze raking Victoria. "Perhaps I do."

Jed had to force down the ire that assaulted him as he watched this. He spoke carefully, concentrating on his need to do what was right for Victoria. "Let's go back to the beginning."

Sinclair smiled, seeming willing to respond to Jed's overture. "Certainly. I have nothing against you, McBride. It is obvious to me that you and Victoria are close. I am prepared to accept that."

Jed could feel Victoria's gaze on him. He dared not even risk a glance at her.

Sinclair held out his hand. Briefly Jed shook it, before the motion of their horses broke the firm grip.

In spite of himself, Jed forced himself to respond to Sinclair's overtures as he now struck up a polite conversation with him. Sinclair also included Victoria, obviously valuing her contribution to the subject at hand.

Soon Jed found that he was at least able to converse with the man on a civil level. To his further surprise, as the discussion progressed, the topic turned to horses and the breeding of them. Jed soon learned that Sinclair was clearly an expert on the subject. Jed himself knew something of the matter, although he would never have chosen to make his living that way, because it was what his father had done. Horse lore was the only thing his father had ever taught him of value, but Jed had no interest in following the drunkard's example in any way.

As they talked, much of what his sire had told him came back to him. He and Sinclair soon began to compare the merits of the many equines that were to be seen in the park on a Saturday morning.

Victoria watched the two men with growing vexation. Ian had come to her home with the express notion of taking *her* riding. For the past hour, he and Jedidiah had chatted and discussed horses as if they were old friends.

Somewhere inside her she knew that she should be glad Jedidiah had decided to be courteous to Ian. Jedidiah's previous disapproving silence had begun to wear on her equilibrium. Still, she could summon no feelings of happiness or even relief when he made peace with Ian Sinclair.

Victoria knew that if she was the least bit candid with herself, she would have to admit that her present disquiet was not due to her irritation with Jedidiah McBride. It came from another source entirely. As they rode along, she'd realized that if Ian did indeed mean his proposal, she should, for the good of everyone concerned, accept him.

Her marriage to Ian would free Jedidiah to get on with his life as soon as his child was found. His resentment at looking after her was becoming all the more obvious. Why else would he react so poorly to Ian? Yet she hesitated.

She cast an unknowingly wistful gaze toward Jedidiah as he pointed out the weak withers on an otherwise notable chestnut mare. He looked a devastatingly strong and all-confident male sitting tall in the saddle of his Thoroughbred stallion. The slight breeze ruffled his sun-streaked blond hair and tossed it into his sea-green eyes.

Victoria sighed.

Only a short time later, she pleaded fatigue and the two men escorted her home. Ian Sinclair refused the refreshment she offered to him, saying he had another engagement. Strangely, she was not the least bit sorry to see him go. The strain of maintaining a casual attitude was telling on her, and she wished desperately to be alone to think.

Jedidiah had other plans. As soon as they entered the house, he spoke her name in a tone that told her he had something of import to say. "Victoria."

She halted her progress toward the stairs. "Yes." She refused to look around, not wishing to face him just now. She did not want to discuss his actions this day, nor Ian's reasons for coming to see her, nor anything else, for that matter.

His voice was coolly civil. "May I speak with you for a moment?"

She stiffened, but the request was given so courteously that she felt it would be churlish of her to refuse. Still without looking at him, she nodded. "In the library?"

"Thank you," he replied, and followed as she led the way.

Victoria did not take a seat, and neither did Jed. She hoped this interview would not be prolonged.

Jedidiah began immediately. "Victoria, I want to say that I was wrong to behave as I did earlier today. I hope I have managed to rectify any harm I might have caused you with Sinclair. I was simply concerned for you, because of his reported reputation." He paused for a long moment, then went on. "He seems a decent man, and I am certainly not one to slander him."

She had suspected that Jedidiah was acting so oddly because of his promise to protect her, and his words confirmed it. "As I said to you before, I believe he has spent a great deal of energy rebelling against his father. I do not know what brought on the feud, but I feel Lord Sinclair is ready to try to put it behind him."

She paused then, wondering. Jedidiah's acceptance of Ian made her wonder if she should just tell him that she was thinking of marrying the man.

Considering his continued sense of responsibility toward her, Jedidiah had a right to know that he would soon be free of his obligation to her. The unexplainable sadness she felt at this thought made her voice sound raspy to her own ears. "Helping to run the Thorn estates would give

him a new direction for his energies. And might just make
him a better man.''

There was a long silence that seemed to stretch on forever. Then, finally, in a tone that was completely devoid of
any hint of emotion, Jedidiah said, "So it has already gone
that far. You are thinking of marrying him?"

She raised her head high. "He has asked me to do so."

"I see. And you did not bother to tell me."

She forced herself to look at him then. She could not begin to imagine what emotion darkened his eyes. "I was not
sure he was serious in his proposal. His actions today have
made me believe he was. Until then, I had not thought of
what I might say in reply."

"And now you are thinking about what you might say?"
His expression was so remote that it chilled her. She felt as
if she were lost, abandoned, on a winter night. Had they
ever been so close that they had shared the most intimate
act any two people could?

She forced herself to reply evenly. "Yes."

He stared at her for so long she thought she would surely
go mad from the tension of it. She could not look away.

With an unintelligible sound, Jedidiah turned and left the
room. A moment later, she heard the front door slam
closed.

Victoria could only stand still in stunned disbelief at the
violence of his reaction. Whatever could be the matter with
him? He had admitted only moments before that he might
have been wrong about Lord Sinclair's character. What
then was the cause of his disapproval now?

She'd have thought he would be glad to know he might
soon be rid of her. She felt that with her out of the way he
would be free to concentrate on his own problems. The reluctance she felt to tell Jedidiah about the proposal had
been because of her own ill-fated feelings for him.

Victoria could not hazard a guess as to the cause of his obvious anger. And had no wish to try. It seemed she could do little to please Jedidiah McBride.

With her head high, Victoria made her way to her bedchamber. Only then, with the door securely closed behind her, did she lie down upon her bed and sob out her anguish—as she had not done since her parents' deaths.

Jed rode on through the cobbled thoroughfares of London, not sure where he was going or why. After a time, the streets became narrower, the buildings tall and extremely close. Many of the people he passed were filthy and bedraggled.

These were the kind of folk he had grown up among. Here or in Bar Harbor, poverty and illiteracy spoke the same language.

Finally he stopped at a tavern and went inside. The interior was dim and smelled strongly of the smoke that curled from the hearth. He seated himself at a table that was wet from a recent washing but still bore the evidence of white streaks of grease.

An unkempt woman of indeterminate age approached him with a gleam in her tired eyes as she took in his fine clothes. Putting her hands on her bony hips, she did her best to look alluring. "What can I get for ye, my fine gentleman? Somethin' special?"

Jed shook his head. "Just ale. And there will be a bit extra in it for you if it comes in a clean tankard."

She nodded quickly and scurried away, accepting his lack of interest without reaction. The woman was back a moment later with a frothing cup. Seeing that it was indeed reasonably clean, Jed passed her a crown.

Her eyes enormous as cannonballs, she scooped the coin into the front of her tattered dress before it could be seen by either of the other two customers, who lolled at a nearby table. She made no sound, only nodded frantically, then scampered off.

Not being surprised at this behavior, Jed turned to his cup. It was probably more than she made working in this hellhole in months, and the other patrons would likely not hesitate to rob her in order to get it.

He wondered if he had been foolish to give so much, thinking of how it would have been welcomed by his own mother. He shook his head. The crown seemed a small sum of money to him now, but how greatly it would have affected his life when he was a child. Perhaps the tavern wench had a child herself.

As he had a child, Jed reminded himself. He wondered again, as he had for an uncountable number of times, what his son was like. Was the boy happy?

God help him, he told himself angrily, his child was what he should be thinking about, his son. But all he cared about was a woman he could not have—did not want. This only served to bring on more feelings of guilt. Deep inside him he was afraid there was a part of him that did not want to complete his quest and find the boy. Finding him would mean never seeing Victoria again.

And if he did not want her, why did that matter so much? Why did his guts ache at the very thought? It was sheer madness.

Jed had to come to grips with his reactions, to behave like a sane man, not some unschooled adolescent. He had known from the start that Victoria would marry. His having made love to her did not change that, gave him no right to ownership of her in any way.

He looked around, saw the squalor of this place, and wondered how Victoria would react to knowing all the truth about him. Already he'd revealed more to her than to anyone. She'd not seemed surprised to learn of his more—Jed's lips curled at the word—*genteel* heritage. Would she be so accepting of his other side, the one that had been forged in the fires of poverty? He didn't believe so.

Yet Victoria could only be what she was. He'd had no right to react so coldly when she told him she was considering marrying Sinclair. Every time he tried to tell her he regretted treating her unfairly, he ended up doing so again. He knew he had to pull himself together and do what was right. How he could do it without giving away his feelings for her? He knew only that he must try one more time.

Leaving the tavern, he traveled back through the less crowded streets, surprised to see that the hour had grown so late. He'd had no idea he'd been riding for so long before stopping at the tavern.

The Georgian mansion on Grosvenor Square was quiet when he returned. The door was opened by a sleepy-eyed male servant. When Jed asked after Lady Victoria, he was told that she had retired.

Muttering a thank-you, Jed made his way to the upper floor. He knew he should go to his room and leave well enough alone for the night. But the memory of Victoria's stricken face and sad eyes drove him to go directly to her bedchamber. He had no intention of doing anything other than apologizing, he assured himself.

When he knocked at the door, a muffled voice bade him enter.

Victoria was seated at her dressing table, a hand pressed to her forehead, her eyes closed. Her hair tumbled down her back to her hips in a curtain of black waves, making him remember the feel of it against his skin.

Firmly Jed told himself not to think on such things. He was here only to make amends.

She spoke without looking around. "I told you, Betty, you may go on to bed. It is nothing more than the megrim."

Jed answered softly. "It's not Betty."

She swung around in surprise, then leapt to her feet, her hand going to the neckline of her pale blue robe. "Why are you here?" Her voice was hoarse.

Jed looked at her closely, taking in her inflamed eyes and pale cheeks. God rot his soul. She'd been crying. And he knew he was the one who had made her cry.

As if his close scrutiny were too much for her, Victoria half turned away, her dark hair falling across her face. Instinctively Jed knew she hated for him to see her this way, hated for him to know she had been crying. She was a proud and independent woman, more so than any he had ever met. That was one of the very things that drew him to her.

Guilt prodded him like a hot knife in his chest. Without any foreknowledge that he was going to do so, Jed held out his arms in silent repentance for the pain he had caused her.

She ran into them.

Jed held her close, his hand smoothing the tousled mane of her dark hair. Closing his eyes, he breathed in the scent of her.

"Oh, Jedidiah, how I have missed you, missed having you hold me," she whispered against his shoulder.

He felt his heart lurch in response. What a fool he had been to try to deny his longing for her. It washed over him like an incoming tide. To be with her, to touch her like this, was his only hope of relief.

"Victoria, Victoria..." He pressed his lips to her forehead. "I'm so sorry for having hurt you. It is the very last thing I want to do." Gently he cupped her chin, turning her face up to his, his eyes telling her how remorseful he was.

Victoria looked at him, saw the tenderness in his eyes, felt its answer deep inside herself. Suddenly she knew, with an unshakable certainty, that nothing would ever be the same. No longer could she deny the truth inside her.

She loved him, with all her heart and soul.

She also knew as soon as the knowledge came to her that it would only end by bringing her pain. Even if he did love her in return, there was no hope for them. Jedidiah McBride would not stay in England, and she could not leave. There was no other to carry on her responsibilities, to see to the good of all the hundreds of people who depended on her.

The loneliness of her decision, the passionless future that lay ahead, made her ache for all that would not be. That was what led her to her next action. The future might indeed be bleak, but she could, did she but have the courage, seize this moment. Taking his hand, she took a step backward, looking up at him with all the yearning inside her.

Jedidiah stood still, staring down at her, clearly trying to understand what she was saying. She glanced back over her shoulder, toward the bed, where it lay in candlelight, the crisp white sheets turned back in invitation.

He looked at the bed, then at her, and swallowed, closing his eyes. He opened them again, and she saw how they had darkened to jade. "Victoria, I... That is not why I came here. You don't have to... I did not expect..."

She hushed him with a finger on his warm lips. "Shh... I know. You don't have to say a thing."

Again she stepped backward, pulling him with her.

Jed could no longer resist. This was what he had thought about night and day since the first time they were together. Even knowing that she would likely marry Sinclair, he could not deny her or himself.

Victoria felt it the moment his resistance left him, and she nearly sighed her relief aloud. Already she was trembling at the knowledge that Jedidiah would touch her once again, bring her to that furious peak of fulfillment. And, oh, how much pleasure she would know along the way...

The promise of it was already growing in his eyes as his gaze moved over her in an almost tangible caress. He followed her with sensuous deliberation.

She backed up until her legs came up against the side of the bed, her gaze never straying from his. When she could go no farther, he did not press her backward, onto the softness of the mattress, as she had thought he would.

Instead, he reached out to lift the curtain of her hair away from her neck, his lids heavy as he watched her. And Victoria felt her own droop downward. She sighed as he bent his head and began, very delicately, to kiss and nibble at her sensitive nape. Victoria felt a swell of tingling delight shudder through her.

She tilted her head back to allow him better access as he moved around to the front of her neck, her breath coming more quickly with each caress. Then he was moving down, ever so slowly, to press his lips to the tender skin just above the scooped neckline of her robe.

Victoria felt her breasts swell in anticipation as he nuzzled at the edge of the soft velvet. She reached up to pull it open, allow him full access, but he stopped her with a hand. "No. Let me."

She could not take her eyes from his face as he parted the delicate fabric, drawing back first her robe, then her gown, with infinite languor. It was as if he would savor this moment forever. This only served to heighten her own sense of expectancy, and her heart thumped so hard against her ribs that she thought he must surely feel it. When at last she was laid bare to his gaze, he simply stood there, his fervent gaze drinking in the sight of her till she could stand it no longer. "Jedidiah . . ." she murmured.

He looked into her eyes, his own dark with desire. "I had thought nothing could be as beautiful as I remembered you to be. But you are all I recalled and more."

She reached for him, turning her mouth up for his kiss. He took her against him, molding the slender length of her to the hard contours of his body.

When her own hands moved to touch him, she was frustrated by the barrier of his clothing. Then, somehow, without breaking the contact of their lips, he was bare to her questing fingers. The first time they made love, she'd had little thought for anything save the pounding of her own blood. This time, being fully aware that they could not be together again, she was hungry to learn all she could of this man. This love of hers.

She smoothed her hands over the hard muscles of his chest, read the contours of his shoulders with her fingertips. He was so beautiful. A divine creation shaped by a loving hand, for God could be nothing less than loving if he had made Jedidiah McBride.

He groaned as she slid her palms lower over his flat belly and she felt the muscle tighten beneath the skin. Amazed and excited that she had brought about this kind of reaction in him, Victoria was emboldened to dare more. She allowed one hand to glide down into the tangle of thick curls at the base of his stomach, and he quivered.

Then, looking up into his eyes, she pressed still lower, closing her fingers over the length of him. He pulsed in her grip, and his lids closed as he gasped, "Victoria!"

When she tightened her grasp in reaction, he reached down to still her. "No more. I want to pleasure you."

A shiver of excitement rippled through her as he pressed her back into the softness of the mattress. His mouth claimed her eager one in a long, fierce kiss before he moved down to nuzzle her breasts. Her heart stopped as his lips closed on one turgid tip, and it was her turn to cry out his name. "Jedidiah!"

This time, when the liquid warmth grew in her lower belly, Victoria knew how the sensations growing inside her would culminate, knew Jedidiah had the power to carry her beyond herself, to unutterable fulfillment. She put her hands up to hold his head to her, feeling the silkiness of his sun-streaked hair against her skin. He was hers—for this moment, at least—and she would allow herself to do as she pleased. Tomorrow she would know no regrets for having held back.

As Jedidiah raised up on his haunches to look down at her, his gaze hot with desire, she studied him again with unashamed admiration. He was beautiful, more so than she had ever imagined a man could be. His chest and shoulders were a burnished gold from exposure to the sun, and lower, where the sun had not gilded him, he was a dark cream. Smooth skin lay taut over hard muscles that flexed and rippled as he moved. His manhood rose, proud and attentive, from the thatch of curls at his groin. Through hardship and toil, his body had been honed to the peak of what a man could be.

Victoria rose up on her knees, kissing his chest with tender care, feeling the honey flow inside her anew. Jedidiah held her to him, running his hands through her dark hair, then down over her smooth back, to the gentle curves of her bottom. When his hands closed around those two firm mounds, she moaned, arching toward him, aching to have him fill her.

As if sensing her need, Jedidiah urged her gently down, positioning himself above her. She held out her arms, holding him to her as he kissed her once more, his tongue mating, melding, with hers until she squirmed with need. Then he was above her again, parting her long, slender legs.

As he entered her, Victoria cried out his name, "Jedidiah," and he stilled above her. His eyes met her confused, tormented ones as she wondered what was wrong.

To her utter amazement, there was an expression of teasing playfulness that accompanied the flush of passion on his face. He whispered, "Jed."

Her confusion turned to understanding when she realized his intent, to have her call him by the name he favored. She smiled back at him, devilment running through her, in spite of the raging hunger inside her. "Jedidiah."

He smiled back, descending in one long, slow stroke, then stopping. "Jed."

She closed her eyes on the pleasure and agony of having him lie so still. But, summoning her will, she replied. "Jedidiah."

Again he began to move, and Victoria soon abandoned herself to the fierceness of the storm raging inside her. She arched and wriggled beneath him, matching her rhythm to whatever one he set as the sensations built and built to the breaking point.

Until again he grew still.

She looked up at him, biting her lower lip in frustration. She saw the sweat beaded on his own lip, the strain of holding back on his face. She also saw the determination in his eyes. He held her gaze with his as he sank deep, in one slow, excruciatingly pleasurable stroke, then drew back. "Jed," he whispered hoarsely.

Writhing beneath him and unable to prevent herself, Victoria swallowed to moisten her dry throat and nodded. "Yes. Jed."

He closed his eyes and thrust deep inside her, the delight exploding in ecstasy even as she cried out, "Jed... Oh, yes, Jed..."

And then he was pulsing inside her, calling out her name in a hoarse murmur. "Victoria, sweet Victoria..."

She held him to her, reveling in his response as much as she had in her own.

He rolled to lie beside her, pillowing her head on his chest, his hand on her hair. Victoria sighed with exquisite euphoria.

Jedidiah had toyed with her at the end, made her understand the strength of his will. Once, not so very long ago, at Briarwood, he had told her that she would not always get her way with him. Well, if the teasingly erotic game he had just played with her was his way of proving it, she would not mind his doing so again.

She wanted to stay just where she was for hours, to soak up the joy of being here with him. But the hours she had spent crying, coupled with the physical languor he had just produced in her body, made her eyelids droop with sweet exhaustion....

Jed held Victoria while their breathing quieted. Leaning over to look at her, he saw that she had fallen asleep. Her face was completely relaxed in repose, her lashes thick and dark against the flush that lay along her cheekbones. That flush had been brought on by his loving. A wave of tenderness as strong as a gale-force wind thundered over and through him. The absolute unexpectedness of the emotion made it all the more devastating to his peace of mind.

Never had he expected to feel this way about any woman. What it meant, he did not know, only that the sensation was more powerful and compelling than anything else in his life—including his need to find his unknown son.

Jed suddenly realized that if not for the differences in their lives, the very extremes of their positions in society, he might have allowed himself to fully explore his feelings. He might have paid court to her and seen where that might have lead them.

Even as the realization hit him, he knew that it was impossible.

If he had not been good enough for Nina, Victoria was as far above him as the moon. He'd told her about his upbringing, the true humbleness of where he came from. Victoria, to her credit, had not treated him any differently because of it. It was one of the things he admired about her, that in spite of where she came from, who she was, she accepted each person on his or her own merits. But he did not think she truly understood the wretched truth of it. There was no way a lady like her could.

And it was he who could not accept the part of himself that might make him acceptable to her kind. He cursed the Malone blood that tainted his veins. A coldhearted inability to forgive was far worse than the ignorance born of poverty.

For a brief moment, Jed's arms tightened involuntarily around her, and she snuggled closer to him even in her sleep, making his heart ache in his breast. Deliberately he loosened his hold. Not for any reason would he allow anyone to hurt her—not even himself.

Slowly, and with a regret that was nearly incapacitating, Jed drew away. He reached down and pulled the rumpled bed linens up, finding himself tucking them carefully around her, though he cursed himself for taking the risk of waking her.

Then he turned, squaring his shoulders with determination, and pulled on his clothes. He would conquer his desire for her, and this would not occur again. It could not, for Victoria's sake.

But even as these thoughts went through his mind, a distant voice was telling Jed that if he didn't keep his feelings at bay, his whole way of life would be compromised.

After a nearly sleepless night, Jed woke to see Winter standing at the foot of his bed. He was holding the shirt Jed had tossed on the floor when he returned to his room, numb and aching with guilt over what had happened.

Even as Jed watched, he raised the garment to his nose and frowned. Blanching, he realized that Victoria's rose scent must still be clinging to the shirt.

As if sensing that he was being watched, the gray-haired man turned toward the bed. They exchanged a long measuring look. At last the older man said, "May I speak freely, sir?"

Jed raised his arm to rest it under his head. "Yes."

"Lady Victoria is different, my lord. Far above the rest."

Jed nodded stiffly. "She deserves the best."

Winter considered him for a moment. "She deserves whatever will make her happy." He began to fold the shirt.

Jed watched him, not willing to make any reply to that. He could only wonder at the pointed expression on the man's face. Obviously the servants were not blind to whatever was going on between himself and the lady.

Was Winter implying that Jed could make her happy? If he was, the man could not be more wrong.

Chapter Thirteen

The next morning, Sinclair arrived early, dressed for riding. Jed, who was having coffee in the sitting room, was not surprised to see him. He did his best to appear glad to see the other man, though, in spite of his realizations the night before, it was difficult. He set aside the copy of the *Post* he was reading and motioned toward the laden tray. "Would you care for coffee?"

Sinclair accepted readily. "Yes, I believe I would. I've sent up my card with a request for Lady Victoria to go riding with me again."

Jed shrugged. "I see." He was more than slightly apprehensive about how Victoria might react to him after last night. She might have come to the conclusion that she never wanted to see him again, but he was determined to face her. He had no intention of abandoning her until she no longer needed him.

Sinclair nodded as he put sugar in his cup and stirred. "Would you care to go along?"

Coolly Jed replied, "I would be happy to join you." He could not even begin to speculate on how Victoria would respond to his accompanying them again.

He had no intention of allowing the two to go off alone together, though he assured himself it had nothing to do with jealousy. Sinclair would get no opportunity to steal the same liberties that Jed had taken with Victoria. The thought of Ian—or any man, for that matter—doing so brought a wave of nausea that surprised him with its intensity.

Jed forced it down, telling himself not to think about her being with another man. He must focus on his responsibility to make sure the lady was safe and protected from harm until her marriage was assured.

Jed met the other man's friendly expression without guilt. He did, in fact, through a great effort, manage a polite smile. He picked up a copy of the *Times* and offered it to Sinclair.

Ian shrugged, and took it. It seemed he had decided to accept Jed in the role of protective cousin. Which was just the part Jed intended to play from now onward.

After only a short time, Sinclair dropped the paper and spoke with animation and knowledge of the new horse he had just purchased for the purpose of breeding. Jed looked at him with interest. Gone was the pose of the bored aristocrat. The more he saw of Ian Sinclair, the more Jed realized Victoria was right to believe there was something worthwhile to him.

Victoria arrived in the sitting room half an hour after Sinclair, looking pale and uncertain. Jed could not bring himself to meet her eyes, though he could feel her searching gaze upon him.

His offhand greeting to her was completely overshadowed by Sinclair's effusive one. When Ian rose and took her hand for a moment, Jed had to fight the feelings of possessiveness that pierced his heart, keeping his features schooled in a polite mask.

The moment he sensed her attention switch to Sinclair, his greedy eyes focused on her, taking in every detail of her sweet curves, as they were revealed by the close-fitting riding habit of amber velvet she wore. The sheer veil of the matching hat framed her beautiful face and shadowed her heavily lashed eyes. The creamy line of her cheek and jaw were revealed in startling perfection.

When she shook her head in answer to something Sinclair had said, her tongue darted out to wet her lips. Jed felt an almost painful tightening in his lower stomach as he recalled the feel of that tongue on his flesh. A rushing sounded in his ears as other, even more evocative images filled his mind and fired his senses.

He closed his eyes, battling his reactions to her with all his will. It was some moments before he realized that Sinclair was speaking his name.

"Mr. McBride, shall we go?"

"Jed," he replied automatically, the word reminding him of the way Victoria had succumbed so sensuously to his desire for her to say his name. Jed swallowed hard. He now realized that accompanying them was a mistake, did not know how he would get through it without revealing his feelings. Even so, he could not bear the thought of Ian being alone with her.

He would simply have to control himself. "Of course." He rose and went to the door, being careful not to look toward the object of his desire. He was infinitely aware of her where she stood at Sinclair's side, her presence like a shining beacon to his senses.

Once they were mounted and heading for the park, Jed began to get some command over himself. He was somehow able to make perfectly rational replies to Ian's friendly efforts at conversation.

Victoria said very little as they rode along. She felt a trace of bitterness when she realized that neither of the two men seemed to notice. They appeared quite content to carry on their own conversation.

But deep inside she knew that she did not care to talk. All that mattered was the swelling waves of pain inside her.

She glanced over at the man in question, took in the remote expression he wore, and shivered with sorrow. Seeing him like this reminded her, quite forcefully, that the sea captain felt no sentiment toward her.

If he did, it would be impossible for him to withdraw from her so completely. Thus, she knew that the best thing for her would be to push all feelings for him to the farthest, darkest part of her soul. She must never again acknowledge that those emotions existed.

Victoria simply was not sure how this was to be accomplished. Each syllable that fell from his lips, each movement of his strong hands on his horse's reins, reminded her anew of how dear he was to her. How much she would miss him when he went away.

She became aware of someone speaking her name. "Victoria."

Immediately her eager gaze went to Jedidiah, but he was studiously checking the buckle that held the bridle on his horse's head. Her expression changed to disappointment.

"Victoria." This time her gaze found the source of the sound. Ian Sinclair. He was looking at her with a frown of both puzzlement and concentration. He glanced over at the stony-faced Jedidiah, then back to her.

Victoria blushed, her attention focusing on her gloved hands. Dear heaven, had she given herself away? She glanced back at the nobleman, and his knowingly arched brows told her that she very well might have. Desperately she tried to think of some way to rectify the situation.

Nothing came to mind. She was too caught up in her own pain at Jedidiah's rejection and the utter hopelessness of the situation.

Victoria was shocked from these devastating thoughts by Jedidiah's shout of alarm. "Good Lord!"

She looked up to see him spurring his mount away from them. Ahead of him was a sight that made her blood freeze in her veins. A bay gelding, its reins trailing, reared and pranced above the prone body of what looked to be a child.

Jedidiah reached the scene quickly, leaping from his horse to place himself between the flying hooves and the child. He turned on the animal, waving his arms wide. This made the horse rear up again, and for one heart-stopping moment Victoria feared Jedidiah would be struck, but the horse veered at the last moment, racing away across the grass.

Ian Sinclair arrived immediately behind the other man.

Recovering from her shock quickly, Victoria prodded her own horse forward. When she reached the spot, she dismounted to join the men where they knelt beside the child. It was a young boy of probably twelve or thirteen years of age. He appeared to be unconscious, but she could see no sign of blood, no twisted limbs.

Victoria pulled off her gloves and leaned over to touch his still face, which looked so pale against the emerald-green grass. His skin was smooth and warm against her palm, but he did not respond.

She looked up then as a shout sounded behind them. A stout man on a similarly colored stallion was bearing down upon them. He continued to gallop toward them at a breakneck pace, pulling on the reins in the last moment, dismounting even as the horse reared in reaction.

He rushed over and drew the still-unconscious child up into his arms, feeling the fragile neck for a pulse. "Oh, son, thank the Lord you live." Unashamed tears sparkled in his brown eyes.

Victoria felt tears sting her own eyes at the man's unabashed show of emotion for his child. Such paternal devotion was not often so openly displayed. She felt an instant affinity with the stout gray-haired gentleman.

Immediately she introduced herself. "I am Victoria Thorn." She gestured toward each of the men in turn. "These two gentlemen are Mr. Jedidiah McBride and Lord Ian Sinclair. We saw what was happening to your son and came to see if we could be of any assistance."

He nodded, without paying more than cursory attention to the introductions. Most of the man's concentration continued to be centered on the boy. Absently he offered, "Squire Harry Fairfield."

As he said the name Fairfield, Victoria's gaze flew to Jedidiah's face. Fairfield! Heavens, that was Nina's name! Judging by the shock and disbelief on the sea captain's countenance, he was not oblivious of the coincidence.

Jed's gaze focused on the child in the man's arms. He could not allow himself to think that this might mean anything, that this might be the Fairfield he was looking for. But even after twelve years, Jed remembered that Nina's housekeeper had been very definite in her report that Miss Nina was marrying a Squire Fairfield.

His gaze ran over the child's face. Good God, but the age must be about right. His own son would be eleven. The boy was a bit large for eleven, but then, Jed had always been big for his age. The hair was blond and straight, the brow smooth and wide. The boy's nose was straight and strongly formed, even at this age. There might be a resemblance in those features. It was hard to tell, with the youthful fullness still in the downy cheeks. And there was a marked difference in the mouth, it being somewhat fuller than Jed's, but what did that mean?

Was he looking at his own son?

God help him, he could not think properly. What a surprise it was to see the boy here like this. All the people he had questioned, the leads he had followed, all had ended in nothing.

Then, today, when he was least expecting it, he'd been where he needed to be at just the right moment. He might have actually saved the life of his own child—his son. Jed curled his fingers in the grass beneath his hand, smelled the crisp scent it gave off, felt the brush of the breeze against his cheek, looked into the clear blue sky and knew this was real. He felt a soaring sense of wonder that this world was indeed a miraculous place. He gazed down at the boy again, trying to bring himself under control.

The child might not be his, he told himself sternly. It might turn out to be a coincidence, this man's name being the same as Nina's, her having married a man with the title of squire, the child's features being somewhat like his own.

Despite all the rational things he tried to tell himself, his gaze roamed with avid hunger over the child's face again. He tried to remember if Nina had had a mouth like that. He couldn't recall. The face that overshadowed all others in Jed's mind was Victoria's.

He glanced over and saw the veiled excitement and compassion in her gray eyes. He realized that she was thinking the same things as he.

Perhaps, then, it might be true.

Her heart turning over in her breast, Victoria watched as Jedidiah reached out to run a trembling hand over the child's blond hair. The squire appeared not to think that there was anything odd about Jedidiah's reactions, as he made no comment. She could only assume he was too worried about the boy's condition to notice.

Victoria looked at Jedidiah and saw the dazed expression on his pale face as he examined the child. Turning her own attention to the boy's face, Victoria saw again what seemed to be uncanny similarities in the lines of the jaws, the shapes of the two noses, the curves of the cheeks.

It was then that she was fully struck by what was happening. This might be what he had been searching for. This child might very well be Jedidiah's son. If she hadn't been kneeling, Victoria would have had to sit down to keep from falling.

Squire Fairfield cried out, drawing her gaze back to him. "Son, speak to me, son!"

As if in answer to the pleading in the man's voice, the boy's lids fluttered and he opened his eyes. Eyes the color of a sunlit sea.

She had only ever known one other person with eyes that color. Her gaze flew to Jedidiah's face, to see that he had blanched to the color of cream.

Victoria forced herself not to react, but to try to concentrate on the child's condition. His expression was somewhat dazed as he said, "Father..."

Fairfield clutched the boy close for a moment, before holding him away to look into his eyes. "Are you all right? Do you know where you are?"

The boy scowled, and Victoria was rocked by the familiarity of the expression, again glancing briefly at Jedidiah to see if he noticed. His reaction of shocked amazement had not changed. It was as if he could not accept what he was seeing.

She turned back to the young boy as he answered his father with an exasperated tone. "Of course I know where I am, Father." Then his attitude altered, and she saw the real affection he felt for the man come through as he reached up to cover the hand that lay on his chest. "Don't worry, Father. I am fine." He looked around then. "But what about Shadow? Is *he* all right?"

Ian Sinclair spoke from behind them. "I take it this is Shadow."

Having only now remembered the nobleman's presence, Victoria turned to see him holding the young gelding by the reins. Obviously Ian had gone to fetch the animal. Judging by the look of him, the horse had suffered no ill effects.

"Thank goodness," the boy chimed.

The squire interjected gruffly, "You will not be riding that animal again."

The boy looked to him with pleading eyes. "Father, it was not his fault. A stray hound ran beneath his legs, barking. It frightened him." He struggled to sit up, his face filled with stubborn mutiny.

Even in temperament he reminded her of the man she so loved.

The squire scowled, obviously not wanting to give in. But when he answered, his face softened. "I will not have him put down." At the child's happy grin, he held up a hand in warning. "But you shall not be riding that animal again unless the trainer deems him fit, after much more training."

"Yes, Father." The reply was subdued enough, but the gleam of happiness in the boy's eyes did not abate.

Victoria looked to Jedidiah again. All this had taken only a few short minutes, and he had said nothing since hearing the squire's name. He simply stared at the child and the man. It was clear to her that he was having some difficulty in holding back, but did not want to leap in before he was sure he had some right.

She wanted to offer some sign of comfort. She did not. Everything she knew of Jedidiah McBride told her he would not welcome any overt sign of sympathy. The sea captain was a proud man, and would be determined to travel this road alone. Still, she longed to help. "Cousin Jedidiah, perhaps there is something we can do to assist Squire Fairfield and *his* son?"

Jed swung around to face Victoria, her words penetrating some of the shock he was experiencing.

The squire spoke again, drawing his attention. "Andrew and I are quite grateful for what you have done already. The boy had ridden on ahead of me while I got down to tighten the girth." He held out his hand to Jed. "I saw everything that happened, sir, and want to thank you for your quick thinking and bravery."

Jed took the proffered hand, even as his mind reeled over this new piece of information. His name was Andrew, God help him. Andrew was his own second name, and Nina had known that. "I..." He shook his head. "I did nothing. I'm only glad the boy is all right."

Squire Fairfield shook his own head. "That is not the way it appeared to me, sir. And my gratitude stands." With that said, the portly man rose and reached down to help the boy to his feet. "Son, we must be getting you back, so I can have the doctor sent for."

Jed stood with them, feeling Victoria do the same.

Andrew frowned. "Father, there is no need for the doctor." But when he pulled away to try to stand on his own, he swayed slightly, reaching out to steady himself.

Without thinking, Jed reached toward him, then drew back when the boy leaned back against the arm Squire Fairfield put around his shoulders. A painful surge of disappointment rushed through Jed. His hands dropped to his sides. He had to remember to keep a tight rein on himself. Even if he did turn out to be Jed's son, Andrew did not know him, would not welcome such attention from a stranger.

Even as he stood there thinking this, Squire Fairfield began to lead the boy toward his own horse, easing him carefully into the saddle. He then looked to where Sinclair still held the reins of the bay gelding. He shrugged helplessly. "Could I beg your further assistance? I do not want the boy to ride alone right now."

Victoria moved to stand beside Jed. "Of course. We would be glad to help." Her words were polite, but Jed saw the strain on her face.

If all this did turn out to be nothing more than a bizarre coincidence, the Fates had a very poor sense of humor indeed. In spite of his earlier elation, Jed knew that it could all be a coincidence. Life had taught him it could be incredibly cruel when you least expected it.

With gratitude apparent in his voice, the gray-haired man said. "I must add a word of thanks to you, dear lady. It is not every day that you meet three such kind Samaritans as yourselves." He glanced around to the three of them with a smile of genuine appreciation.

Jed could not meet the kindly brown gaze. He had expected to fully dislike the man who had stolen his son, however unknowingly. He had thought he would be a haughty, bored aristocrat.

To discover that this man was anything but made him unexplainably uncomfortable. Jed pushed the feelings to the back of his mind as he mounted his stallion.

He and Victoria followed directly behind the squire, who was in a hurry to return to his home. Sinclair brought up the rear, still leading the gelding.

Jed looked back at the nobleman as he sat in heavy silence behind them, and realized Sinclair had something on his mind. His face was a mask of contemplation, and he was studying the unknowing Victoria with grave concentration. Only once did he glance Jed's way. As their gazes collided, he raised his brows noncommittally, giving Jed little indication of his thoughts.

As they left the park and headed to a slightly less fashionable area of the city, Jed pushed Ian from his mind. There would be time enough to deal with that later. Right now, he knew, he must think about where he was going.

For the first time, he wondered if he was about to see Nina. She might very well be there to greet her husband and son. How he felt about seeing her again, he no longer knew. His gaze went to Victoria. The raging anger that he'd felt toward Nina, anger that had driven him so relentlessly, had been replaced by an emptiness that was devastating in its intensity.

He found himself looking at the squire and Andrew, the boy resting back against the man in complete trust, the man glancing down at him in obvious concern every time they experienced the slightest jolt.

Jed turned away. It was his right to have his own son with him. No one, no matter how personable, would keep him from what was his.

After a time, they arrived at a comfortable-looking three-story house. It was not a mansion such as Victoria or her circle lived in. But the neat white house, with its many windows and gables, exuded a welcoming warmth.

As soon as they halted in front of the house, a manservant opened the door and came out to greet them. Taking in the fact that the boy was mounted before Squire Fairfield with grave concern, he raced to the man's side. "My lord, has something happened?" He looked to the other three, as if wondering who they could be.

"My son has taken a tumble from his horse," Harry Fairfield informed him before he could go on. "Please go along and see that the doctor is sent for immediately."

Jed watched as the man turned to hurry back into the house. He got off his own horse as the squire dismounted, then helped the boy down.

Before Jed could offer to do anything, a bevy of folk streamed through the front door, looking concerned and fearful. All of them, three men and two women, were talking at once. When they saw young Master Andrew leaning against his father, one of the women, a gently rounded matron of middle age in a mobcap, came forward to clutch the child to her.

The other younger woman and the three men began to question Squire Fairfield at once, none of them making the least amount of sense. He raised his hands in exasperation and affection. "Please, dear family and friends, let us go into the house. I have asked Farley to send for the doctor. But it is certainly only a precaution. Andrew has seemed to improve even as we were riding home."

There was another flurry of speech, this time giving the general impression of relief. The matronly woman now kissed Andrew on his cheek.

For his part, Andrew seemed nothing so much as embarrassed by this attention. Jed could not help feeling sorry for him. A boy of his age would certainly not take such fussing with good grace were he upon death's very door.

Squire Harry Fairfield turned to Jed then, his expression bright with sincerely felt emotion, also taking in the still-mounted Victoria and Ian. "My friends—and I do count you that now—I can only tell you once again how grateful I am that you came to our aid this afternoon. I owe you more than I can ever repay."

Jed could only bow. "You are very welcome, sir. We were happy to be of assistance." He looked to the other two, and watched them nod in agreement. Nina was not among the group who stood looking at them from the front steps, but Jed found he did not have the heart to pry any more into the squire's life just now. The man had had a terrible shock today. He did not need Jed to tell him that the child he believed was his might not be.

Jed spoke quietly. "I think we will leave you now, so that you can get things under control here. I hope you will not mind if I call back to see how the boy is doing."

"Of course not." Squire Fairfield surprised him by giving him a friendly pat on the back. "Any time." He paused then and smiled at the woman who was still hugging Andrew too tightly. "Or better yet—my sister is giving a party this evening, and I am sure she would be utterly delighted if you would consent to attend."

The lady nodded enthusiastically. "Anyone who has been a friend to my brother is a friend to me."

As she spoke, a servant came forward and took the horse from Ian Sinclair, who was shaking his head in regret. "I must beg your pardon here, Squire Fairfield. I have a previous engagement that I cannot break." He glanced toward Jed meaningfully. "Though if Mr. McBride and Lady Victoria are able to attend, I would be most grateful to hear news of how young Andrew is faring."

The squire expectantly looked to Jed, who replied, "I would be very happy to accept your invitation if Lady Victoria is able to do so." He knew a sense of relief. He had been given a further opportunity to find out if this might indeed be his child without having to completely disrupt their lives.

Victoria nodded her agreement. "We would be most pleased to attend."

The squire smiled cheerily. "I'm sure the doctor will have come and gone by then. And with a clean bill of health for my boy." His eyes grew misty for a moment, and Jed felt an unexpected tugging at his heart. He pushed the feeling away. He owed this man nothing.

Harry Fairfield continued, oblivious of the other man's thoughts. "He's my heart, that boy. Nothing can happen to him. It's just a tumble he's had, and nothing more. Never should have agreed to let him have that horse, but it's so hard to deny him, his mother being ill and all."

Jed's stomach somersaulted. In her letter, Nina had said she was ill. But he controlled himself, holding in his suspicions, determined not to act without proof.

Jed made a hasty goodbye and mounted his horse. Victoria and Sinclair followed him as he rode from the house. Squire Harry, having no idea of the possible repercussions of this day, waved them away with a smile.

Victoria could not help being aware of the way Ian Sinclair was watching her. But right now she could hardly bring herself to worry about that.

All she could think about was that she and Jedidiah would be returning to that house this very evening. They would likely learn whether or not the boy Andrew was actually Jedidiah's son.

They would also meet Nina. Victoria glanced over at Jedidiah, who rode a few feet to her left. He was lost in thought. Was he, she wondered, thinking about the same thing she was? Was he wondering what his reactions to seeing the woman would be?

What disturbed her was Jedidiah's anger toward Nina. Could such resentment exist where there were not strong feelings? And when he saw her again, would he realize those feelings were not hatred, but something else? Could he still love this woman? Would he ask her to go to America with him?

The pain of acknowledging the question was horrific. Even as she felt this, Victoria understood that it was none of her concern. Jedidiah would love where he saw fit. He had his own life to live, as she had known from the very beginning. He had never pretended otherwise.

She looked over at the man who was so in her thoughts. With the strain of the past hour on his face, he was even more attractive to her. His expression was marked by determination, and a hopeful vulnerability heretofore unknown in this proud, strong, resourceful man. She was even more drawn to him because of it.

Frustration made her prod her horse to a faster pace. Damn him!

When they reached her home, Victoria replied with the barest of civility as Ian Sinclair made his excuses and left them at the door. She wanted nothing so much as to find out what Jedidiah McBride was thinking. What his plans might be.

He seemed almost startled when she asked him to come into the library with her the moment they entered the house. He made no comment, simply looking at her as if suddenly remembering her existence.

This only served to make Victoria more disheartened. Already he was forgetting her.

Calling on all her inner strength, she squared her shoulders, holding her head high. Then, immediately, before she could lose her courage, she said, "You do think that Andrew might be your son."

Jedidiah looked down at her, his expression remote, his eyes unreadable. "Yes, I do."

"What will you do?" She could not bring herself to mention Nina.

He frowned at her, as if surprised by the question. "If he is my son, I will confront his mother and tell her I mean to take him to America with me."

Even though she'd known this, the words sliced through her like a freshly sharpened blade. She forced herself to go on, to learn the rest, the worst. "Do you mean to do that this very night?"

He looked away, his eyes focusing on the evergreen tree outside the window. "I don't know. I had not allowed myself to think that far into the future." He turned to her then, his expression searching. "Why do you ask?"

She met his look evenly, though it cost her dearly. "I need to know what you will do. I am not yet married, or even certain of my choice."

His face hardened, and he swung around so that she could only see his profile. "I see. Well, you have no need to worry about that. I will stay until you marry Sinclair." He glanced at her briefly, and for a moment she thought she saw sadness in his gaze, but it was gone before she could be sure. "That is what you mean to do, isn't it—marry Sinclair?"

She raised her chin, staring at the gold trim on the drapery without really seeing it. "Yes...that is...I believe so." She took a deep breath before going on. "I am not quite certain, but it seems very likely. He's a decent sort of man."

"Well," Jedidiah answered with a shrug, "that settles it, then. We've each made our plans."

"Yes," she replied, "we have." She turned to go to the door. "Well, it is good that it's all been settled. "I think I'll go up now and have a rest before getting ready for the party."

She would not let him see how much she was hurting. How she knew she would continue to hurt, long after she was nothing but a faint memory in his mind.

Chapter Fourteen

Victoria was ready long before the time to depart for the party had arrived. However, she needed time to put aside her own feelings for Jedidiah McBride. She had in fact, by the time she met him in the foyer, managed to convince herself that she could do so. Her equanimity was destroyed when Jedidiah brushed her bare arm as he lifted her light evening cloak to drape it around her shoulders.

Victoria felt the current of physical sensation that raced between them, and caught her breath at its intensity. All her efforts to convince herself she could live without him went flying by the wayside.

Jedidiah's reaction to the contact was instantaneous. He jumped back as if stung. What made her heart sink was the look of resentment in his green eyes. He attempted to hide it by turning away from her and moving quickly toward the door, but it was too late.

She felt the hurt of his disapproval sink into her soul. Yet somehow, through the fog of her pain, she knew she did not want him to see how devastated she was.

Why, Victoria wondered, would he feel so resentful toward her? Was he disturbed by his reactions to her because of their very inconvenience to him? Now that the end of his quest appeared to be in sight, he would want to put any attraction to her aside. He would soon find another woman to warm his bed, for that was all she had been.

Calling on the strength and pride of the many generations of Thorns who had faced adversity with courage, Victoria raised her head high. She must, for the sake of her name, at least, salvage some modicum of self-respect in this.

It was only with an expression of assumed hauteur that she was able to endure sitting across from Jedidiah on the drive. He seemed too lost in his own thoughts to even notice, but Victoria did not let down her guard.

When they arrived, they were greeted by an effusive hostess. Her mobcap of the morning had been replaced by another one that was made of a gauzy fabric and bore several ribbons of the same shade as her pale pink gown. She took Victoria's hand in hers. "My dear Lady Victoria, I am very sorry for our lack of manners earlier in the day. We were never properly introduced. I am Mrs. Eliza Rochester. And this—" she indicated the portly gentleman at her side "—is my husband, Mr. Dexter Rochester. None of us understood who you were until you had gone and Harry told us your name. I must tell you how very honored we are to have the daughter of the duke of Carlisle as a guest in our home."

Mr. Rochester's contribution was an expansive "Quite right, my dear. Very pleased to have you."

Victoria shook her head, very aware of the man at her side, wondering what he would be making of such an effusive greeting. Glancing toward him, she realized that she needn't have worried. His intent gaze was trained on the small foyer behind their hostess. It, and the stairs that rose upward were empty.

Was he then so eager to see if his Nina was here? She forced herself to concentrate on making a reply to her hostess. "Oh, please, Mrs. Rochester, there is no need to apologize, and it is I who am honored to be here. Your first concern was, understandably, for the well-being of your brother's son. I do hope all is well with him.''

"Oh, you are very gracious, my lady." Eliza Rochester nodded her head, setting those ribbons astir. "Andrew is doing quite well, and none the worse for the tumble he took. The doctor says he will be fine once the megrim subsides."

Jedidiah spoke up. "I am very happy to hear that."

The woman turned to him, her eyes now growing damp with emotion. "And Mr. McBride. Henry has told us all." She reached up to wipe a tear away with the edge of her lace handkerchief. "How can we ever repay you for risking your own life to save that of our dear Andrew? What would we do without him, especially with our dear Nina so unwell."

At the mention of Nina, Victoria felt Jedidiah stiffen beside her. It was true, then. Andrew was Jedidiah's son. Even though she'd known it must almost certainly be true, the realization pummeled her.

She could hear the barely suppressed emotion in Jedidiah's voice when he spoke up beside her. "Is Ni—Mrs. Fairfield here tonight?"

Before anyone else could answer, Harry Fairfield's enthusiastic reply erupted from the stairs above. "No, Mrs. Fairfield is not here." He hurried down to them. "She is unable to travel at this time." A hint of melancholy tinged his tone before he went on cheerily, "I have a splendid idea. Why don't you both come out to the country and meet her? I know she will want to thank you personally for what you have done. Especially as she is from your own country, Mr. McBride." He beamed at them like a benevolent uncle.

Jedidiah answered quietly, but with complete conviction. "We would be happy to accept."

* * *

The house was only a day's journey into the country. Under any other circumstances, Victoria would have enjoyed the drive. The warm weather had brought the daffodils and lilies from the ground, their faces turned with wanton abandon toward the sun. She felt that she had bloomed with just the same ebullience from Jedidiah's lovemaking.

Her gaze went to him where he sat across from her and Betty, reading a copy of the *Post*. He seemed no more interested in the changes wrought in her than the sun did in the flowers.

Betty's presence in the clarence was welcome. The maid was able to relieve some of the tension, without being aware of it, with her cheery commentary on the fineness of the weather and the unexpectedness of the trip to the country, which she was very happy about, being tired of London already.

Winter had remained in London, as Jedidiah had been adamant in stating that he would not require the man's services. He'd added that they would not be there long.

She knew the American was telling her he would soon be on his way. She also knew he would not be leaving alone. Poor Squire Fairfield was riding in his own brougham just ahead of them, unaware that his life was about to be irreversibly altered.

It was with growing sympathy toward the squire that Victoria saw the end of their journey some hours later. The Fairfields' home was charming, a comfortable-looking brick structure with a sharp roof, dormers, and cutout stone windows. The windows ran the length of the three stories, the top row being gabled and having sculpted white casements. Ivy clung to the walls, and decorative shrubbery graced the drive.

They were greeted by a smiling male servant in a black coat and trousers and a crisp white shirt. "Squire Fairfield." He stepped out of the way for his master to enter the front door.

Andrew bounded in and began to remove his coat. "Has Mrs. Rhodes been baking?" Victoria watched as he sniffed the air, which was filled with the scent of fresh-baked bread. The squire gave him a disapproving glance, and he subsided, though she could see that his natural ebullience had not been tamed, but only leashed, for he grinned sheepishly.

Obviously accustomed to his young master's impetuous ways, the servant addressed the squire. "It is so good to see you home, sir." His polite but curious gaze took in Victoria and Jedidiah as they followed Fairfield into the entrance hall.

Harry turned with a sweep of his hands. "As you see, we have guests. Lady Thorn and Mr. McBride are to be treated with the utmost courtesy and hospitality."

The servant bowed. "Of course, my lord." He then took his master's hat and gloves, before doing the same to Jedidiah. Victoria unclasped the light, short cloak she wore over her traveling dress of burgundy-colored silk and handed it to him, as well.

"Would you be so good as to fetch Mrs. Rhodes?" the squire directed.

"Of course, sir." He bowed and left them.

Andrew looked up at his father. "May I go and see Mother now?"

"Yes," Henry told him. "I shall be up shortly myself."

The boy bounded up the stairs that dominated the entrance hall just as a woman emerged from a door to their left. She came forward with a smile, her hands folded before her plump middle. "Sir, we are so glad to have you home."

"And it is good to be here," he replied, then turned to his visitors. "Mrs. Rhodes, these are my friends, Lady Victoria Thorn and her cousin, Mr. Jedidiah McBride. Would you be so good as to look after them for me? Please see that they have suitable accommodations, and anything else they might require." He turned to them. "I hope you will not think me rude, but I ask you to excuse me for the moment, as I would like to see my wife. I must give her the medication I brought from the doctor in London."

Victoria nodded. "Certainly. We do not think you in the least rude."

Jedidiah bowed, his face expressionless. Victoria could only wonder at his thoughts as he said, "I agree. We will see you later, I'm sure."

He smiled at them. "Oh, for tea, most definitely. Nina will want to meet you as soon as I tell her what you have done for us."

To Jed, it seemed as if years had passed since they were left in the hall with the housekeeper. In fact, it had been only one hour. He stopped himself then, realizing it had in fact been many years that he had been waiting to face Nina ever since she had deserted him. Now the moment had come.

He squared his shoulders and followed the manservant down to the garden, where tea was being served. He had been through so many changes of emotion in the past two days that he was numb. Trying to imagine what it would be like to finally see Nina again was impossible.

At seventeen, he had felt he loved her more than life itself. Now he knew that had not been true. The feelings he had for her had been a mere shadow of what real love could be. This certainty came from an understanding that he could never really love anyone as shallow and unfaithful as she had been. He knew now that real love was more than physical. It grew out of true respect and admiration. How he had come to this understanding, he was not quite sure.

He was led out through a set of French doors to a flag-stone patio with two enormous oak trees growing on either side. These provided shade and a sense of intimacy. There was a lace-covered table with a silver tea service set up on it and several wicker chairs grouped around it. Only two faced him, and Victoria was sitting in one of them. She rose as soon as she saw him, her expression unreadable.

Jed looked from her to Harry Fairfield as the other man also stood and came forward with his hand outstretched. "Ah, Mr. McBride, you're here at last. Come and meet my sweet Nina."

Suddenly feeling as if time had slowed to a crawl, Jed moved around the end of a rattan lounge that rested in the shade of one of the oak trees. And there she was, lying before him. His eyes took in every detail of her appearance, her too-white complexion, her sunken cheeks, her with-ered frame, no bigger than a child's. Lord, he thought, she really is ill, and was surprised by the pang of sadness he felt.

He looked into her face, and was further surprised by what he saw. There was a defiant expression in her dark eyes as she faced him. It was as if she were waiting for him to denounce her to her husband and child, but refused to be cowed.

He thought of Andrew. If nothing else, he had learned the boy was close to both of his parents. How would Nina's inevitable death affect him?

All these thoughts ran through his mind in the beat of a heart. He listened as Squire Fairfield introduced him. "My dear, this is the man I told you about. The one who was so brave in risking his own well-being to save Andrew from harm."

She held out an incredibly small hand, her eyes having taken on a pleading expression. "You have no idea how very grateful I am to you Mr....McBride. My family, my son, mean everything to me.''

He felt a stab of sympathy. As he took the cold fingers in his. He told himself not to let her get to him this way. She had duped him, cheated him, taken the one thing that might have made a difference in his life, that might have made him feel as if he had someone. Why should he care about her now?

But something held him back, kept him from denouncing her there and then. Yet he could not completely refrain from giving her an inkling of his pain. ''Mrs. Fairfield, I have met *your* son. He's quite a boy. Given an opportunity, any man would be proud to claim him for his own.''

She jerked her hand back, and at the same moment a violent fit of coughing seized her. The spasms racked her too-slender frame. With shaking hands, she pressed a handkerchief to her lips to try to muffle the sounds.

Harry Fairfield fell to his knees beside her. ''Nina, my heart...'' The agony on his face showed that he would have taken this upon himself to spare her. When finally the attack settled somewhat, Nina met her husband's gaze with a pitying one of her own. Her free hand reached out to cup his cheek tenderly. ''Oh, Harry, what a trial I am to you.''

Jed found himself unable to keep watching them. He had not expected to see such deep and moving affection between them. In his memory, Nina was a cruel and selfish being who would do whatever she must to gain her own ends. This new image of her did not add up with the one he had held for so long.

He did not know he was seeking Victoria until his eyes found her. She was looking from him to the Fairfields with compassion and something else he could only have described as regret.

At that moment, Harry Fairfield drew his attention by saying, ''I am going to take my wife up to her room now. I think she needs to have some more of the medication the doctor sent. It will soon have her feeling stronger.'' The desperation in his voice was obvious, in spite of his cheery words.

Jed watched as he lifted Nina easily into his arms and carried her into the house. The situation was not the way he had thought it would be. Nina seemed neither unloving nor cruel. Andrew was completely happy and well adjusted, his concern for his mother's health aside. It appeared that Harry Fairfield had been as good a father as any boy could ask for.

He wanted to turn to Victoria, to take her into his arms and relieve his frustration and sadness in her warmth. He knew he could not do that.

With an unknowingly wretched groan, Jed turned and made his way across the patio to the garden. He had to be alone to think.

Victoria watched Jedidiah leave with a feeling of utter despair. It was obvious from his reaction to seeing Nina again that his feelings for her were not as dead as he had believed.

When Victoria came down to tea, she'd been shocked to see Nina Fairfield. That she'd once been a beautiful woman was still apparent in the delicate features of her face and the doelike quality of her dark brown eyes. Now her face was too thin and shadows hollowed her eyes and cheeks. Her amazingly lustrous dark hair, which had been carefully arranged in the latest style, seemed too heavy for her slender neck to support.

Victoria had seen the agony and indecision on Jedidiah's face as he looked at his lost love. Did he see her as she had been when they were young? There had been such bitterness in his voice as he spoke of Andrew. Was he thinking of all the things he had missed, of how his life would have been if Nina had stayed with him? Was he wishing they could share what little time she might have left?

Victoria could only believe he was. Obviously finding out that Nina was so ill had completely destroyed any hope Jedidiah might have harbored that they could be together. That did not mean he didn't wish things were different.

The thought was more painful than Victoria would have imagined.

Jed wandered across the grounds, uncaring of where he was going. Thus it came as a surprise to him when he heard someone call out his name. "Mr. McBride."

He turned and saw young Andrew racing across the grass. The sun shone on his blond hair, and he wiped a golden lock from his eyes as he came to an abrupt halt in front of Jed. He smiled a friendly, curious sort of a smile. "Mr. McBride, I thought you would be having tea with Father and Mother."

Jed looked at the boy, took in his long, strong limbs, his relaxed, confident stance, his direct gaze, and was swept by an overwhelming sense of pride. He had fathered this human being, this fine male specimen. In the most fundamental way, they belonged to each other.

He forced himself to act casually, for he did not want to bring the truth out until he had talked to Nina. Why this was so, he wasn't sure. "Your mother was not feeling well."

Andrew's expression darkened with sadness for a moment. "She has not been well of late. Father is quite worried, as am I."

"I'm sure you are." Jed spoke gently, in view of Andrew's concern.

With the resilience of the young, Andrew changed the subject. "I usually take tea with them. But Mother thought it might be more restful for you and Lady Victoria to have it without me." He grinned with devilish amusement.

Jed felt himself smile in return. He couldn't help it. The boy had an infectious sort of a temperament. "I would not have been bothered by you," he said honestly.

Andrew's grin widened. "It's quite all right. I have been to the stables to see my horse, Shadow. The trainer is working with him."

"How is he doing?" Jed hoped Andrew was not trying to get back on the animal before it was truly ready.

The boy scowled now. "I think he's doing very well indeed. I wanted to ride him again now, but Father will not hear of it. He says he'll be sold if I even so much as mention it again, until he says it's safe."

Good for him, Jed thought. It seemed as if Harry Fairfield, though extremely loving, was not overly indulgent. The boy was certainly a credit to him. But Jed did not want to think about that. He would have been a good father, if given the chance.

Again Andrew changed the subject. "Father says you are a sea captain." His sea-green eyes glowed with admiration. "How exciting that must be, to sail the seven seas, fighting pirates." Andrew waved an imaginary cutlass.

Jed had to look down for a moment to keep the boy from seeing the amusement this brought. "There isn't much pirating going on these days. It's really much more routine than that. Many of the ships are steam-powered now, and don't even have to wait for the wind to take them."

"Is your ship steam-powered?"

Jed shook his head. "No, steam hasn't managed to come up to the speed of the fastest wind vessels yet."

Those eyes locked with Jed's. "Is yours one of the fastest?"

Jed shrugged, but his pride was evident in his voice. "You could say that. My ship, the *Summerwind*, has won its share of races."

Andrew's expression became more openly admiring, and Jed had to fight down the urge to reach out to him, to say he was his father. He pushed the inclination aside. His gaze was assessing as he asked, "Would you like to go to sea?"

Andrew looked out across the greensward, his gaze focused on high seas and wind-filled sails that only he could see. "Would I like to go to sea?" Then he sighed and turned back to Jed. "No, my mother is ill, and I would not want to leave her."

Jed's heart turned over in his breast. God, what a fine, loyal young man he was. He looked into those eyes the same color as his own and marveled that any being could be so much like himself. And yet so different. Where Jed knew he was detached and watchful, Andrew was open and warm, inquisitive and spontaneous. Nina, as wrong as she had been to keep Andrew from him, had given the boy a good life.

That didn't mean she should get away with what she had done. Didn't he have a right to know his own child, his flesh and blood? Didn't Andrew have a right to know his own true father?

Jed knew he had to talk to Nina. He had the feeling that only then would he be able to come to grips with the confusion that held him hostage.

At dinner that evening, Victoria addressed Squire Fairfield directly, being careful not to look at Jedidiah, who sat across the table from her. "I find that I have business to attend in London, sir. I hope you will not think me rude if I make my departure in the morning."

Harry Fairfield turned to her with surprise. "I hope I have done nothing to upset you."

She shook her head, feeling Jedidiah's intent gaze upon her. Victoria refused to look at him, could not do so if she was to follow through with her intentions. "No, of course not. You have been most kind. I simply must see to some things that I have neglected." She took a deep breath. "It is my hope, though, that you would allow my cousin to stay on. I believe he is gaining much from your fresh country air."

She watched as Squire Harry gave Jed a long, assessing look that he seemed totally unaware of. The American was now studying his wineglass with intense concentration. Suddenly she wondered if the squire might be coming to suspect that something was wrong. The unspoken message that Jedidiah and Nina Fairfield had exchanged on meeting one another had been obvious to her. Perhaps she was not the only one.

She put the thought aside, reminding herself as the squire nodded slowly that Jedidiah was making his own way here. She had no say in it.

Harry Fairfield spoke evenly. "Of course you must stay on, Mr. McBride. I would be happy to put the brougham at your disposal at any time you wish to take your leave."

Jedidiah glanced up, replying in an emotionless tone. "Thank you, sir. I am very grateful for your consideration."

Victoria forced herself to meet his gaze as he turned to her. It was as cool and distant as the moon. He arched a brow as she stared at him in consternation, and she drew herself upright. She would not let him see how hurt she was, how much she cared. The sooner she was away, the better.

Victoria was just moving toward the large bed, with its ruffled pink counterpane, when a knock sounded at her door. Victoria pulled her robe close about her, wondering if Betty had come back to offer her assistance again. Victoria had sent the girl away once, not being in the mood to listen to her chatter.

She opened the door, holding a candle before her. "Please, there is no need..." She halted, her heart giving a double beat, as she saw Jedidiah McBride standing there. "Cousin... Mr. McBride."

He looked at her for a long, indefinable moment, his lips curled sardonically. "Mr. McBride. Are we back to that, after everything that has happened between us, Victoria?"

She swallowed, wanting to tell him how much she cared, that she loved him more than life itself. But she dared not, had no right to do so. She looked into the candle's flame, willing herself not to react. "I... Yes. I think it would be best now, under the circumstances. Don't you?"

He paused for a time, then glanced around self-consciously. "Do you mind if I come in? Anyone might see us if I keep standing here in the hall."

Victoria nodded, stepping back. "Of course." He would not want Nina to think there was anything between them.

She watched as Jedidiah came into the comfortably furnished chamber and shut the heavy oak door. He then turned and looked at her thoughtfully. Victoria forced herself to remain passive under his scrutiny, though she wanted to turn away, afraid those fathomless eyes of his would see how very responsive she was to his presence even now.

He surprised her with his next words. "You are going back to London to tell Sinclair you will marry him."

She was still for a moment. The idea had not even entered her head. Guilt assaulted her, for she'd not given Ian the least thought since sending him a note telling him she was going to the country. But she would not tell Jedidiah that. She wanted him to feel he was free of her. "Yes," she replied. "As we have discussed previously, it is for the best." Even as she said it, Victoria knew she was telling a falsehood. She could not marry Ian, not feeling as she did about the man before her.

A muscle flexed in his lean jaw. "I...I thought as much." He hesitated, then went on. "I came here to say thank-you. I appreciate everything you've done for me. Without you, I would never have found Andrew. He is all that I imagined and more. Quick of mind, strong, loving, imaginative." She could hear the awe, affection and amazement in his tone as he spoke of the boy, and it moved her more than she could have said.

She took a step closer to him, unable to put into words her joy that he would share his feelings about the child with her. "He's quite a boy, Jedidiah. How proud you must be."

He looked into her eyes, his own sad. "I can hardly take credit for his upbringing, though, for that was not my doing. It is Harry Fairfield who has raised him as a son to be proud of."

"But you will have a hand in his future," she said, turning away so that he would not see her sorrow. "When you take him back to America, he will come to know you as he always should have."

Jedidiah hesitated for a long moment, then nodded. When he spoke again, his voice was oddly distracted. "Yes, when I take him back to America. He'll come to know me then."

She barely heard this, as the pain of his leaving hit her afresh. She turned her back on him. "I shall miss you, Jedidiah. I am glad we have known one another."

"Victoria." She heard him directly behind her, but she could not bring herself to look around. "Victoria." When still she did not answer, he put a hand on her arm. Even that slight contact caused her stomach to contract with need.

She closed her eyes, willing the feelings away. They had never been more unwelcome to her. Her voice was husky with emotion when she spoke. "Please, Jedidiah, you must leave now."

Gently but determinedly, Jed turned her toward him, reaching down to lift her face to his questing gaze. What he saw in her eyes made him catch his breath, for there was no denying the sadness, and desire, in her eyes.

They had been through so much, awakened each other to a depth of passion that few ever know. Never had it been so very difficult for him to say goodbye to anyone, but he knew he must, for her sake. Jed could not stop himself, leaning forward to kiss those soft pink lips this one last time. But as soon as his mouth met hers, he—they—were lost.

Victoria reached up to pull at the buttons of his white linen shirt.

He felt an explosion of heat in his loins that shocked him. All the things he had tried to convince himself of, that he could resist his desire for her, that he could forget what they had shared, all meant nothing in the face of this incredible, raging need.

Jed reached up to push her robe back from her shoulders, his mouth descending to a delicate bare shoulder as he did so. He then moved up to press hot kisses to her throat as she threw back her head, her fingers twining in his hair.

Victoria had no time to think, did not want to do so. Her need and love for this man overrode every other thought in her mind. There was nothing but Jedidiah, his smooth, hard-muscled shoulders beneath her hands, his lips on her heated flesh.

She pulled at his shirt even as he reached down to draw her nightgown over her head. They were separated for a mere fraction of a moment, but she was still eager and grateful when they came together again, her bare body pressing tightly to his.

He bent to suckle her aching breasts, and she found it difficult to breathe at all, the pleasure of it was so great. A trail as hot as boiling tallow shot directly to the core of her. She gasped aloud, arching her back.

The sound of her passion only drove him on, and Jed knelt to caress her belly with his mouth and tongue, feeling it quiver at his touch. He moved on, lingering in the dark patch of curls that guarded the gate to her womanhood.

Victoria could bear it no longer. All the pent-up longing she'd known over the past days erupted into a blaze of passion so hot that it scorched her through to her very soul. She bent over him, her knees so weak she could hardly stand. "Please, Jedidiah, please, no more. I must have you now."

Jed needed no more encouragement than this. He stood and pulled her to him. His hands trailed down her back as his lips found hers and she gave him a kiss that near drew the blood from his veins.

"How I want you..." she whispered hoarsely, her breath mingling with his.

His hands moved of their own accord, reached down to close over the firm mounds of her bottom. She leaned against him, standing on tiptoe as she encouraged him. He kissed her open mouth as he lifted her against the hard, aching need of him.

To his surprise, she reached up to clasp his shoulders and wrapped her legs around his waist. He slid into her as if she were made for him, the perfect sheath for his eager blade.

He closed his eyes on the sheer pleasure of it, his knees weak. He took two steps, holding her up against the door as she cried out his name. "Jed..." Her lips rained kisses on his face and neck, and he drove into her again and again, striving to quench his loneliness and need with her sweet body. Only now could he feel right, for never was he whole without her.

She met him eagerly, gasping out her own passion as she reached the peak of fulfillment. "Oh, yes, Jed."

Her ecstasy triggered his, and he found himself shuddering against her body, calling her name, "Victoria," as the fierce passion they shared exploded in a cascade of glittering pleasure.

Chapter Fifteen

As the ripples of pleasure ebbed away, Victoria sagged against Jedidiah with a sigh. But with the ebbing of pleasure came the heartbreaking sorrow of reality.

Her chest tightened until it was difficult to breathe as the pain hit her full force. Why, oh, why, had she done this?

Inside her, Victoria knew it was because she loved him. It was a force she had no power to resist, and if she was honest with herself, she knew she did not want to resist.

It was Jedidiah who had made the choice that they could not be together. Not Victoria. Were it her right to say, they would never be apart again.

She saw no reason why they could not be together, marry, start a family and continue the Thorn line. It was what she desired above all else. This man, the one who held her so close against him even now, whose beloved breath stirred her hair, he would not let it be.

Damn him, she cursed silently, a sob catching in her throat. She jerked away, upset with him for hurting her and with herself for being hurt.

Jedidiah leaned over to look at her, his expression confused. "Victoria?" When he saw the resentment on her face, he scowled. "What is the matter?"

The ridiculousness of the question caused her indignation to turn to fury. "What is the matter?" She faced him squarely, folding her arms across her chest. "I will tell you, sir, what is the matter. You are."

He took a surprised step backward, even as an answering anger rose to spark in his eyes. "Me? What have I done? If you think I came here to..." He gestured widely.

Victoria could not even find it within herself to be embarrassed at this reference to what had just taken place between them. She was far beyond mortification, feeling as if her only chance at happiness were slipping through her fingers. Deliberately she moved toward him, her hands on her hips, with only the dark fall of her hair to cover her nakedness. "That is not the problem. The problem lies in your stubborn refusals to see that we are good together, that if we tried we might be able to make something together." There, it was said, and she wasn't going to be ashamed for laying herself bare.

He was shaking his head, that dreaded icy cast setting his features, and her heart sank even further. "No, you don't understand, Victoria. Do you remember the day I came to your room, the day you had been crying?" He didn't have to remind her that it had been the second time they made love. The knowledge of it was there in her eyes.

At her nod, he went on. "I had gone into the city, to a part I'm sure you've never been. The conditions there are dreadful."

She interrupted. "I may have been there. My father founded a home for wayward girls. I continue to support it."

He sighed with frustration. "Do you see what I'm saying? Your father founded a home. You continue to support it." He put his hand over his heart. "I lived among those people. Not in London, but in Bar Harbor, where I grew up. It was dirty and sordid and rough." He motioned toward his shirt and trousers, where they had been tossed on the floor. "I am an impostor in those fine clothes, making small talk with aristocrats. Even the wealth I have gained was started through the goodwill of Sebastian Cook. If he hadn't left me a half interest in the business, I would still be nothing more than a laborer, working in his factory.''

She moved to stand as near to him as she could, willing him to listen to what she had to say. ''But you are not a laborer working in his factory, Jedidiah. He left you a share in his business because your ideas saved it. He would not have done so if you didn't deserve it. He was simply a fair and honest man.'' She stabbed him in his bare chest with a finger. ''You are unique, Jedidiah McBride, no matter how you fight against it. No one besides you would ever question your worth.''

He frowned. ''But Nina—''

''Was a fatuous girl.''

''My mother's family?''

''They have never met you. Your grandfather is clearly as stubborn as yourself.'' Her lips twisted. ''Stubborn and foolish—it is a disastrous combination.''

He clasped her upper arms. ''Don't you ever say that I am like him in any way. I know it was his rejection that killed my mother. She loved him, and he could not forgive her for loving my father.''

Her voice was strong with her convictions. ''You cannot escape the fact that a portion of the man's blood flows in your veins. It has shaped you as much as early poverty, which is what has made you so strong and independent. Everything that has come before is a part of you, Jedidiah. You are stubborn and outspoken, but also good, kind, brave, intelligent and well mannered, and nothing less. It is you who cannot accept all the parts of yourself, so you believe that others will not. You do not want to be like him? Then follow your own path. Choose to set your arrogance and prejudice aside.''

He leaned over so that her face was mere inches from his, his gaze seeming to reach into her soul as he searched for the truth in her. "And so, Victoria, tell me, you who care so very much what society thinks of you and of the reputation of your ancient lineage. Even if it is true and you have no difficulty with the humbleness of my beginnings, do you believe that your society would accept all the things about me? Would they invite me into their drawing rooms if they knew that I had played in the gutter?"

She refused to flinch from his scrutiny. "The answer to that is obvious. Some would care a great deal. My only rebuttal would be to say this—they would certainly not approve of everything about myself, either." She indicated her present state of undress with a sweep of her hand. "What matters is that I do not care where you came from. I accept you for who you are, without reservation."

He looked at her for a long moment, then stepped back, letting her go. "You are wrong, Victoria, and incredibly naive. You would not feel the same when the passion you feel for me has cooled."

Victoria stared up at him, seeing him retreat into the shell that he had erected around himself, with a regret so painful it made her throat ache. He would not allow her to reach him. Turning away, she began to gather up her discarded garments. "It is you who are wrong, Jedidiah. You are too attached to the beliefs that have kept you safe against the world to let them go. And I pity you for that."

It was only a moment later that she heard the door open and close softly behind her. She swung around quickly, but it was too late.

Jedidiah was gone. She swayed, reaching out for the carved bedpost, then sank to her knees beside it.

God help her, he was gone.

* * *

Jed stood beside the window, his gaze trained on the night outside, seeing nothing in the darkness. His sight was turned inward, on the misery in his heart.

For a moment, when she tried to convince him that they could have something, Jed had felt himself wavering. What heaven she had offered by making him believe that they could be together, that he could have the right to hold her in his arms. Even when he set aside his pride and reticence to reveal the whole truth of his past, she'd not turned away from him. But Jed had forced the impossible hopes away.

Victoria was not thinking clearly. He knew that what he had told her was true. Once her passion cooled, she would come to see that she had made a dreadful mistake in having a relationship with him.

That was something Jed could not face. He wanted Victoria for more than an affair, wanted . . .

With the force and violence of a storm at sea, the truth came crashing down around him.

Love.

He loved her, loved her with all his heart and soul, wanted to be the father of those children she had spoken of. Jed did not know how it had happened, or when passion had changed to this all-encompassing emotion that made every other he'd experienced in his life pale by comparison.

And that made his rejection of her arguments all the more necessary. Jed was not willing to settle for passion alone. He needed all of her, or nothing.

Victoria had not said anything that made him believe she felt the same. It was true that she was open in her desire for him, that she had said they could be together. But she had not spoken of love or marriage.

Why would she? he asked himself ironically. She was going to marry Sinclair. She'd told him so herself.

His face twisted bitterly. In spite of all her talk about accepting him as he was, she did not want him as a husband, to walk beside her and share her life. That, unfortunately, was what he wanted most.

Jed swung away from the window, flinging himself down on the bed. He would get her out of his mind, and go on with his life as he had planned.

In the morning, he would see Nina. She would not put him off again. He had to talk to her about Andrew, to make her understand that he had a right to be a father to the boy. It would be hard for them all, but there was no other way. Hadn't it been just as hard for him, finding out that he had a son and not been a part of his life?

He rested his arm across his eyes, willing himself to go to sleep. He would need his rest. Everything would change for him as of tomorrow.

Victoria would be gone.

Dawn was lighting the sky when Jed at last fell into a fitful sleep. When he woke, the light from the window told him it was no longer early.

Hastily he rose and changed from his crumpled clothing into clean brown pants, a fresh white shirt and a brown jacket. Feeling only slightly less like a buck that had been mauled by a bear, he made his way downstairs.

When he questioned the manservant, Jed was told that the squire and young Master Andrew were out riding, and that Lady Victoria had left for London.

With all his might, Jed fought the fresh wave of loneliness that gripped his stomach. When the man inquired as to whether he would like breakfast outdoors or in the morning room, Jed declined either. He did not believe he could manage any food just now.

He drew himself up straight, taking a deep breath, telling himself that the pain of Victoria's absence would ease in time. He could only pray it would be soon, though there was little hope in him of that.

He forced himself to concentrate on the present.

Nina.

He was told that Her Ladyship was resting on the terrace. Jed muttered a thank-you and made his way there with determined steps. This was his chance to speak with her alone, and he was not going to miss it.

When he came to halt beside her lounging chair, Nina looked up with resignation, but no surprise. "I knew you would come." With difficulty, she pushed herself up higher on the pillows.

He shrugged, not sure how he felt, now that the moment to confront her had arrived. "How could I not?" She was such a pitiful figure, trying to face him with what little strength was left in that fragile body.

She motioned toward one of the wicker chairs near her own. "Please, sit down."

He spoke immediately, not wanting to allow the doubt that assailed him to stand in his way. "I have come for my son."

Her dark brown eyes met his with unashamed pleading. "I know, and you have the right. I should not have kept him from you. I cannot even bear to think about my own life without him. But, Jedidiah, please, can you not see that you would be hurting him more than anyone? He loves his father ... Harry ... and has known no other sire."

He looked away from her, not wanting to hear this, not wanting to acknowledge the hot agony of this truth inside himself. It was not fair, not right, that he should always be alone. Didn't he, Jed, deserve someone to love and care for, someone who would love and care for him? He stood, shaking his head like an angry lion. "No, Nina. It isn't right. I would have been a father to him. Would have loved him and taught him right from wrong with every bit of care that your Harry has." He banged his fist against his chest. "I was robbed of the privilege, and now he looks to another man as his father. Am I to be punished for your sins for the rest of my life?"

She sat forward, her face as white as fresh snow. "Jedidiah, I am the one who has wronged you here. I freely admit my transgression. I stole what was yours, without regard to the injustice of it. I was young, and very selfish. I was afraid of what people would say about me if I told about the child and married you. I knew I was pregnant, and was desperately afraid of what might become of me, when I met Harry. He was visiting relatives in Bar Harbor. He seemed...taken with me, and I, knowing that this could be my chance to save my reputation and future, I encouraged him. In the end, we were married—but I did not set out to hurt you."

Jed looked down at her fragile form, searching for the rage he had once felt toward her, but all he could summon up was a jaded sort of pity. "So you used him as you used me."

She hung her head. "Yes." Then she faced him again. "But only in the beginning. Harry is older than myself, and not incredibly handsome—well, I did not think so then—but he is kind and wise and loving. In the end, I could only fall in love with him. He was, is, more precious to me than I could ever have imagined."

He watched her closely, listening for any hint that she might be lying to him. He could ascertain none, but he still pushed away the sympathy that rose up inside him. "What has this got to do with me, Nina? Why should I let your desires and feelings matter to me?"

She put her hands on the arms of her chair and leaned toward him, her desperation giving her strength. "You should not care about me, Jedidiah. In fact, you have no reason at all to do so. I will not be long in this world. It is

Harry and Andrew that matter to me, and I hope Andrew does to you. You must see that when I die, Andrew will need his father."

Still Jed fought to deny the untenable truth. "I am his father."

She shook her head. "He has known no father but Harry. Can you imagine what it will be like for him to be taken away from here, from the life he has known?" She sagged back against the pillows, having exhausted her small store of energy. "He would not thank you for that."

"He would come to see that I loved him in time, and would even come to understand why I had to take him. We have already struck up a bond of sorts."

Her burning, fevered eyes met his. "At what cost, Jedidiah? Do you hate me so much that you are willing to go so far to get revenge? I deserve it, but neither Harry nor Andrew does. And, God help us all, Jedidiah, you cannot punish me without punishing them."

The next breath she drew exploded in a harsh burst of coughing. Her whole body spasmed as she held a lace-edged handkerchief to her lips.

Without even knowing he was going to do so, Jed found himself holding her, rubbing her back gently until the attack eased. He could not help but see how pathetic she had become, how close to death she walked.

All these years later, here he was, offering her what little comfort he could as she pleaded for the one thing she had learned meant anything. Her family.

Nina had discovered that much, at least. This realization made him wonder what he had learned. When she subsided against the cushions and closed her eyes, Jed asked, "Is there something I can get you?"

She shook her head without opening her eyes. "No, just allow me to rest for a moment."

He sat down, feeling helpless and confused. Was Victoria right? Was he keeping himself from belonging to anyone?

He thought of the Cooks, of how they had taken him in when he needed someone. They had loved him as if he were their own, Sebastian giving him a half share of the business when he died. And Peter, Sebastian's real son, had welcomed him with open arms, had said he deserved it. Jed had never felt quite worthy, quite secure. He had driven himself in his work to the point of obsession. On more than one occasion Peter had thrown up his hands and said, "Enough, Jed. We have enough."

Only when he received the letter from Nina had he felt he had just cause to leave the work behind. His obsession had been transferred to this new cause, that of finding and taking his child. He'd felt that this might finally be the thing that could fill the hole inside him.

Here he was, on the verge of having what he had sought so desperately, suddenly realizing that it would not answer his emptiness. Was it possible that the solution to his loneliness was inside him? Could he change his life by risking his safety and reaching out for happiness?

Jed ran his hands over his face, not sure what he should do.

At that moment, he heard the sounds of footsteps approaching. He looked up and saw Harry Fairfield come through the French doors.

When he saw Jed, the man's expression became grim, and he wondered why. Then, as soon as his gaze came to rest on his wife, the squire blanched and rushed to her side. "Nina, love, are you all right?"

She opened her eyes and gazed up at him with abject devotion. "Harry, you worry too much."

Jed spoke up. "I did not know what to do. She started coughing. I asked if I could help, but she refused."

Harry Fairfield looked at him for a long moment, then smiled gently. "Of that I am certain. You have been very good to us, sir. You have, in fact, given me what I hold most dear."

Jed found that he could not look away from the other man's gaze. Then it hit him, with the force of a cannon blast. Harry had guessed, guessed that Jedidiah had fathered his son. He knew the truth, and made no recriminations against his wife. In fact, the knowledge seemed to have affected him not in the least, as far as his love for Nina and Andrew was concerned.

Jed looked at the other man, understanding as he did so that this was a depth of love and forgiveness he had never experienced. The Cooks had treated him well out of pity. At least not until he met Victoria. Only she, of all the people he had known in his life, had ever shown such generosity toward him, forgiving him when he wronged her.

It was true that she had not mentioned love or marriage. Neither had he.

Did he have the courage to do so? Could he risk rejection and hurt by coming forward and telling her of his feelings?

Could he not? Jed no longer saw how he could go on without at least trying.

He looked toward the man who knelt beside his sick wife. In order to know any peace, he must allow these people to go on with their lives. Jed stood, as did the squire. "I believe I have caused you and *your* family enough disruption." He indicated Nina, who was watching him warily, too weak to try to convince him anymore. As he continued, her face changed and tears of gratitude filled her dark eyes. "You have enough trouble for any man, without my adding to it."

At that moment, Andrew came bounding out onto the terrace, water seeping from wet clothes, his blond hair plastered to his head. "Father, Mother, I caught a fish." Those green eyes were bright with excitement. "He tried to take my pole with him, but I went in the pond after it."

Harry Fairfield looked at the boy with unreserved adoration. "I can see that, my young man. Perhaps you should have changed before treading on the carpets."

Chastened, Andrew bit his lip. "Uh, oh, I really should have." Then his inherent exuberance gushed forth again as he rushed to Jed's side. "What do you think, Mr. McBride? Isn't he a fine fish?"

Jed's throat ached with the realization that this boy would never know he was his father, but he forced himself to speak as normally as he could. "He certainly is a fine fish." Unable to stop himself, he reached out and ran his hand over that wet blond hair, so much like his own. "The finest fish I've ever seen, caught by the finest... fisherman."

With the greatest effort of his life, he brought himself under control. "I'll be saying goodbye now. It was very good to meet you."

Andrew gazed up at him in disappointment. "Will we be seeing you again soon?"

Jedidiah shook his head. "I wouldn't think so. You and your father will be wanting to concentrate on helping your mother. That is the important thing."

Protectively, Andrew moved to Nina's side. "Perhaps you are right." He looked down at her, his expression puzzled and concerned. "Mother, are you crying?"

She shook her head, her gaze meeting Jed's as she smiled in gratitude. "No, not crying. The sun was in my eyes, that's all."

Jed knew that he had done the right thing, but he did not know how much longer he could hold up if he continued to stand there and look at the three of them, so much a unit, so very distinct from him. In a tight voice, he said, "If you will excuse me, I must go and pack.'' He nodded to each in turn. As his eyes lit lastly upon Nina, he saw her mouth the words *Thank you.*

Jed knew he shouldn't, but he couldn't stop himself glancing toward his son. Andrew stood tall, his green eyes, so much the mirror of his own, meeting Jed's one last time, before the pain slicing through his gut forced Jed to turn away. He strode into the house, not daring to look back.

An hour later, Jed was astride the horse he had borrowed and on his way to London. He had refused the loan of the brougham, feeling he would be much quicker on horseback. If he made haste, he was sure, he could be in London by nightfall.

He refused to even question the wisdom of his actions. Rushing headlong into this was the only way he felt he could follow through. There was only one way to find out if there was any future for himself and Victoria.

No matter how difficult it might prove, he would go to her and lay his heart on the line. He would tell her that he loved her. He would ask her to marry him.

He could only pray that her answer would be yes.

Chapter Sixteen

Victoria had not gone on to London, as she'd led Jedidiah to believe she would. She arrived at Briarwood two days after leaving the Fairfields'.

Having thought that being in her own home would help ease the ache of her misery at being parted from the man she knew was the only one she would ever love, Victoria was disheartened to find that even here she could not escape the anguish of losing him. Everywhere she went there were reminders of Jedidiah.

In the dining room, she imagined him seated across from her, his enigmatic eyes on hers. In the sitting room, she envisioned him standing tall and handsome in the light of the windows. He was everywhere, and try as she might, she could not make him leave her thoughts.

Even the servants seemed to feel his absence, though he had been with them only a short time. One by one they asked after his return, and each time she told them he was returning to America, her broken heart ached afresh.

Even though it was her first day back at Briarwood, Victoria threw herself into her work. She knew it was her duty to spend long hours going over the items that had been neglected in her absence. Her need to immerse herself in her work was not connected in any way to the man she so badly needed to put from her mind. It was when she came across the paperwork that transferred several boilers to the possession of one Captain Jedidiah McBride that she broke down in a deluge of tears.

For years she had not allowed herself the release of crying, and now it seemed that was all she did. She held a lace handkerchief to her face to muffle the sounds of her grief.

Victoria looked up with a guilty start as a knock sounded on the oak door of her father's study. Wiping her eyes hastily, she straightened her spine and called out, "Enter."

"My lady..." the liveried manservant who opened the door began. "There is a gentleman here to see you. He says it is quite urgent and personal."

Hope surged up in her chest, for a breathless moment. Then she pushed it down. Surely the man would have recognized Jedidiah. She forced herself to speak normally. "Did he give his name?"

"He said only to tell you that it was Ian."

For a brief moment, she closed her eyes. "Of course." Taking a deep breath, Victoria looked at him. "Where is he?"

He bowed. "In the green sitting room, Lady Victoria."

"Tell him I will attend him shortly." With a nod of thanks and dismissal, Victoria stood and drew herself up to her full height. She should have expected Ian to take some action. Her note had told him little. She had planned to write to him, to explain that she could not be his wife, but she had not done so.

The deed could no longer be postponed. Victoria wished only that Ian had not come all this way to see her. How very awful she was, to have made him go to this trouble simply to learn that she would not have him.

Ian stood when she entered the room. He came toward her slowly, his gaze intent. As always, she was struck by his sensual presence and his dark good looks, and she wished she could care for him. She could not.

Victoria halted him before he could speak. "Ian, please do not say anything. First, let me tell you how very sorry I am for the way I have treated you. It is unconscionable. I would understand perfectly if you wished to withdraw your proposal because of it."

He continued to study her for another long moment. "Should I, Victoria? Is that what you would want me to do?"

She held his gaze. "Yes, Ian, that is what I want you to do. You deserve more than I would ever be able to give you."

He looked away. "It is McBride, isn't it?"

Past lying now, feeling that she owed this man truth, if nothing else, she nodded. "Yes."

He smiled stiffly. "I thought as much, but I wanted to hear you say it. He's a fine man. Where is he? I would like to offer my congratulations. I hope you will invite me to the wedding."

She raised her chin high, refusing to acknowledge its trembling. "Cousin Jedidiah and I are not going to be married, sir. He is on his way back to America."

His taken-aback expression quickly dissolved into a frown. "Then he is a fool."

Pride would not allow her to show this man just how much she was hurting. Victoria looked at him, again feeling sorry that she could not care about him. But it was Jedidiah McBride who had captured her heart, and nothing could change that. "Ian, you are a good man. I hope that, despite everything, we can be friends." She held out her hand.

He took it. "I would like that, too. And remember, if you ever need anything, or change your mind..." He smiled ruefully and shrugged.

She could not help smiling gently in return. "That is very kind of you, but I don't think I will be changing my mind.

Again I must say you are worthy of far more than I would
be able to give you."

He shrugged again.

To Victoria's relief, Ian made his excuses a short time
later, saying he had other pressing business to attend to. It
was obvious he understood that she felt somewhat awkward over what had happened between them.

Victoria sighed as she watched him leave, his sensitivity
making her wonder for a brief second if she had made a
mistake. The thought was quickly dispelled. She could
marry no one right now, not with the wound of Jedidiah's
leaving so fresh and aching inside her.

She looked around the empty room, and suddenly realized that she had to get out. There were too many memories of the sea captain in this room, in this house that had
once been her refuge. Now it felt like a prison.

Going to her bedchamber, Victoria quickly changed into
a riding habit. Mary was the one person who might understand. Although she did not want to burden her friend with
her own problems, especially with her father so ill, Victoria had to at least see her.

Her mare was somewhat restive as they started out across
the parkland, but she soon settled down. It was a beautiful
day in early April, and Victoria suddenly realized that only
a month had passed since Jedidiah McBride rescued her on
the roadside.

Yet her life had changed irrevocably.

Not wanting to think about that, or anything to do with
the man, Victoria urged her horse to a gallop. The wind
whipped the bonnet from her head, but she did not even
slow as she sped over the grounds. Somehow, some way,
she had to get him from her mind, had to find a way to be
content in herself again, to wipe his touch from her soul.

Perhaps it was because of her preoccupation with these
thoughts that Victoria did not sense that something was

wrong. Perhaps it was because Reginald Cox had grown more clever in his plans to take her.

One moment she was seated on her horse, racing though the trees, the next she was looking up from the ground. The air rushed from her in a painful gasp, and her back was on fire with the force of the landing. At first Victoria could think of nothing besides trying desperately to suck air into her starved lungs.

As soon as she saw Reginald's face appear above her own, a new sensation gripped her: fear. With Jedidiah gone, she had no one to come to her aid. She'd not even thought to bring a groom.

Cox smiled. "Victoria."

She did not reply, making a great show of breathing deeply. Heaven help her, what was she to do? Obviously the madman would not listen to any reasonable arguments to let her go, or he would not be here.

He turned to someone just out of sight. "Get the carriage." She could only assume that he must have again enlisted the aid of the imbecilic Lloyd Jenkins. That made two against one, no matter how inept they were.

Telling herself she could not allow him to see how badly shaken she was, Victoria simply lay there. Her mind churned as she tried to think of some way out of this, while giving her body time to right itself.

Lord, what a fool she had been to let this lunatic go free after his attempted abductions of her. Jedidiah had been right in thinking she should have him arrested.

He spoke again. "Victoria, surely you have recovered somewhat by now. I am very sorry for having to resort to such lengths. But you did force me." He bent to help her up.

Using surprise as her ally, she drove her clenched fist into his nose. Reginald rocked backward, crying out in outrage and pain as blood gushed from the offended organ.

Quick as a cat, she pushed him with both hands and scrambled to her feet. He reached out to grab her, but she sidestepped him neatly and raced toward her horse. The escape attempt would have succeeded quite well, if the horse had not stepped on the trailing skirt of her riding habit.

As Victoria pushed at the animal to try and free herself, Reginald was upon her. He grabbed her from behind, giving a cry of fury as she bit his hand. "That will be quite enough!" he shouted.

The next thing she knew, there was a blinding pain in her head, then nothing....

Victoria woke slowly, feeling the pounding in her head with a groan. When she opened her eyes, she at first did not know where she was, nor did she understand why she felt as if the seat beneath her were moving. Casting her gaze around her, she met that of a grinning Reginald Cox.

The events that had preceded this came flooding back to her. And with them came a sense of horror.

Glancing around the interior of the conveyance with feigned disdain, Victoria said, "Really, Reginald, a rented hack?"

His smile disappeared like a hedgehog down a hole. "I . . . I . . ." he sputtered. "I did not want to be seen in my own coach. I had to be anonymous, of course."

She raised delicate brows high. "Of course. It is also quite possible that you no longer own a coach." At his guilty start, she pressed on, surprised to have struck a nerve so easily. "Is that the problem, Reginald? Have you completely run out of money? Is that why you persist in these ridiculous attempts to marry me against my will? Have you run through your entire inheritance so quickly?"

He frowned darkly. "A few thousands pounds a year doesn't go very far these days." His eyes hardened as he looked at her. "But you wouldn't know anything about that, what with your vast wealth." He grinned again, like a fool in a play. "And that, my dear Victoria, is why I must have you."

She stared at him coolly. "I will not marry you, Reginald. I will say that you are forcing me. No minister would go forward with the deed."

This did not seem to trouble him in the least, and she began to know a growing sense of apprehension. He only made this feeling worse when he went on. "You see, my dear Victoria, I have paid handsomely, with nearly the last of my funds, to make certain that a blind eye is turned to, shall we say, any hint of reluctance on your part."

She forced herself to remain calm. "I will not live with you. As soon as the ceremony is over, I will have it annulled."

"Will you now?" He leaned forward. "I do not think so, because I do not intend to let you out of my sight until I am quite certain that you carry my child." At her start of horror, he shrugged. "I know enough about you to know that you would not want to harm your own child by creating a scandal."

Unable to reply with any pretense of composure, Victoria turned away from him. What, she asked herself, was she to do now?

Jed arrived at the Georgian mansion in Grosvenor Square late into the night. He had ridden hard after leaving the Fairfields', uncaring of fatigue or hunger, knowing only that he must get to Victoria before she could say yes to Sinclair.

The house was dark, and he waited for what seemed hours before someone came to answer his knock. Mrs. Dunn appeared in the barely opened portal, the candle she held casting eerie shadows over her face and the entrance hall behind her. When she saw that it was him, she flung the door wide. "Mr. McBride, what a surprise to see you!"

Jed wasted no time on pleasantries. "I must see Lady Victoria. It cannot wait until morning."

The housekeeper frowned in confusion. "Sir, I would be happy to do anything you ask, but the lady is not here. She sent a note telling us that she was going on to Briarwood. It arrived late this afternoon. We assumed you would be with her. Winter has gone off with your things and hers."

Jed ran an agitated hand through his hair, reeling from the shock of discovering she was gone. All the way, he had kept telling himself that this was what he must do, that he had to get to her and tell her how he felt. He had been so single-minded in his need to see her he had not thought of any other possibility.

She was not here. It felt as if someone had doused him with cold water.

He turned and left the house, unheeding of Mrs. Dunn's worried query as to where he was going in the dead of night. Where else on earth would he go but to Briarwood? That was where the woman who mattered most to him on earth was to be found.

Victoria refused to even speak to Reginald during the next hours on the road. It was with some surprise that she felt the hack come to a halt shortly after night fell. She looked over to her abductor in an unspoken question. He said, "We must stop here for the night."

Victoria felt her heart swell with hope. She might find some way to escape.

As if he had read her very thoughts, Reginald told her, "Do not be foolish, Victoria. I am willing to hurt someone if it becomes necessary. Don't think you can involve anyone else in this." He reached into the pocket of his coat and removed a pistol.

Disappointment made her sag back against the seat. She righted herself immediately, refusing to give up hope. If she was observant and patient, perhaps she would still be able to find some method of freeing herself.

When they alit, Victoria saw, without surprise, that Lloyd Jenkins was driving. He did not meet her gaze as she looked up at him, and she had the distinct feeling that he had somehow been coerced into helping his friend. Yet she did not see how his lack of enthusiasm could help her when she felt the barrel of Reginald's pistol prod her lower back.

He motioned toward the door of the dilapidated inn with his free hand. Slowly she passed beneath a sign that hung from one hinge and bore the words Gray Gull Inn. That name, and the sharp salt tang in the air, told her that they were not far from the sea.

Having decided to bide her time, Victoria made no effort to thwart Reginald as he asked for two rooms, one for himself and his wife and another for his brother. But her lips curled as he signed Mr. and Mrs. Stockton with a flourish.

He never removed the weapon from the small of her back until the innkeeper, a short, balding man with shifty eyes and a restless habit of rubbing his hands together, left them alone. She saw the little man go with relief. He had given her such a lecherous glance that she was almost grateful for Reginald's presence. Even if she had been of a mind to seek the innkeeper's assistance, she did not believe she would get any help from that quarter.

Moving away from Reginald, Victoria ignored him, peering about the room to see if she could find any ready avenue of escape. There seemed to be none. The only furnishings were a bed, a rickety table and wardrobe and a roughly made chair.

Just then the door opened, and she swung around to see Lloyd enter. Reginald addressed him immediately. "Your room is across the hall."

Lloyd looked not at her, but at his cohort. "I... Uh, yes, thank you. I just thought you would want to know that the horses are stabled for the night."

Cox smiled with complete self-assurance and settled himself in the chair. "Good. It looks as though everything will go according to plan. I told you there was nothing to worry about, didn't I?"

Lloyd's gaze flitted to Victoria and away. "You did, Reggie, you did. You were right when you said McBride wasn't at Briarwood with her. Things certainly would have been different if he were around."

Victoria's stomach twisted with renewed loss, even as Reginald scowled. He spoke with what she knew was bravado. "I'm not so sure of that, Lloyd. I'm not intimidated by the man."

Victoria could not withhold a choking gasp of disbelief. As Reginald turned to glare at her, she coughed and said, "My throat is dry." She didn't feel there was any point in making him any more riled than he already was. It would be better if he began to believe she was resigned to her fate. He might then become less vigilant.

Reginald waved an airy hand at his coconspirator. "Why don't you make yourself useful? Go down to the common room and see if you can round up anything decent enough to eat and drink."

Lloyd hesitated. "How do you want me to pay?"

Reginald scowled. "Out of your own pocket, of course. I've told you, you'll be reimbursed handsomely once the lady and I are wed."

Ducking his head in submission, Lloyd left the room. Watching him, Victoria could not help thinking what an imbecile he was to allow himself to be intimidated by a waste of a man like Reginald Cox. Unlike Jedidiah, they had been given every advantage, and had turned out all the worse for it.

Yet she knew she must lay some of the blame for her current circumstances at her own feet. She had been foolish to believe that Reginald would come to his senses and leave her alone simply because he had been reared among good people. Obviously, evil, like good, knew no social boundaries. Her heart ached afresh for the man she had lost.

She went over to stare out the window, angry with herself and sickened by both Reginald and the weak-minded Lloyd.

It was with some surprise that she felt a hand on her arm only a moment later. She turned to see Reginald standing behind her. He was looking at her with an expression that made her blood slow in her veins. An expression of lust.

He seemed unaware of her revulsion as he allowed his gaze to roam over the snug-fitting bodice of the amber velvet riding habit, then down to her waist and hips. He licked his full lips. "Oh, Victoria, but you are beautiful."

She shook her head, stepping backward involuntarily. "Reginald, you are not to touch me."

He smiled and closed the distance again. "And why should I not? You are to be my wife by this time tomorrow. It would behoove me to begin my efforts to get you with child as quickly as possible."

"Oh, heaven, please," she whispered silently, "do not allow him to do this." It was more than she could bear to think of him touching her after she had been with Jedidiah. The thought of Reginald doing those things to her was completely repulsive.

"What about Lloyd?" she asked in desperation. "He will be back shortly. Surely you would not wish for him to find us that way."

He frowned pensively. "Perhaps you are right. You will be my wife soon. And I would not wish for *my* wife to be made a spectacle of." He eyed her lingeringly. "But later, when we are alone, I will not be dissuaded."

As Reginald moved away, she turned her back on him, her knees threatening to give out on her. Somehow she kept herself erect, knowing that she could not allow the cad to see how frightened she was. He seemed to thrive on the weakness of others.

Luckily, Lloyd returned only minutes later, and Victoria turned her attention to the business of eating. Without a word to either of the men, she collected a steaming-hot meat pie and a glass of wine and went to sit on the bed. The hot pastry and wine might have been vinegar and dust, for all that she tasted them, but she forced herself to consume the food. If an opportunity for escape presented itself, she would need her strength.

In a depressingly short time, the two men had finished. Victoria, who was lingering for as long as possible, felt Reginald's hot gaze upon her with trepidation.

At last he spoke up, his patience obviously having run out. "Well, I think it's about time you were getting along to your own room, Lloyd."

Lloyd cast a nervous glance at Victoria. "Do you think you should stay in here with her, Reggie? You aren't married yet."

Reginald took a deep breath and let it out slowly. "Lloyd, as I told you when we were discussing our plan of action, someone must stay with Victoria to watch her so she doesn't get away. Since I am to be her husband, it is only natural that I should be the one."

The shorter man nodded jerkily. "Yes, you are right, Reggie. I just want to say again that marriage is one thing, and forcing yourself on her another. She is a gentlewoman."

Reginald stood, putting his arm around the other man's shoulders as he led him to the door. "How right you are, my friend. I agree with you completely. Victoria's virtue must remain sacred until we are declared man and wife."

Though he still appeared a bit uncertain, this seemed to reassure Lloyd enough for him to leave the bedchamber without further discussion. When he was gone, Reginald turned to her.

Mockingly he said, "I don't know what it is about you, Victoria, but you seem to bring out the protective instincts in men. First your esteemed Mr. McBride, and now Lloyd. I must say I find it quite touching, if a bit irritating."

As he came toward her, one slow step at a time, Victoria tried to fight her fear and despair. If only Jedidiah was here to rescue her, to take her in his arms and make her feel safe. But he was not. He was on his way to America with Andrew.

She had no one to rely on but herself. It was she, Victoria, who would have to think of some way out of this nightmare.

As Reginald Cox came within inches of her, Victoria held up her hand to press him back, her palm against the wool of his tweed coat. "Please, wait! I... We have been traveling all day without stopping." She looked up at him meaningfully. "I must have a moment of privacy."

He stood still, his brow creased as he listened to her. Then understanding dawned. "I see." He shrugged. "It is a reasonable request. I'll allow you to have your few moments of privacy, but do not forget that I will be right outside the room. You'll have no chance to leave it."

She nodded quickly. "I will not try."

As soon as the door closed on his back, Victoria went into action. Making as little noise as possible, she went to the wardrobe, which stood to the left of the door. Using the wall for leverage, she set her back to it and pushed with all her might. The ancient piece of furniture was heavier than she had thought. At first it only teetered, and she nearly gasped her frustration aloud, but the need for silence was great and she held it in. Once again she pushed, straining until her eyes ached with the effort.

And then, to her utter amazement and relief, the heavy old wardrobe toppled over, to rest directly in front of the portal. There was an immediate cry of alarm from the man outside.

The door handle rattled as he turned it and pushed against the heavy oak panel, but it did not budge. Elation rippled through her.

"Victoria," she heard him say in a threatening tone, "let me inside. This will get you nowhere. You cannot escape."

She made no reply, rushing to the bed to strip back the covers. A wave of disappointment swept through her when she saw the tattered condition of the sheets. She had hoped to tie them together and lower herself out the window, but they would never hold her weight.

Hearing more than one voice outside the door, she rushed over to see if she could make out what was being said. She recognized Lloyd's voice. "Why do we have to break the door down tonight? Why don't you just leave her until morning? She can't get out."

Reginald replied heatedly, "I want in."

Lloyd answered him slowly. "You said you only wanted to stay in there with her to make sure she didn't get away. You weren't lying to me were you, Reggie? I couldn't go along with you to Scotland if I thought you had done anything really wrong."

When Reginald's answer came, his tone was much more subdued. "Of course, Lloyd, you are right again. Tomorrow will be soon enough to get her out of there. We wouldn't want to upset our landlord by dragging him from his bed at this hour, which would surely happen in the commotion of getting her out of there.''

Their voices trailed away, and she heard the sound of a door closing.

Thank God for Lloyd, she thought, as relief washed through her like a spring rain. She didn't know what she could do, but she now had till morning to think of something.

Once more Victoria moved to the rumpled bed. Carefully she examined the bed linens again. They were just as thin as she had first thought.

Going to the window, she looked out into the dark night, realizing that if some other avenue did not present itself she would be forced to try it. Falling to her death might indeed be preferable to marrying Reginald Cox.

Opening the pane with difficulty, she studied her surroundings. The inn had surely been built in the time of Elizabeth, for it was of that style of construction. There were no gables or trellises or awnings to aid her in climbing.

Despondency flooded her as she stood there, sobbing a prayer to the night that somehow deliverance would come. She forced the window closed, as the mist that was gathering was unpleasantly damp.

Chapter Seventeen

Jed was near to dropping with exhaustion when he arrived at Briarwood. Only one night had he stopped to rest, and precious little sleep had he gotten even then. He could think of nothing besides Victoria and the fact that she had not gone to London, but had returned to Briarwood. What it meant, he was too tired and confused to understand. He could only ride.

One of the footmen, Charles, answered the door. He first drew back in shock, then threw up his arms in open joy at seeing him. "Oh, Mr. McBride, we're so glad to see you. Lady Victoria's horse came back without her this morning. No one's been able to find her, though we've combed the woods, and are still doing so."

Jed grabbed the poor man by the lapels. "Good Lord, what are you saying?"

"It's the lady, sir. She's gone. Without a trace."

Jed released him, running his hands over his face as he tried desperately to think.

Then it came to him with a certainty that left him weak. "Reginald Cox. But where has he taken her?"

"Where would he take her but to Scotland, and Gretna Green?" Charles spoke up.

Pulling himself together, Jed faced the servant. "I'll need a fresh horse, some water. And tell Mrs. Everard that I will require some food, something I can take with me and eat as I ride."

When the servant had left to do what he'd been told, Jed went up to his former room, and on impulse changed into his seafaring garb. The garments were loose, and would offer freer movement when he throttled Reginald Cox.

He also washed thoroughly, wanting to be as fresh for this new journey as he could be. He had to stay alert and strong to be of any use to Victoria when he found her.

From the back of Jed's mind came a determined voice that told him he would find the strength to choke the life from Reginald Cox if he was half-dead. He could not doubt the truth of it.

In no time, he was back on the road, the few servants who were not out searching the woods for their lady calling out to him their encouragement and their faith in him. In spite of his anxiety and fatigue, he couldn't help being touched by their belief in him.

Never had he felt more of a sense of belonging than at Briarwood. The people's trust in him only made him all the more resolved to get to Victoria before it was too late.

Having asked about the most direct route to Scotland, Jed followed that road. He did not think Reginald was clever enough to employ any complicated strategy in order to foil a possible rescue attempt. He would want to get Victoria to Gretna Green, and safely wed, as speedily as he could.

Leaning low over the horse's back, Jed urged him to a gallop. He would get there in time!

What remained of the daylight hours passed in a blur for Jed. He would not allow himself to think about anything besides staying in the saddle and on the road. He ate the meat-and-cheese sandwiches Mrs. Everard had made for him without even slowing. Only when the horse lagged with thirst did he stop for a moment at a stream to let him drink.

It was sometime after darkness had fallen that Jed came to an inn along the side of the road. It was a run-down structure, with a crooked sign that swayed in the breeze that blew in from the Irish Sea. In the light from the lantern that hung over the door, he could see that a silvery fog had settled over the scene.

Jed slowed his horse. He had not seen any other habitation for some time, and wondered how long it might be before he did again. Should he trade horses here, so that he could continue on a fresh one?

Victoria became very still when she saw a horse and rider come to a halt outside the inn. Even in the darkness, there was something familiar about the man, his erect carriage, the way he held the reins in obviously capable hands. Then as he moved forward, into the lanternlight, she gasped aloud.

Jedidiah. She did not know how or why he was here. She knew only that he was the answer to her prayers, not just for her immediate safety, but for her happiness.

As he hesitated, she fumbled with the window. It stuck. Frantically she began to pound on the glass, calling his name. Jedidiah did not seem to hear her, for he turned his horse toward the road once more.

With no consideration for any possible injury she might sustain, she hit the window with her fist, putting all her strength behind it. The glass shattered, raining down from the casement, even as she screamed his name in desperation. "Jedidiah! Jedidiah, I am here!"

As he looked up, she cried out again, even louder, waving her arms. "Jedidiah!" Now Victoria heard the sounds of shouting from outside her door.

Reginald and Lloyd.

When they began pounding and banging at the door in an effort to get inside, Victoria realized they were no longer concerned about waking the landlord. She looked back out the window and saw Jedidiah running toward the inn.

At the same time, the wardrobe began to slide, albeit slowly, as the door was forced open. She ran across the room, pushing with all her might, hoping to buy a bit more time. But she could not hold the two men.

In a matter of moments, Reginald was grabbing her roughly by the arm. "Come with me," he growled, and half dragged her out into the hallway as she fought to resist him.

Other people, in various states of undress, had come to see what was going on. The innkeeper ran down the hall toward him, pushing the others aside. "Just what is going on here?" he bellowed, in a surprisingly strong baritone for such a small man. "You'll be paying for any damage done to my property."

Reginald ignored him, simply tossing a handful of coins on the floor. "Get the hack!" he shouted to Lloyd, then followed behind him, his progress being delayed by the fact that he had to half carry the reluctant Victoria.

As Lloyd cried out in pain and surprise from ahead of them on the narrow stairs leading to the lower floor, Reginald turned to drag her back in the direction from which they had come. Desperately he addressed the innkeeper, who was busily gathering up the money. "Is there a back door?"

The man pointed to a door just to their left. "'Tis for the housemaids."

Not having the least care for why it was there, Reginald smiled in satisfaction and pulled Victoria after him. The doorway lead to an extremely narrow set of winding stairs. There was barely room for one of them to traverse the stairs at a time. Reginald had to force her down in front of him.

Victoria continued to fight him with every step, and he finally ended in picking her up and holding her against him with his arms about her waist.

When she heard a loud voice shout, "Victoria!" from above, her heart soared. "I'm here!" she screamed. "I'm here!"

Cox let out a growl of anger. "Shut up!" His hand contacted painfully with the side of her head. The world spun for a moment, then righted itself.

They came to a door. With his hands full, Cox obviously felt no compunctions about using her as a battering ram, for he shoved her against the portal, putting all his weight behind the effort. She grunted, as the door swung open.

Instead of continuing to run, as she had expected, Reginald dropped her and spun around, reaching into his pocket at the same time.

The gun.

There was no time to shout a warning as Jedidiah sprang through the opening. In spite of the fact that his green eyes were hard with rage, his lips twisted with bitter determination, she had never seen a more welcome or beloved sight. He was like the Archangel Michael, tall, powerful, glowing with righteous rage and undeniably handsome, come down from heaven to save her. His lethal gaze came to rest on Reginald with pleasure. The gun in the madman's hand seemed not to faze him in the least.

Reginald Cox indicated his pistol. "I've hoped for this moment," he said with bravado, though Victoria could hear the fear he fought to disguise.

Showing absolutely no hesitation, Jedidiah growled, coming toward him, even as Victoria watched the coward raise his gun. Without pausing to think, Victoria threw herself against her abductor.

Reginald fell, and she with him. The gun discharged, and her heart stopped as she tried to right herself. When she sat up, she saw that Jedidiah was pulling Reginald up by both arms. The small man was shouting in hatred, even as he struggled to free himself. Jedidiah hit him squarely in the face with his fist, then hit him again, even as blood burst forth from his nose. He continued to hit Reginald until he went limp in his hands.

Jedidiah let the other man fall to the floor. He then stood panting, his whole body shaking with the force of his emotions.

Only when Victoria put her hand on his arm did he turn to face her. A soft cry escaped her when she noted the trickle of blood that ran down her beloved's arm. "You're hurt!" She reached toward him.

"It's nothing to worry about. The bullet just grazed me," he told her impatiently. His green eyes studied her carefully. "It's you I'm worried about. Are you all right? They didn't harm you?"

She shook her head. "Only my pride."

At that, he pulled her into his arms, and she went joyously. "I was so frightened for you," he whispered, holding her head against him, his warm breath in her hair.

"You came for me," she whispered, her voice husky with emotion.

His arms tightened around her. "I couldn't leave. I had to see you again, but when I went to the house in London you weren't there. I went immediately to Briarwood, and they told me you were gone." He paused for a moment as he relived the pain of that moment. "I knew it had to be Cox. It was the footman Charles who realized where he had taken you."

She held him with all her strength. "Oh, Jedidiah, I am so glad."

"Hold up there." They looked up when the innkeeper's voice interrupted them. He stood in the open doorway, glaring at them, for a moment, then came forward into the room, which Victoria now saw was the kitchen of the inn. "What is going on here?"

Jedidiah stepped back from Victoria, but did not release his hold on her. "This man has kidnapped Lady Victoria Thorn. You will send for the authorities." When the man hesitated, Jed took a step toward him. "Now, or I will know the reason why."

The innkeeper's demeanor changed with magical speed. "Aye, my lord, as you wish." He hurried over to drag the still-unconscious Reginald to the door. "I'll just take him out into the common room, where he can be watched until the law comes."

Jed nodded. "That is a very good idea. Do the same with his friend."

"Aye, my lord." He exited with Reginald. Victoria felt not the least compunction about Jedidiah's directive to call the authorities. Reginald deserved no more consideration than he had shown her.

She turned and smiled up at Jedidiah, who pulled her close against him once more. "I'm afraid we will have to spend the night here," he said. "I'm too damned tired to go any farther tonight."

She rested against him happily. "I have no fear that anyone else will trouble us. You have shown them what will happen to them if they do." Her eyes darkened, her gaze rising to his mouth. "Let us go to the innkeeper and take a room."

Jed looked down at her, more tempted than he could have said. But he had something he wanted to tell her first. "No, Victoria, I can't do that." At her look of shock and disappointment, he hurried on. "What I mean to say, Victoria, is that I do not want to take you like this, here in this place."

She tried to make herself believe he was right and honorable to say this. "I see." She nodded as agreeably as she could. "You want to wait until we are somewhere else, somewhere that Reginald has not been."

"No." He tightened his arms around her. "That is not what I mean." Then, to her utter amazement, he released her, slipping down upon his knee and taking her slender hand in his large ones. "What I mean, my love, my life, my soul, is that I do not want to *take* you, here or anywhere else. When I touch you in that way again, I want you to be mine in every way. What I am trying to say, Victoria, to ask, is, will you marry me?"

At her gasp of surprise, Jedidiah looked up at her closely. For a long time, she gave no answer, her eyes closed, too overcome by the unbelievable happiness that rushed through her with the force of a summer storm. Then, at last, she opened her eyes. Tears clouded the misty gray depths as she whispered, "Oh, my love, I will be your wife."

He stood and drew her back into his arms, holding her against the hard length of his body. In risking his pride, which was nothing, he had gained the world. His throat was tight with emotion as he whispered, "Thank God, you love me."

"But, of course I do," she said, holding him to her, creating a fresh wave of joy in his heart.

Suddenly she pushed back, looking up at him in question. "What about Andrew, your business, your life in America?"

Briefly his eyes darkened with pain, but then they cleared as he once again realized the rightness of his decision to leave Andrew's life undisturbed. Briefly he told her what had happened at the Fairfields'.

She reached out to brush a tender hand over his cheek. "You are such a dear, kind man to think of your son before yourself."

He held that hand against his lips, wondering what he had ever done without her. He had not been truly alive.

He smiled into her eyes. "As for Cook and McBride, I think we'll be opening a branch in England. Possibly in a heavenly little place called Carlisle."

She threw her arms around his neck and kissed him, but he drew away to look at her again. "There is just one more thing. About our children."

She watched him closely.

He held her gaze with his own, wanting her to know that he meant what he was about to say, that he had made the decision without regret. "I want our children to have the name Thorn. McBride is not a name that has ever meant much to me. Yours is one they can be proud to carry."

She shook her head slowly. "Jedidiah McBride, your name means something because it comes from you. You alone are good enough to give it nobility. I do not wish to see the name of Thorn disappear after all these centuries, but I wish for our children to bear the name of their father whom I love and honor more than the breath I draw. Could we not settle on Thorn-McBride? It would be an appellation of great honor, for me and them."

He crushed her against him, tears clouding his own eyes. "What did I ever do to deserve you, Victoria?"

She held him to her, glorying in his strength. "You loved me."

*   *   *   *   *

IT'S THAT TIME OF YEAR AGAIN!

launches its
1997 **March Madness** celebration
with **four** of the brightest new stars
in historical romance.

We proudly present:

THE PHOENIX OF LOVE by Susan Schonberg
A reformed rake strikes sparks with a ravishing Ice Queen

HEART OF THE DRAGON by Sharon Schulze
A fierce warrior forsakes his heritage for a noblewoman on the run

EMILY'S CAPTAIN by Shari Anton
A Southern belle is ensnared by a dashing Union spy

THE WICKED TRUTH by Lyn Stone
A dauntless physician falls victim to the charms
of a beautiful murder suspect

**4 new books from 4 terrific new authors.
Look for them wherever
Harlequin Historicals are sold.**

You are cordially invited to a

HOMETOWN REUNION

September 1996—August 1997

Bad boys, cowboys, babies. Feuding families,
arson, mistaken identity, a mom on the run...
Where can you find romance and adventure?
Tyler, Wisconsin, that's where!

So join us in this not-so-sleepy little town and
experience the love, the laughter and the
tears of those who call it home.

WELCOME TO A
HOMETOWN REUNION

Gabe Atwood has no sooner rescued his wife,
Raine, from a burning building when there's
more talk of fires. Rumor has it that Clint
Stanford suspects Jon Weiss, the new kid at
school, of burning down the Ingallses' factory.
And that Marina, Jon's mother, has kindled a fire
in Clint that may be affecting his judgment. Don't
miss Kristine Rolofson's *A Touch of Texas,*
the seventh in a series you won't want to end....

Available in March 1997
at your favorite retail store.

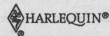

FREE VALENTINE'S BROOCH!
$9.95 U.S. retail value

This Valentine's Day Harlequin brings you
all the essentials—romance, chocolate
and jewelry—in:

VALENTINE *Delights*

Matchmaking chocolate-shop owner Papa Valentine
dispenses sinful desserts, mouth-watering
chocolates...and advice to the lovelorn, in this
collection of three delightfully romantic stories
by Meryl Sawyer, Kate Hoffmann and Gina Wilkins.

As our special Valentine's Day gift to you, each copy
of *Valentine Delights* will have a beautiful, filigreed,
heart-shaped brooch attached to the cover.

Make this your most delicious Valentine's Day
ever with *Valentine Delights!*

Available in February wherever
Harlequin books are sold.

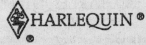

HARLEQUIN ®

Heartbreak RANCH

Four generations of independent women...
Four heartwarming, romantic stories of the West...
Four incredible authors...

Fern Michaels
Jill Marie Landis
Dorsey Kelley
Chelley Kitzmiller

Saddle up with Heartbreak Ranch, an outstanding
Western collection that will take you on a whirlwind
trip through four generations and the exciting,
romantic adventures of four strong women who
have inherited the ranch from Bella Duprey,
famed Barbary Coast madam.

Available in March,
wherever Harlequin books are sold.

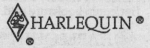

HARLEQUIN ®

®

Look us up on-line at: http://www.romance.net

HTBK

LOVE *or* MONEY?
Why not Love *and* Money!
After all, millionaires
need love, too!

How to Marry a MILLIONAIRE

**Suzanne Forster,
Muriel Jensen
and
Judith Arnold**

bring you three original stories
about finding that one-in-a million man!

Harlequin also brings you
a million-dollar sweepstakes—enter
for your chance to win a fortune!

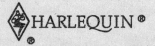

HARLEQUIN ®

Harlequin and Silhouette celebrate
Black History Month with seven terrific titles,
featuring the all-new *Fever Rising*
by Maggie Ferguson
(Harlequin Intrigue #408) and
A Family Wedding by Angela Benson
(Silhouette Special Edition #1085)!

Also available are:
Looks Are Deceiving by Maggie Ferguson
Crime of Passion by Maggie Ferguson
Adam and Eva by Sandra Kitt
Unforgivable by Joyce McGill
Blood Sympathy by Reginald Hill

On sale in January at your favorite
Harlequin and Silhouette retail outlet.

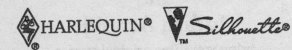

From the bestselling author of *Scandalous*

Cam Monroe vowed revenge when
Angela Stanhope's family accused him
of a crime he didn't commit.

Fifteen years later he returns from exile, wealthy
and powerful, to demand Angela's hand in marriage.
It is then that the strange "accidents" begin. Are the
Stanhopes trying to remove him from their lives
one last time, or is there a more insidious,
mysterious explanation?

Available this March at your favorite retail outlet.

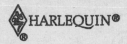
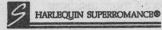